Love Me Tomorrow

PRAISE FOR *LOVE ME TOMORROW*:

"Emiko Jean is so smart. I wish I'd had this idea.
Perfect for fans of *To All The Boys I've Loved Before*."
Jenny Valentine, author of *Us in the Before and After*

"Written with Emiko Jean's signature warmth and wit,
this deeply moving rom-com proves that love isn't only real,
but also its own kind of magic. I adored every word."
Ann Liang, *New York Times* bestselling author of
I Hope This Doesn't Find You

"*Love Me Tomorrow* has Emiko Jean's signature humour,
banter, and heart. The romance sizzles, and the suspense
kept me turning the pages. What a beautiful, unexpected, and
heartwarming adventure I went on with the characters.
Another winner from one of my favorite authors!"
Gloria Chao, author of *American Panda*

"If you're a rom-com fan like me who adores love letters,
has crushes on book boyfriends, and adores a main
character who is funny, smart, and tough,
Love Me Tomorrow is your perfect read."
Jennifer Chen, author of *Anatomy of an Ex*

"This magically moving, quickly paced
tale is an ideal escapist read for fans of high-concept
love stories and time-bending shenanigans."
Publishers Weekly

"Charming, funny, time-traveling romance."
Kirkus

Love Me Tomorrow

EMIKO JEAN

SIMON & SCHUSTER
London   New York   Amsterdam/Antwerp   Sydney/Melbourne   Toronto   New Delhi

First published in Great Britain in 2026 by
Simon & Schuster UK Ltd

First published in the USA in 2026 by Sarah Barley Books,
an imprint of Simon & Schuster Children's Publishing Division,
1230 Avenue of the Americas, New York, New York 10020

Text copyright © Alloy Entertainment, LLC and
Emiko Jean 2026. All rights reserved.

This book is copyright under the Berne Convention.
No reproduction without permission.
All rights reserved.

The right of Alloy Entertainment, LLC and Emiko Jean to be identified as the author of this work has been asserted by them in accordance with sections 77 and 78 of the Copyright, Designs and Patents Act, 1988.

1 3 5 7 9 10 8 6 4 2

Simon & Schuster UK Ltd
1st Floor, 222 Gray's Inn Road
London WC1X 8HB

For more than 100 years, Simon & Schuster has championed authors and the stories they create. By respecting the copyright of an author's intellectual property, you enable Simon & Schuster and the author to continue publishing exceptional books for years to come. We thank you for supporting the author's copyright by purchasing an authorized edition of this book. No amount of this book may be reproduced or stored in any format, nor may it be uploaded to any website, database, language-learning model, or other repository, retrieval, or artificial intelligence system without express permission. All rights reserved. Inquiries may be directed to Simon & Schuster, 222 Gray's Inn Road, London WC1X 8HB or RightsMailbox@simonandschuster.co.uk

www.simonandschuster.co.uk
www.simonandschuster.com.au
www.simonandschuster.co.in

The authorised representative in the EEA is Simon & Schuster Netherlands BV,
Herculesplein 96, 3584 AA Utrecht, Netherlands. info@simonandschuster.nl

Simon & Schuster Australia, Sydney
Simon & Schuster India, New Delhi

A CIP catalogue record for this book is available from the British Library.

PB ISBN 978-1-3985-5571-6
eBook ISBN 978-1-3985-5572-3
eAudio ISBN 978-1-3985-5573-0

This book is a work of fiction. Names, characters, places and incidents are either the product of the author's imagination or are used fictitiously. Any resemblance to actual people living or dead, events or locales is entirely coincidental.

Printed and Bound in the UK using 100% Renewable Electricity at CPI Group (UK) Ltd

For all the girls who don't believe love can last

PROLOGUE

There used to be a photograph of the day my parents were married on our mantel. The frame was white abalone, the picture a close-up of them pressed together in an orange booth of a doughnut shop. In it, they hand-fed each other maple bars in lieu of wedding cake, their ring fingers newly anointed with plain silver bands purchased at a pawn shop.

Money was tight. Dad was writing his first book; Mom was cleaning houses. A big wedding wasn't in the budget, so they headed to the courthouse. A judge married them between speeding ticket hearings. Afterward they skipped hand in hand to Bavarian Bliss and asked the baker to snap their photograph.

When I was little, I'd hold the picture, rub their faces with my thumbs, and ask them to tell me the story again. "How did you two meet?"

Clearly, they adored each other.

So it was a mystery to me when it all fell apart, why the love went away.

There were probably signs. But at age eleven, I had failed to catalog them. I didn't see the bridges catch fire and start burning—"whiplash" is the right word for the morning my parents sat me down and said they were separating. Dad moved out the same day.

Months passed by. The rain started in Seattle. Dad didn't come home. In fact, he signed a new lease, moving from his temporary executive apartment to a more permanent residence—the Glenn. That day Mom was in the kitchen, trying hard not to cry. I don't think she wanted me to see her sad. Our brokenness settled in.

I wanted to fix her, fix our family, and I believed I could. I slipped out the back door and biked across town, tears spilling and mixing with the rain while I pumped my legs all the way to the Glenn. To apartment 27.

It was nearly evening when I knocked.

Dad answered, surprise flashing in his expression. Leaves swirled, blowing into the entryway and settling as he let me in.

I sat on his new couch, something velvet and hard that still smelled like factory chemicals. It wasn't at all like our cozy furniture at home that had absorbed the smells of made-from-scratch meals and the weight of our bodies after Friday-night movie marathons.

I felt so out of place. And Dad looked so out of place. It was like nothing in this apartment could ever hold the imprint of me or us.

"Please," I begged on a rough gasp. "Come home."

I made messy promises. To always brush my teeth, to go to bed on time, to clear my plate after dinner, to remember to empty my lunch box. I promised to be good, to be better.

I cried, and Dad cried too. He held my hands, wiped my tears, and gently told me, "No. I'm sorry, honey. I can't."

And I understood then what it was like to love and lose.

This was the landscape of heartbreak, and from that day forward I vowed never to step foot into it again.

A door slammed shut then, only to be pried open my senior year of high school.

Everything would change that year.

The year of the notes.

CHAPTER ONE

It began with a wish.

Wait.

Not exactly. I take that back. It began with granny panties. Yeah, that's more like it.

Looking back, I, Emma Nakamura-Thatcher, would say my love story began with a set of full-back underwear.

It was summer, a random weekday afternoon, and I had landed in the place I'd spent most of my teenage years avoiding: the lingerie department with my mother. Suffice it to say a part of me did not want to be there. And that part was all of me.

Chin tucked down, I hummed along with the Muzak, skirting the outer aisle, checking out bralettes with matching lace panties. Deeper in, my mom dug through a bargain bin. I did my best to project a not-with-her vibe.

"How about these?" Mom clutched a pack of generic-brand undies. Strands of black hair clung to her forehead. She was working up a sweat. Outstanding. "They're on sale. Half off."

Blood rushed to my face. I zipped to my mom's side, cataloging the humiliation fallout. There were two other people in the lingerie department: a golden-ager in thick glasses examining undershirts, and the girl behind the register, who exuded cool—magenta bangs, tiny nose ring, thick winged eyeliner.

Luckily, neither of them noticed Mom's excitement, which wasn't in her smile but in her eyes, intense and damn near rabid.

"Well?" Mom asked at my approach.

I studied the pack of underwear in Mom's hands, then shifted to the bin. "I dunno," I murmured, picking through the piles and considering other options. My hand closed around an alternative—red, lacy, dead sexy.

What kind of girl wore this type of underwear? A pretty, adventurous girl.

Was I that girl? Nope. Not even close.

I was seventeen years old, ate the same thing for lunch every day, and had been kissed two times.

The first kiss was in middle school. In eighth grade, with Liam Huxley on a playground. I was in a swing, he bent down, and our noses bumped. He tried some tongue, and honestly, not impressed. I darted away and avoided him the rest of the year, easy since we were in different halls, he in A and I in B—practically worlds apart. The fates continued to smile down on me when we went to different high schools.

The second kiss was at the beach. With Brandon. No last names. He was a local, lived in town, and I was on vacation with my mom. We spent the whole weekend sneaking off into the sand dunes. Hidden in the blades of the high grass, I learned a lot. Five out of five stars. I was someone else there—a different Emma, inhibitions eroded away by the roar of the tide and the salt in the air. Insert wistful sigh here.

Liam and Brandon were easy to leave. Each relationship had

a limited shelf life. And as a classic risk-averse kind of girl, I didn't drink after the sell-by date.

"Emma?"

I blinked. "Sorry. What?"

Mom shook her head. "I said not those." Her face was makeup-free, her hands chapped from the chemicals she used to clean houses. "They look synthetic." She plucked the red scrap of lace from my hands, rubbed her thumbs over the crotch, *over the crotch*, and inspected the label. A tongue cluck followed. "One hundred percent polyester. You need cotton underwear. It's breathable." Mom tossed the panties back into the bin and fisted the full-backs. "We'll get these."

Well. That settled that. I trailed her to the cash register.

"Find everything okay?" The checkout girl scanned the pack of underwear, eyes flitting to Mom. A gold pin applied to her crop top stated her name: Camille.

"Yes." Mom dug around in her purse, the leather aged and worn away at the handles and bottom. "We don't need a bag. I brought my own." She produced a crinkled plastic sack and placed it on the counter.

A few years back the State of Washington had passed an eight-cent charge to curb the single use of plastic and paper bags. Ever since, a whole cupboard in our kitchen had been dedicated to one large plastic bag filled with a bunch of rolled-up smaller plastic bags, the size of a watermelon and the density of a tumor.

A corner of Camille's mouth tugged up, and I dropped my gaze in a quick burst of embarrassment.

All set, Mom handed me the plastic bag, and I folded it against my body.

As we left, I was careful not to make eye contact with anyone. Part of my high-level degree in blending in.

This was my life: safe, predictable, easily forgotten.

The parking garage was packed when we got to Mom's car, an old Volvo with crank windows and fabric seats whose glory days were circa 1999.

I unlocked the doors and climbed into the driver's side. Mom followed, settling into the passenger seat. The interior smelled of coffee and old cereal.

I was backing out when Mom announced, "I registered you for the Sherwood Institute last night."

"What?" I braked hard.

The van waiting behind us honked.

Mom frowned at me. "Pay attention."

I eased my foot off the brake and drove ahead. "How do you even know about Sherwood?"

Mom crossed her arms. "Mr. Lebanon emailed me. He was wondering why you hadn't finished your paperwork. I said you hadn't mentioned any paperwork. We hopped on a phone call. The Sherwood Institute is an excellent opportunity, Emma."

I couldn't argue with that. Sherwood was a performing arts college-prep program and hosted after-school intensives every fall. Space was limited, the spots competitively vied for. At the end of the program, there was a performance where each student played a solo. Scouts from major music institutions and universities were invited to watch and sip warm punch at a mixer afterward.

I should have been thrilled when Mr. Lebanon, my music teacher, mentioned Sherwood in the spring. He'd recommended me and sent in a video of my last recital. The admissions committee had replied with an avid yes, but my pragmatic self couldn't mirror their enthusiasm. I was bound for community college or the University of Washington. Somewhere close to home where I'd study business or education—a solid track to a future job.

"You love to play the violin," Mom rolled on.

Again, I could not argue. The first song I ever played was "Hot Cross Buns" on the recorder in kindergarten. I was obsessed. It was "Hot Cross Buns" in the living room. "Hot Cross Buns" under my covers at night. "Hot Cross Buns" in the empty bathtub, because even then I could sense where the best acoustics were in the house.

Under duress and marveling at my sudden obsession, my folks took me to the Music Factory. Dad placed his hands on my shoulders and said, "Choose." I ran my fingers over the flutes, plucked the strings of guitars, beat drums, and stopped in front of the violin. My world went still and quiet, as if I'd been summoned.

I've been playing the violin ever since.

"Mr. Lebanon believes you may be able to get a scholarship to music school."

I watched Mom sift through her purse to find a tube of Voltaren, and my decision to stay home firmly settled. She needed me.

The last few months her hands had gotten worse. I'd had to help out more around the house, sub in for cleaning jobs when her fingers wouldn't straighten. There was no way I'd leave her in order to chase some impossible dream of playing the violin in college, only to submit to the constant grind afterward. Full-time professional violinist gigs were as scarce as toilet paper during the pandemic.

I kept my eyes on the road, my mind on deflection. "I can't believe you talked to him."

"He's a nice man, and he has a nice voice. Is he a singer? I bet he can sing."

I did not care for her dreamy tone. "Ew."

She went on, emboldened. "I bet he has kind eyes, too."

I opened my mouth and shut it abruptly, slapped into awareness. Mom's smile died too. The mood in the car plummeted to zero degrees. Coming up on our right was the Glenn, an apartment complex built around an old park with a burn-your-skin-off-in-the-summer metal slide. It was also where my dad had lived during the divorce.

Damn it.

I'd forgotten to take the detour.

In my peripheral vision I could see Mom, her jaw locked tight. A silent memory passed between us . . .

Me riding my bike in the rain, begging Dad to come home. Mom was frantic when she finally found me, drenched and sobbing on Dad's new couch, yellow price tag still attached. The three of us huddled in that apartment, trapped in a deep crater of misery.

Mom waited until the Glenn was in the rearview mirror before speaking. "You're going to Sherwood."

Spine rigid, I flicked on the blinker to turn left and started to try to convince her that Sherwood was not in our best interest. "Mom—"

She sliced her hand through the air, not a fan of my attitude or of being challenged. "End of discussion." She stared out the side window. "Trust me. I'm doing you a favor."

Life is a series of choices. Unless the choice is made for you.

CHAPTER TWO

I was still in a huff when we pulled into the driveway.

My parents had bought our house, a fixer-upper, before I was born. Fast-forward years later, and the 1940s bungalow was still a fixer-upper. The outside was peeling paint, brick, and chipped shiplap. The inside was lath and plaster walls, antique brass lights, and pinewood floors still sticky with glue from when my dad pulled up the carpet—beware of the rusty nail near the top stair.

"I'm going across the street." Mom dropped the tube of Voltaren into her purse. "Here. Take my bag inside and let Theo and Jiji know we're home."

I fumbled with the keys, still not talking.

Mom jabbed my side. "Did you hear me?"

"Yes. Got it. I'll take your purse inside."

She gave me a final doubtful look and climbed out of the car.

I found Theo in the kitchen, digging around in the cupboard where we kept cereal, cookies, and canned goods.

"Hey," he said, nose deep in, T-shirt stretching taut over his shoulders. "How come I can't find the Oreos?"

I used to call Theo "Teddy" because as a kid, he resembled my favorite stuffed bear—round cheeks, rectangular glasses, button nose, tight, curly hair.

He was anything but now.

His transformation had happened all at once. First went the braces, followed by a six-inch growth spurt. Then came the contacts. When I saw him without glasses, it threw me for a loop, like I was seeing him naked. Each part of his face exposed—shrewd eyes, sharp jaw, sardonic grin. I realized then, Theo Beckett was cute.

I dumped the keys, Mom's purse, and the shopping bag on the counter.

Theo was my age and had lived next door since before I could remember. Somewhere in the bowels of the Becketts' family room closet was a box of compromising photographs of the two of us. Highlights included splashing in the bathtub at three years old, bubbles to our ears; dressing up as a bottle of soy sauce and a pot of rice for Halloween when we were four; and last but not least, waiting outside the emergency room at age eight—when Theo had to get a stitch after I stabbed him with a fork for taking the last slice of double-pineapple pizza. The maiming did not work. He still stole my food.

"You can't find them because I hid them." It was easier speaking to his turned back.

"Unscrupulous woman." He shut the cupboard and turned. Crossing his arms, he shot me a dimpled grin, and my heart flipped over with a sigh. "You are inherently distrustful," he added, then jerked his chin toward the bag on the counter. "Need help bringing anything else in?"

More than a few times Theo had skipped out his front door,

seeing Mom and me struggling with groceries. He'd haul them in, glasses slipping down his nose, winded by a jug of milk.

But that was before.

I could not square that boy, my childhood best friend, with what he'd become: a hot nerd hybrid with a 4.2 GPA who was on track for early admission to Caltech. All the while reading thick books with dragons on the covers, running a couple of miles a day, and spending the rest of his time playing online games, cursing into a giant headset, threatening to punch opponents in the nuts.

"No. This is it. Where's Jiji?" I asked.

"Dozed off on the couch." Theo pointed over his shoulder with his thumb.

I peeked through the saloon doors, an addition from the previous owner in the seventies, into the living room.

Jiji, my grandfather, was sleeping sitting up, chin tucked to his chest, eyes closed, lightly snoring. A news network was on, volume set to blow your eardrums out. Jiji didn't like wearing his hearing aids. I crept into the living room and turned the noise down.

The sight of Jiji, sleeping in the late afternoon, sunlight pooled on the floor around him, only intensified my determination to stay close to home after graduation.

My grandfather had come to live with us during the divorce. He was there to help, to look after me. But around when I turned fifteen, Jiji started eating less and sleeping more. These days I covered him with blankets, made his meals, brought his medication to him with a full glass of water. He was mine to take care of now. I didn't mind. At all, actually. Love and duty were the same in this instance.

"I fed him mozzarella sticks and chicken nuggets," Theo said when I faced the kitchen again. "He did *not* think it was funny when I pointed out the meal was distinctly monotone."

A few plates were in the sink, and I loaded them into the dishwasher. "Thanks for keeping an eye on him."

"No problem. I love him. Even though I am sure he does not love me. When I sat at the table with him, he told me, 'Not so close.'" Theo lowered his voice to mimic Jiji's deep baritone.

I wiped my hands on a towel and faced him with a wince. "I'm sorry."

Jiji could be ill-tempered. He hated the internet and refused to understand why people didn't drink regular coffee anymore. He grew visibly agitated at the idea of parkour being a sport. Most of the time he pretended he didn't speak English.

Theo laughed, grinned wide. "It's no problem."

I gave him a begrudging smile. "The Oreos are behind the Raisin Bran."

His look was a mixture of impressed and proud. "Clever."

Theo hated raisins and had sworn against eating shriveled, dried fruit ever again after choking on a prune at his grandmother's house.

He whistled low, finding the cookies. "Regular. I was hoping for Double Stuf. We're really cutting corners here now." He tucked the package under his arm and checked his watch. "I've got to head out. I have a raid in half an hour."

With that, I recognized him again and remembered what we were to each other: friends, and sometimes, good-natured enemies.

Last summer I'd sat on the floor day after day, watching him play games, practicing my violin while he searched for a golden acorn. I'd played "Ode to Joy" when he unearthed it. I'd ramped up the tempo as his avatar grew wings and lifted into the sky, bathed in a celestial light.

I followed him out the door. "Have fun foraging for nuts and berries."

Theo stopped in his tracks and reversed course until we stood toe to toe. He was a good head taller than me now and had to look down to find my eyes. His were hazel, and up close you could tell where the brown blended to green—dirt into moss.

He tsked. "That sounded super condescending, Emma. Especially for someone who dresses like an elderly gentleman who perpetually feels a draft." He pressed the Oreos into my hands, our fingers brushing. I stifled a flutter in my belly. "Normally, I'd take these, but your outfit is so sad, I'm going to have pity and leave them with you."

I frowned.

He was right that I was a fan of old things—music, vintage clothing, people.

The mustard shirt I was wearing belonged to Jiji. My grandmother had chosen it for him. I still remembered that Christmas. Watching Jiji kneel by the tree and unwrap the shirt, his face caught in the crosshairs of joy and love. Behind him, my grandmother smiled. Mom and Dad and me, too. Our happiness glowing brighter than the tree. I was seven. This was before my grandmother died of breast cancer, before my dad packed his bags and drove away.

How nice it would be to go back to that moment. I might stay in that Christmas morning forever. It was the last time we were a family. The last time I felt truly whole. Solid. Unbreakable.

"My outfit isn't so bad." I glowered at him.

He quirked a lazy smile. "Wow. Not so bad. Way to set the bar high."

His thumb moved, and my gaze dragged to his hands, now touching mine. Silence pulsed between us.

Abruptly we pushed away from each other. He cupped the back of his neck, hung his head. "Um," he said. "I gotta . . . I'm going."

He was out the door before I came to.

CHAPTER THREE

"Plainclothes police." Jiji nodded at a lanky man stripping the meat from a yakitori stick with his teeth, keeping his eyes leveled on the crowd.

We'd come downtown for Tanabata, the festival of stars. The Seattle Japanese Garden was festooned with brightly colored paper in the shapes of kimonos, cranes, streamers, and lanterns. Sticky-fingered, mochi-eating kids darted over wooden bridges. Couples strolled arm in arm. The mood was chaotic, buoyant.

I loved it.

I turned to Jiji. Despite the homicidally hot weather, Jiji shuffled alongside me in glaringly white, thick-soled tennis shoes, a lightweight Members Only jacket, and a slightly oversized driving cap, like he was daring the sun to give him heatstroke.

Officially, my grandfather used to work for a phone company. Unofficially, he worked for an organization subcontracted by the US government. He often dropped hints at a second life beyond that of the loving father and husband who worked nine to five.

Evidence Jiji was an international spy:

When my mom was a kid, Jiji disappeared for long periods. Nobody knew where he went. My grandmother had a number to call only in case of emergencies. When he returned, it was often with gifts from other countries—Spanish silver, Murano glass, Russian nesting dolls.

Mom also said Jiji once sat through an entire dinner with a suitcase handcuffed to his wrist. He didn't mention it. Nobody asked about it.

He often pointed out where hidden security cameras were located and how to lose a tail if you were being pursued.

His favorite movie was *Bridge of Spies*, but mostly to poke holes through the plot and details, like pointing out that the actual CIA building looked "nothing like that."

When I was younger, we played a game where we pretended to be lost in a forest or jungle, any sort of hostile landscape. Jiji taught me how to build a fire, boil water for drinking, and forage for food—e.g., the wild blueberries growing near an abandoned house down the street. As long as I was dry and warm, I was safe.

And last, I once found a note, hidden in a box of keepsakes at the back of his closet, from a former secretary of state thanking Jiji for a "personal" favor.

"Cool," I replied as we passed the suspected plainclothes cop, moving deeper into the garden. I knew better than to ask him to elaborate. Jiji had a weird way of turning your questions back on you. Mind tricks.

"Hai," he agreed.

"You okay? Want me to grab your cane from the car?"

Jiji waved a hand. "Eh."

My grandfather was sparse with words. But spend enough time with him, and you learned to interpret his "ehs." In this case, *No thank you.*

"Emma?" My name floated by on my left. The voice was slightly familiar, high pitched, and unsure.

I turned.

A woman stopped in front of me. She pressed her hands to her chest, nails painted bright pink. "Candice Johnson. From Prospect Street."

Prospect Street. Right. The Johnsons. We cleaned their house. They had three kids. A playroom that appeared as if a hurricane of vomiting cows had passed through. Garbage cans near overflowing. And ornamental Buddha heads everywhere.

She smiled hesitantly at me. People were funny about stating directly that they had a maid, and danced around the actual words. Instead of *It's Candice Johnson, you clean our house*, it's *Candice Johnson from Prospect Street*. Dot, dot, dot.

"Hi." I pasted on a friendly smile, part of my work uniform. "Candice. Of course."

She pulled on a man wearing old water-stained Birkenstocks and a Grateful Dead T-shirt. "This is my husband, Trent. You remember Emma, right?" she said to him. "She and her mom come to our house on Thursday afternoons."

"To clean," I clarified.

"Right," Trent was saying. "Nice to see you, Emma." He rocked back on his heels.

Silence ensued. Behind them, their towheaded kids bellied up to a calligraphy table and used the brushes as swords.

"Oh," I said into the thick, expectant quiet. "This is Jiji. My grandfather."

Their smiles grew. Both bowed to Jiji. "It's nice to meet you."

Jiji kept his back straight, his presence commanding. "Based on the man's slouch, receding hairline, and pale color, I suspect he has a vitamin deficiency," he said in Japanese.

I pretended to translate. "He says it's nice to meet you."

Candice's smile doubled in size, as did Trent's. "Isn't this festival fantastic? We come every year. Trent and I went to Japan before we had kids and loved it."

"The food. The land. The people, all so beautiful," said Trent with great fanfare.

"Eh," Jiji grumbled, and wandered away. Translation: *I've had enough*.

"Where are you from?" Candice's eyes searched my face.

Their kids were kicking pea-sized gravel at one another now.

"Me?" The word came out on a squeak, reflecting how awkward I felt. "I'm from here. I mean, I grew up in Seattle, the same as my mom. My dad is white." Though people never cared about that. "My great-great-grandparents left Japan when they were married."

"Fascinating." Trent examined me like an artifact, eyebrows raised. "Why did—"

My phone rang, and I pulled it from my pocket. Dad was calling. "Sorry, I'd better take this." I waved the phone at them. "Nice seeing you."

I jogged off and answered. "Dad."

"Honey?"

I moved to a quieter section. "I'm here."

Jiji was near the tea pavilion, hands behind his back, speaking to a volunteer.

"How are you?"

"I'm good," I said, chipper.

"Where are you? It's very loud."

"I'm at the Japanese garden with Jiji. It's Tanabata. I should probably go. Can I call you back?"

Jiji was on the move, strolling over some moss-covered stones toward the bamboo grove. I followed him at a distance, heart tripping with worry, wishing he'd use a cane.

"I wanted to see if you would come to dinner at my place in a few weeks." He gave me the exact date and time.

I jolted, surprised at the invitation, which was so far away, more than a month, and sounded weirdly formal.

Dad and I had a pretty good relationship. He was around a lot, considering. I used to go to his house every other week, but since high school started, we hung out more on Fridays or Saturdays. Weekends were easier. Usually we got takeout and watched movies, eating on the couch.

I chewed my lip, thinking. "Um, sure, I can do that."

"Great," he said brightly. "I want you to meet Madison. I think we're at that point. She's out of town visiting her sister for a couple weeks. Then her daughter goes on this annual trip to New York with her dad. Anyway, it's kind of impossible to get everyone in the same place at the same time. That's the soonest they're both available."

I slowed my steps, digesting that information. Dad had had a few girlfriends over the years. Nothing long-term. But I'd been hearing Madison's name for a while—maybe six months, give or take a few weeks. She had a daughter around my age and was an ER doctor.

I had mostly heard about her in passing and hadn't paid much attention. I would nod vaguely when he chattered about what they'd been up to. Like, *Cool. Awesome. Middle-aged dating, such a thrill.* But now it seemed I should have paid more attention. Now my dad and Madison seemed serious.

I agreed to the time, hung up, and stayed put for a moment. It's not that I didn't *want* Dad to have a relationship. I wanted him to be happy. So why the weird, heavy feeling in my stomach? Why the wariness at the thought of Dad falling in love again?

Tamping down the sense of foreboding, I sought out Jiji. He'd positioned himself at a foldout table.

"You really left me hanging back there with the Johnsons." The sun had lowered in the sky, and everything was tipped in gold and pink. "Whatever happened to 'never leave a man behind'?"

Jiji ignored me. Pen in hand, he dashed out words onto a strip of bright-colored paper. Other pieces hung from the stalks of bamboo, gently flapping in the wind. They were tanzaku, wishes—the heart of Tanabata. My grandmother's favorite holiday.

This was why we came. For her.

I had only hazy memories of my grandmother, glimpses captured in flickering yellow light and silent like an old home movie. When she smiled and cupped my cheek. Playing the piano in their old house in Sacramento. Because she'd loved music too.

She'd been a gentle spirit, the love of Jiji's life.

Jiji finished writing and drilled a finger into the table, indicating I should make a wish too.

I stuck up my hands. "I'm good." Wishes weren't my thing.

"For your grandmother."

Smooth move. Very well played.

I grabbed a pen and a strip of paper, scowling at the blank tanzaku. The Tanabata legend—the one about Orihime and

Hikoboshi, that cautionary tale dressed up as romance—pressed against my thoughts. She'd been fine alone, weaving at the edge of the universe, until her father, the king of the heavens, decided loneliness was something that needed fixing. So he arranged a marriage for her with a cow herder. And maybe it did ruin them, that love. It made them forget themselves so completely that Orihime's threads became floods and Hikoboshi's cows trampled through heaven.

The king's punishment, casting them back to opposite banks of the Milky Way, almost seemed merciful. One meeting a year. The seventh day of the seventh month. Just enough to remember what burned between them, never enough to let it consume everything again.

I wish, I wrote, and paused. The pen trembled against the paper as my thoughts turned toward my grandparents—how Jiji still carried my grandmother in his bones. To my parents, who'd adored each other until they didn't. And then to Dad with Madison, ready to try again despite all evidence that love was just a prettier word for eventual grief. Did love always die out, fade away? I hoped not, but hope felt thin against history.

I wish for proof, I continued, the words bleeding dark against the bright paper. *Show me that love is real. That love can last.*

"Ready?" I hooked my arm through Jiji's, and together we walked toward the bamboo, the memory of my grandmother thick on our skin.

We tied our wishes to the tallest leaf within reach and stepped back. I smacked a kiss on his bicep through his jacket, wanting him to live forever. He patted my hand, like, *There, there, that's enough. Your emotions are overwhelming.*

Waning summer heat pressed against our heads. A gust of wind swept through the garden, whipping the tethered paper around. Another, more violent gust followed on its heels. Festival-goers ducked, hands over their heads, as specks of dirt flew through the air.

But something drew my attention up. A shooting star darted across the sky. Impossible this time of day, but I swore I saw it. An arc of light gone in a blink.

Now I wonder if it might have been Orihime, winking at me, secretly smiling. Ready to split the universe open and stitch something new.

CHAPTER FOUR

Summer dwindled, senior year fast approached, and Mom sent me to Yarrow Point, a ritzy town outside Seattle, for a cleaning gig. Here the homes were estates, an apple cost twelve dollars, and the dogs were purebred. Note the two Weimaraners walking across the street, jaunty tails piercing the air.

I parked my LeSabre, Jiji's car gifted to me after he couldn't drive anymore, alongside the curb and squinted up at the house. It was one of those modern marvels made of metal and glass, pretty typical for the area. The windows showcased a straight shot through the gray-and-lavender living room to the pool in the backyard. Beyond that, Lake Washington glittered in the sun like a precious gem.

Yep. This was how the other half lived.

I hauled myself up the driveway, set my buckets down at the doorstep, and punched out a text to Theo: **This house is huge. Any interest in helping me clean today? I will not split the money with you. But you'll get the pleasure of my company for an afternoon.**

Theo replied ten seconds later: **Hard pass.**

When Theo and I were little, our moms shared childcare.

I'd go with Theo and his mom during her French lessons. Theo would go with me and my mom to clean houses. He'd never admit it now, but he loved figure skating back then. He'd put yellow microfiber cloths under his shoes and "skate" around the houses. He even made us call him Ripp, after Adam Rippon, for a while.

I sent Theo a thumbs-down, slipped my phone into my back pocket, and knocked.

A man decked out entirely in Lycra and one of those aerodynamic helmets opened the front door.

One of the owners, I presumed.

Air-conditioning blasted me in the face, and I swooned internally. Our house didn't have AC except for a box unit we kept in the living room window. Marble floors, heated toilets, and imported cabinets from Italy did nothing for me. But central air-conditioning—try living without it, and you'll have a new appreciation for HVAC systems.

The man tapped his left lobe, indicating earbuds, and pointed down the hall. "Bill, you SOB. How are you?" he boomed, clip-clopping past me and out of the house to stand beside a bike with a skinny seat in the driveway.

All right, then.

I picked up my bucket and stepped inside. "Hello?" I called, winding my way into the kitchen to find a middle-aged woman wearing little gold hoops in her ears and minimal makeup.

"Hi. You must be Emma. I'm Jennifer." She smiled, dusting a hand over the island, a seamless slab of dove-gray marble. "I spoke with your mom on the phone about the house, and she said you could give me a time estimate when you arrived."

I gripped the bucket and assessed the space. "If the rest of the house is in the same shape as these rooms, probably around six hours."

Disappointment tried to furrow Jennifer's smooth forehead. Botox, most likely. But super well done. Kudos to her and her dermatologist. "Do you think you could do it in four? We're having company, and the caterers will get here around then."

"Sure!" I chirped. Because there was only one correct answer to the question—an enthusiastic yes. *No problem. I'm excited. Best day of my life, I promise. It totally won't take a miracle.*

"Great." Jennifer seal-clapped. "I'll give you a little something extra for your trouble."

At that, I swooned anew. Four hours was sounding better and better. I could totally be bought.

Two hours in, I'd cleaned almost the entire upstairs—the primary suite with buttery linens, a guest bathroom outfitted with Turkish towels and a heated toilet seat.

I was hustling.

Wisps of hair stuck to my sweaty face. I paused in a bedroom, positioned under a vent and stretched the collar of my shirt to balloon with cool air. Staring out the window at the turquoise pool and sapphire lake, I wondered what Mrs. St. James might do if I had a little swim. I smiled, just imagining her face. Not that I would ever.

My phone dinged. Mom had texted: **Sherwood confirmed your registration. All set. First session is the second week of school.**

My mouth edged into a frown.

"Hey."

At the deep male voice, I startled. My phone tumbled from my hands, dropping between the nightstand and the wall, landing with a muted thud on the plush carpet.

"Damn it," I swore, and knelt, squeezing my arm behind the piece of furniture.

Footsteps, and the voice again. "Sorry. Let me help." He was close, so close I could smell him—peppermint, tuberose, a touch of musk. The scent of money.

With a grunt, I closed my fist around the phone and yanked. "Got it."

Still in a crouch, I looked up. Way up.

This guy was huge, tall and brawny, blocking off the rest of the room. Slowly he blinked into focus. Jade-green eyes fringed with dark, thick lashes. Equally thick sandy, wavy hair with golden highlights. Tan skin, not from working in the heat, but from drifting on a boat. A yacht tan.

He squinted down at me anxiously. "Are you all right?"

"Fine." Nerves rising, I shot up, only to be immediately struck dizzy. My head would have collided with his chin if he hadn't stepped back. Wobbling, and on the verge of a Victorian-style fainting spell, I steadied myself with a palm on the nightstand.

"Get her a chair," another male voice chimed in.

Over the first boy's shoulder I spotted a near duplicate. His face was cast in sharp angles. He looked broodier, slightly smaller. But they had the same eyes and hair. Twins.

I straightened my shirt self-consciously. "I'm good." To prove it, I swooped down, grabbed my yellow microfiber rag from the floor, and wiped the nightstand. Imagine my great chagrin when he stayed put.

Then again, why should he have moved?

Most of the time, I didn't pay much attention to the rooms as I cleaned. My focus was on dust, the trash, and folding sheets into hospital corners. But then I noted the navy comforter, the large television with video game consoles (which probably cost three months' worth of paychecks), and the sweatshirt, slung over the desk chair, from Clearview Prep—a private school with spectacular views of the sound and a student population whose families had a minimum net worth of ten million.

Definitely a teen boy's room. So, fair. I was in his space.

Still, this teen boy and his clone were clearly violating the house cleaner–client agreement—in which each party carefully skirts around the other, pretending they don't exist. A relationship dynamic attributed to house cleaners knowing the most intimate and secret details of their clients' lives. The couple on the brink of divorce. What families' kids were suspended from school. The newlyweds with an ultrasound photograph pinned to the fridge one week, then a week later stuck to the back of a picture of an angel on their mantel. (I didn't charge them for that clean.) The widow who lived in a near-spotless neoclassical mansion on Seattle's Millionaire's Row, owned a dog that looked more rodent than canine, and always made you sit down for a cup of tea before you vacuumed. Her name was Mrs. Sydney, and I liked her the best.

"I'm Colin," the boy closer to me said.

"Let's go," his brother grouched, basketball tucked under his arm.

Colin stepped back as if to leave, and relief rushed through me. That's right. *Go.*

But then he paused. Stayed put. "That's Sebastian, my brother. He's kind of moody," he whispered as if in apology.

"Dude." Sebastian's face twisted.

"He knows it's true. Along with being mercurial, he's also incredibly rigid. When we go on road trips, he marks where all the available restrooms are on the map. Not a single fun bone in his body." Colin smiled lazily, something naughty in his eyes.

"Leave her alone and let her do her job," said Sebastian. "Let's go."

I gave Colin my own smile, tight and restrained. "Nice to meet you both." By which I meant the opposite. It was not nice to meet them or to be in the middle of their weird sibling dynamic.

"Hold on," Colin said with a glance at his brother. He circled back to me.

Such hubris.

I reached under Colin's desk and dumped the trash into a white bag I'd brought upstairs.

Colin's chin tucked down like he was embarrassed. "Just so you know, all those fast-food wrappers in my garbage are from separate occasions. I usually eat very healthy. Green juice? Yes, please."

Sebastian rubbed his pinched brow. "My God, this is painful to watch."

I scooted toward a set of shelves. Colin kept on my heels. "Do you find my brother funny and charming? I didn't exactly explain it, but to be clear, he's emotionally unavailable and takes his laptop to the bathroom with him." A pillow hurtled through the air, hitting Colin square between the shoulders. Colin smoothed back his hair. "He's also prone to fits of violence."

"Don't worry." I kept my attention welded to the bookshelf, littered with rowing trophies and medals, and ran a cloth over an old copy of *Winnie-the-Pooh*, the only book. I paused at the unexpectedness of it. The spine was well worn. I'd always thought Christopher Robin was kind of sad, a lonely boy with imaginary animals for friends. I was so focused on *Pooh*, this surprising detail in his room, I spoke without thinking. "I find both of you equally unappealing." I stopped and closed my eyes, ears ringing. Well, poop. I'd said that out loud. I opened my eyes.

Colin and Sebastian were both struck still, a wave of cold surprise splashing over their faces. Absolutely befuddled.

Sebastian was the first to react, rewarding me with a cock of the head and a slow smirk, as if to say, *Well, goddamn, look at you.*

Mentally, I spiraled, panic setting in. Mrs. St. James would call my mom once she heard I'd insulted her sons. Mom wouldn't care what excuses I gave, like these two boys were entitled, overprivileged, too-big-to-fail, most-likely-child-emperors-in-their-past-lives jerks. All she'd see were the dollars draining from her account.

I clutched the yellow cloth to my chest. "I'm sorry, I shouldn't have said that."

"Of course you should have." Colin's expression was inscrutable. I decided he was definitely high. "Open and honest communication is the foundation of any good relationship. How can I make myself more appealing if I don't know you find me unappealing in the first place? But then again, I shouldn't have to change who I am for you to like me. It *is* slightly problematic." Not untrue. He pursed his lips, and his brow lowered in deep concentration. "I'd say your name here for effect, but I don't know it."

"Emma," I said. "Your house cleaner. And I'm all done here." My steps were light and quick as I crossed the room, picking up the bucket and trash bag on my way out.

"See you next time, Emma," Colin called at my back.

Sebastian murmured something and a scuffle ensued. As I dashed down the stairs, I glimpsed Colin putting his brother in a headlock and giving him the mother of all noogies. Being an only child, I didn't really get siblings. Also, being a girl, I didn't understand the hypermasculine display. All of it was out of my wheelhouse.

I spent the next two hours carefully cleaning the downstairs, avoiding the brothers. I breathed out a sigh of relief when I heard them leave, the sound of the garage door opening and closing. To make sure they were gone, I peeked out the window. Like a true psychopath, Colin was driving a BMW. Sebastian was in the passenger seat.

Finished with one minute to spare, I collected the envelope and checked inside. Five hundred dollars for the cleaning, plus an extra hundred as a tip. Sweet. I tucked the bill into my back pocket and hauled the white trash bag to the side of the house to dump it. The weather was hot and windy. My hair blew in my face as I opened the bin and lobbed the bag inside. The lid slammed shut with a bang.

I stayed put, cooling down for a moment. It was then that I saw it. A scrap of white paper caught in the hedge. A piece of garbage that had escaped?

I plucked it from the leaves and studied the paper, plain and heavy, the kind Delia—my other best friend besides Theo—and I ogled at stationery stores. Delia was an artist and obsessed with paper. She considered the near-translucent sheets from the dollar store in our household printer a cardinal sin.

I flipped the card stock over. On the back, words had been inked in a messy, boyish script.

> If I'm being honest, I loved you from the beginning.

I pulled in a shallow breath, struck by the words, their intensity.

For one insane second I entertained the idea, imagined being loved that way. An ache clawed up my throat and I swallowed it back—

No.

Words like this weren't meant for me.

I crumpled the note and threw it away, leaving it in the yawning darkness of the garbage can.

CHAPTER FIVE

Before the Glenn, when my parents first separated, my dad rented one of those executive apartments for short stays. You know the kind—prefurnished, economically equipped with the basics. Mom dropped me off every other weekend. I pretended not to see her park down the street and weep. And I definitely never told her that I liked going over there. It was fun, a vacation of sorts. We'd go to the movies. He'd let me buy the candy Mom wouldn't. We'd get takeout from one of the three restaurants within walking distance—Happy Teriyaki, Go Go Pizza, or Best Burger.

Food growing cold, I'd sit at the laminate table made to look like wood, watching as he opened cabinet after cabinet, searching for glasses and plates. "I just can't seem to get the hang of this place," he'd say, then add, "But hopefully, I won't be here for long."

Of course he wouldn't. Soon he'd move back in. Soon he'd be home. Mom and Dad were still wearing their wedding rings at this point. My hope wasn't totally delusional.

Anyhoo, I remember there were four of everything in the kitchen. Four plates. Four forks. Four spoons. Four knives. Four dish towels.

In Japan four is an unlucky number. The way it's spoken sounds like the word for "death." Some buildings in Japan don't even have a fourth floor.

I thought about it after my dad moved out of the executive apartment and signed a four-year lease at the Glenn. The number four. Death. Divorce.

Cut to me now—sitting in my car, parked along the curb at Dad's recently purchased townhouse I'd helped him choose, prepping to meet Madison and her daughter. I heaved breaths in and out, pushing down unease. Change wasn't always my friend.

My dad chose that exact moment to open the front door.

He stood at the threshold, hands in his pockets. Light flooded the front step, and I saw him clearly—full head of hair giving way to gray at the temples, blue eyes that I wished I'd inherited instead of my mother's muddy brown. "Emma," he said loud enough for his voice to carry to the car. "You coming in?"

I opened the car door, smiled, and drew my shoulders up to my ears. "Sorry I'm late."

I'd cleaned the Johnsons' house that afternoon and spent too long on some glittery goop stuck in their carpet. Then I'd cleaned Mrs. Sydney's house. We'd had English breakfast tea and cucumber sandwiches while flipping through an album of photos from her first marriage, to Gary, a stuntman in Hollywood.

I moseyed up the steps to meet my dad.

"Hey," he said, followed by a loose side hug. "Good to see you."

I was carrying an old denim messenger bag, on which I'd sewn a patch that had a violin and read, What the Pluck.

I inched up an eyebrow. He was acting weird. Jittery. "You too."

"Come in. Come in." He moved us into the house and shut the door.

Music played low from speakers positioned higher up on the wall. The air reeked of onions.

"Did you get new furniture?" I didn't recognize the leather couch and glass coffee table. We'd seen each other the past month but had met for lunch or dinner out. I hadn't been over in a while. Too long, it seemed.

"It's Madison's," he said, doing his best to act casual. "Here, let me take your stuff." Dad slipped the bag from my shoulder and hung it on a coatrack.

"Madison's?"

He shifted, hands on his hips, and dropped his eyes. "Madison and I spent the weekend up north. Have you ever heard of glamping? We were sitting around the fire, talking, and we realized we wanted to live together." A nervous laugh burst out of him. "She still has her place. The lease isn't up for a while. We've been slowly moving some of her things in."

I exhaled a weighty breath, remembering a photograph of an astronaut in space staring through the window at Earth, alone and far away. All the lives being lived down there, and the astronaut not knowing what was happening to the people they loved. That's how I felt. The sting of suddenly realizing how much I had missed. When your parents were divorced, you didn't have all of them anymore. That was a price everyone paid, I guess. We spent more time catching up than we used to have to.

He stared at me with concern. "I know this is a lot to take in. You want to walk around the block, just the two of us?"

I sifted through the information—Dad and Madison were

more serious than I thought—then through my feelings, worry and apprehension. Was he moving too fast? No. Not really. They'd been seeing each other for months. I swallowed against the knot in my throat and forced a smile. "It's okay. I'm happy—"

"Hey, Adrian. I know you asked us to give you a few minutes, but dinner is ready and Mom is sweating bullets while smiling, trying to keep everything warm and perfect. She might spontaneously combust."

The most acute, painful awareness slapped me as Madison's daughter loped into the room.

She wasn't a stranger.

Camille, the girl from the checkout counter at the department store where I'd bought granny panties, was standing in my dad's living room.

Right on cue, she straightened and lifted her chin, brightening. "Hey, I recognize you."

"You've met?" Dad looked between us.

"I was shopping with Mom," I interjected before Camille could. Life lesson: When you can, take control of the narrative. "We met for, like, five seconds."

Madison popped up behind Camille and said, "Camille, I told you to stay put."

Then there were four of us.

That number again. Four.

I assessed Madison in seconds. Petite. Brown hair, with a little pug nose. Lines bracketed her eyes and deepened as she smiled at me.

"You must be Emma. I've heard so much about you." She rolled past her smirking daughter, toward me.

"Emma, meet Madison. Madison, meet Emma," Dad said, placing an arm around Madison's shoulders.

"Hi." My wave mimicked a salute.

"And that's her daughter, Camille, whom you've met already, for, like, five seconds," Dad said. Madison's expression turned quizzical. Dad squeezed her shoulder. "Well, it's official," he announced. "We've all met now."

Smiles of various degrees were passed around. Camille's bordered on cynicism. Mine was, I'm sure, pained. Dad's was oblivious, truly joyful. And Madison's, apprehensive.

The evening proceeded accordingly. We sat down at the table set with checkered place mats and coordinating napkins. A hunk of meat loaf garnished with parsley sat on a platter. Next to it was a bowl of mashed potatoes and a smaller dish of peas and carrots.

"Madison cooked all day for us." Dad whipped out a napkin and placed it on his lap. When he'd rented at the Glenn, we'd used paper towels, and once those ran out, dish towels, to wipe our hands and faces.

"With your help," Madison commented. They shared a love-sick look.

I took a hearty drink of water, finding the whole situation surreal.

Dad and Madison were moving in together. I barely knew her. I'd just *met* her. But her daughter, Camille, knew what kind of underwear I wore. So there was that.

"How domestic." Camille snuck out a hand and popped a piece of diced carrot into her mouth.

"Camille." Madison's face pinched with a reprimand.

Silence, and we passed the food around in the thick of it, spoons clinking against the dishes.

"I'm glad we're finally doing this," Madison said once everyone had portions on their plates. Leaning in, she said to me, "Emma, your dad says you play the violin."

I poked at the loaf with my fork. "I do," I responded, lifting my gaze and halfway wishing for the house to collapse. Camille was making some sort of design in her mashed potatoes, an elaborate labyrinth.

"You go to the Seattle Arts and Music Academy?" she asked.

I looked down at my plate and nodded. I'd been attending SAMA since ninth grade. My first day of senior year was next week. Summer had flown by.

"Camille is a writer," Dad offered when I didn't elaborate. He beamed at Madison's daughter.

Dad was a writer too. He was an author who had published ten bestselling political thrillers. He spent his life plotting stories and chasing character arcs. I understood. Sometimes it was the same for me with the violin, compulsive and obsessive—lost in the art. Nothing else quite measured up.

Camille did not chime in.

Somehow I made it through dinner and the rest of the obligatory get-to-know-you questions. I learned a lot. More than I wanted to. Camille went to Ballard High School. Her dad was a graphic designer and had a loft downtown. Camille lived there full-time because Madison was an ER doctor with irregular hours. That's how Dad met her—doing research for a book at the hospital. On it went.

Last bite still in my mouth, I jumped to clear my plate.

"I'll do the dishes." Without waiting, I scooped up Dad's and Madison's plates.

"Thank you," said Madison. "Camille would love to help you."

A clear code for Camille: *Help Emma right now.*

Dad and Madison took their glasses of wine to the porch.

We all needed a reprieve.

In a strategic move, I turned on the water full force. Conversation would be difficult over the noise. In my peripheral vision I saw Camille wander into the kitchen. She searched the cabinets to find a mug, then poured a couple of inches of red wine into it. Super bold.

I checked the porch. Madison and Dad leaned against the railing, staring outward at the wetland preserve. A blue heron circled and landed in the water. Jiji always said blue herons were sent from my grandmother. That they were a sign she was still here, with us. Sometimes I believed it. That the gauzy veil between here and long gone could be lifted.

"That was intense. Did they spring the moving-in-together on you today too?"

"Less than an hour ago," I said over the sound of the water.

"Ouch. Mom told me this morning." Camille's voice had a husky rasp to it. Almost smoky. "This is so awkward. Tell me you hate it as much as I do."

I cleared my throat, placing a dish in the drying rack. "I don't know. There are things I hate more."

If Camille was happy to ignore that we'd met while I was buying underwear, I was happy to oblige. Never happened, as far as I was concerned.

Camille cradled the mug of wine. "Such as?"

"My mother's social media presence, for one. Mosquitoes, for two." I turned the water off and faced her, gripping the edge of the counter behind me.

She eyed me. "Full body searches."

"People using speakerphones in public," I said.

She offered the mug to me. "The word 'moist.'"

I sipped the wine, kind of enchanted by Camille. This worldly, better-than-me seventeen-year-old.

Honestly? The wine was my first taste of alcohol. I found it bitter and sour. Screwing up my nose, I passed the mug back. "Dysentery."

She laughed. "I don't think I can beat that."

"Intestinal infection for the win."

She tilted her head at me. "We should hang out sometime. Here. Give me your number," she said, pulling out her phone.

I rattled off the digits.

My phone chimed with a text.

Hi, Camille had written.

We did the dishes and shared the rest of the wine, passing it back and forth, my cheeks growing warmer with each sip.

CHAPTER SIX

Fascists, Camille texted days later.

I was at school, in Special Projects, basically a free period for seniors, practicing in one of the private studios, a little soundproof booth with a window cut out in the door. Violin and bow set across my lap, I texted back. **Huh?**

Outside, the media room buzzed with first-day energy. Nervous freshmen finding their way around. Teachers well rested and not yet overcaffeinated. All of us giddy about the freshly filled vending machines.

Things I dislike more than that dinner. Fascists, she replied.

I sat back, surprised and a little happy to be hearing from Camille. **Curdled milk,** I typed, and hit Send.

Fruitcake, she replied.

I nodded sagely into the empty space. **Fruitcake is super gross,** I agreed.

I know, right? Celery, too. I don't understand why people eat it. It's like crunchy water.

I snickered. I liked Camille. And I actually kind of liked her mom, too.

You still there? Camille texted. **Did I stun you with celery?**

Loud chewers, I wrote.

Camille texted back with a vomit emoji. Then said, **We should hang for real. There's a party this weekend. Want to go?**

I swallowed and pressed my knees together. Blinking, I thought about families I'd watched over the years, little sisters trailing behind big sisters. We were the same age, but I felt younger than Camille. And if I was being honest, I kind of wanted to be like her. Not in a weird, creepy wear-her-skin sort of way, but to have the same aplomb.

Sigh. If only it were that easy.

Sure, I replied without thinking things through.

Well, shoot.

The truth sank in the rest of the week. In all my years of high school, I had never attended a party. This realization was both embarrassing and a little pathetic. It wasn't because I didn't want to be fun or have a good time. But other priorities had always pushed their way to the front of the line—cleaning houses, academics, violin.

Saturday morning I was in a full-blown panic. How to prepare for my first party? Why had I said yes? It took me five minutes to explain my situation to Delia over the phone.

"Underwear," she'd said immediately. "We start with underwear. That's what matters."

Ten minutes later she was at my door. Already in my hand was the unopened package of nude briefs Mom had bought for me weeks earlier—a purchase I'd been successfully ignoring until now. I'd exchange them for something that didn't scream *I've given up on life.*

"God, look at them," Delia said as we drove to the mall, poking the plastic wrapping with one finger. "What if you get in a car accident? What if you hook up with someone? Do you want them to see those? I'm pretty sure my grandmother has the same kind."

The verdict was final. The briefs had to go.

"I don't think thongs," I said when we'd parked.

Delia paused, considering. Cat hair clung to her oversized black T-shirt like tiny constellations. "What is the point of thong underwear, anyway?" Her voice carried that breathy, slightly asthmatic quality that made everything sound philosophical.

"So there's no panty line?" I ventured.

Her enormous eyes caught the garage's fluorescent light, almost luminous. "Don't you *want* people to know you're wearing underwear?"

The logic felt weirdly perfect. We left the car and headed into the mall. I nudged her shoulder. "Thanks for coming with me today."

She nudged me back. "You bet. I was feeling socially adventurous."

Delia and I had met our first day of freshman year when we were paired together in fifth period for an icebreaker activity. She'd been accepted to SAMA for her collage work. She wielded an X-Acto knife like a surgeon, cutting squares from magazines, newspapers, anything printed, and remaking them into mosaic portraits.

I'd learned early on that her life motto was "I love the idea of going out, but it's just not for me." She was an introvert, a Pisces through and through. This attitude complemented mine, which was to shy away from the spotlight. Both of us operated in the background of student life at SAMA.

Thus, we kept our social circle small. Just us two. With Theo occasionally sprinkled in.

Back at the lingerie department, I double-checked to see if Camille was working. Nope. From there, it all went smoothly and to plan. Picture me, the proud new owner of a variety of undies, bikinis and hipsters, satin and lace. Did I feel awesome? Totally.

Delia's nose was in the bag as she picked through my new purchases. "I really love this pair . . ." She glanced up and froze.

I turned my eyes in the direction of hers and felt all the air get sucked from the room. Ezra French was walking across the mall. Twenty feet away and he was a sight to behold. His presence commanding. Ezra was tall and lanky and wore a vintage motorcycle jacket that stretched over his shoulders. And that hair, thick and tousled like fingers had just been run through it. A series of flutters passed through my stomach and up into my lungs.

Last year he'd been a senior at SAMA and been accepted to every major music college, but he had stayed home for reasons unknown. Our instructors called him a prodigy. I had a flash of him on the stage, sitting in a chair, illuminated in a dusty cone of light, sure hands carefully drawing a bow across his cello. Watching him made me ache with envy. To be so young, talented, and beautiful.

"Meep," went Delia, dropping the bag. Bits of satin and lace spilled onto the mall floor.

Too late, I found my voice. "Delia, no!"

She was already in the vitamin store, and Ezra was walking over, swooping down like an underwear superhero.

"Got it." He stood, bag in one hand and pair of purple panties balled in the other. His light brown tiger eyes lingered on me.

In school he'd sparingly made eye contact. A drug to most girls. Me included. "Hey," he eased out. "I know you. Emma, right?"

Did I mention he had a thing for suckers? Specifically, cherry lollipops he'd eat between classes and let hang between his lips while he played.

I pulled in a breath. Ezra French remembered me. Ezra French had just said my name with his lollipop-sucking mouth.

Mentally, I inventoried myself. I'd chosen to wear a tie-dyed shirt that said, A Fiddle in Hand Makes a Very Fine Man. I'd crossed out the word "Man" and Sharpied "Woman" over it. It was a dumb shirt. So dumb. My heart pounded against my ribs. It was like his voice had reached into my lungs, stealing my oxygen.

He gestured at my shirt and bag, my underwear still in his hand. His sculpted cheeks lifted with a half smile. That's all he ever smiled. Partway. "Band. We were at SAMA together. In ensemble. You play the violin. We did that fundraiser."

Yeah, that. The orchestra fundraiser sophomore year was a pop-up deli, with custom sandwiches made to order. We'd had a line through the cafeteria doors. Ezra had been a delivery boy. Did I mention how many girls liked Ezra? Cynthia Bang, a voice major, had ordered three foot-longs. My job had been manning one of the industrial slicers.

I managed a nod and stumbled out a reply. "Yes." A pause. Which I did not use wisely. Which I did not use to consider what I should say next. Instead I blurted, "I cut the meat."

Ezra's mouth twitched. A slow five seconds passed, and then a full-bodied laugh ripped out of him. I would have liked the sound of it had it not been at my expense.

Horror-struck, and mouth jammed shut, I repeated the words

back to myself in my head. *I cut the meat.* Had I really just said that? *I cut the meat. I cut the meat.*

This was the most embarrassing moment of my life.

Ezra chewed his bottom lip, biting away the laughter. "Your friend—she goes to SAMA too, right? Is she okay?" His lovely brow knit, focusing on Delia, who was positioned in front of a row of vitamins named ColonBlaster.

I swallowed. My tongue felt too big for my mouth. I might have been having some sort of embarrassment-related allergic reaction. "She's fine," I managed to croak out. "Just shy." Swallowing again, I eased myself back into a sense of even footing, regrouped. I even managed a small, albeit probably deranged, smile.

"Got it." He nodded and eased the scrap of purple back to me, like it was no big deal, like he was exceptionally well versed in the care and handling of girls' underwear. "I think you dropped this."

"Thanks." I fought a blush, grabbed the underwear, and scrunched it into my palm. My God. *Please let the floor open up and devour me.*

"No problem." He stuffed his hands in his pockets, hunching his shoulders like he was trying to make himself smaller. One of his Converse shoes was held together with duct tape. He stared at me, his head tilted curiously, suppressing a smile.

Under the force of his gaze, I looked away. No wonder he never made eye contact. That was powerful stuff.

Delia had moved from ColonBlaster to a row of giant protein powder containers. "I should probably go," I said.

He tilted his head. "Yeah, me too. I'm meeting some friends at the movies."

"Don't want to be late," I filled in for him. A normal person would have ended the conversation there, said goodbye. Then perhaps waved and been off. But since we've established that I am a noob, especially when it came to Ezra French, I did the most me thing ever: I bolted, sprinting toward Delia in the vitamin store, Ezra's final parting words—"It was good to see you"—reaching my ears way too late.

CHAPTER SEVEN

By the time evening rolled around, the humiliation bruise of seeing Ezra at the mall had faded, replaced by a new, jittery excitement.

I was by the window, waiting for Camille to pick me up for the party. Jiji was hanging in the living room, national news network on.

A little hatchback plastered with stickers—a monkey winking, a holographic picture of Jeff Goldblum, the PBS logo with the words "Save public programming" next to it—pulled up. I recognized the shape of Camille behind the wheel.

I yelled at Mom that I was leaving and pressed a kiss to Jiji's cheek, which smelled faintly of aftershave. "Don't forget to take your hearing aids out before you go to sleep."

"Eh," he said.

I'd check when I got home.

I skipped out the door and down the steps, and dropped myself into Camille's passenger seat. "Thanks for picking me up." Her car was warm. The heat on. Days were still sunny and bright, but in the evenings it cooled. September neared.

"Sure thing," she murmured, pulling away from the curb.

She'd changed her hair from magenta to neon orange. Maybe I should dye my hair too. Or paint my nails. Did I need to add more color to my life?

"Is what I'm wearing okay?"

I'd chosen the plaid skirt I'd worn to my last violin recital. Skirts were fun. Ergo, I was fun. Delia agreed. I'd snapped a photo and sent it to her for confirmation that I looked ready to have a good time.

"I guess." Camille didn't look at me but did shift to lower the volume on her stereo. "It's sort of retro. I haven't seen anyone wear something knee-length like that in a while."

I decided to take it as a compliment and smiled brightly. "Thanks."

I was also wearing purple underwear. The skivvies Ezra French had so expertly held. But she didn't need to know that.

My phone chimed with a text. I peeked at the screen, at Dad's words. I heard you and Camille have been talking. I'm so glad you two are getting along. Let's meet for breakfast. Next weekend, Saturday?

Camille dipped her chin, motion directed at my phone. "Boyfriend?"

"Ha!" I snorted, and Camille grinned. "No, my dad." The only guy, aside from Theo, who had my number. "He was asking about getting together again."

Camille hummed, thinking. Her cheek facing me had a piercing, right in the middle, a little diamond that sparkled as we passed under streetlights. "Don't you think this is all so wild and weird? The two of them moving in together after a few months of dating? It's like, who are the kids here?"

"Yeah. I had some whiplash the other night. I knew Dad was dating your mom, but I was like, and no offense, who is this woman? I've never met her before, and now you're shacking up?"

"Totally," she agreed, which pacified me immensely. "I don't know if this is a universal divorce-kid thing, but I'd kind of been holding out hope my folks might get married again. It's not like they hate each other. We vacation together."

"You go on vacation together?" I looked at her in surprise, my imagination filled with images of Camille, Madison, and a man with a blurred face on a beach, strolling in the tide at sunset. This was the opposite of my parents, whose hairlines started to sweat anytime they were forced into the same room.

Camille smiled knowingly. "They always seem to come back to each other." She sighed. "But I guess it's not meant to be."

She turned up the music, cutting the conversation.

Which was good, because I was extremely distracted by the ghost of my past rising above me. Through a warped lens in my mind, I saw the executive apartment again. Saw my dad's shoulders slumped in defeat. My stomach bottomed out.

I didn't want to, but I wondered, when it came to love, when it came to Madison and Dad, if heartbreak was a foregone conclusion.

Camille stopped behind a long line of cars in front of a home with a red roof and a peekaboo view of Puget Sound. She pulled down her visor, applied some maroon lip gloss, and offered some to me. I took it despite the enormous questions expanding in my throat. Questions like, *Do you really think your mom and dad are still in love? How often do you vacation together? Why did they get divorced in the first place?*

I spread some of the gloss across my lips, unsure in the dark how the color looked but liking how it coated over my internal meltdown. I decided to back-burner my angst and embrace the night for what it was supposed to be—fun.

We opened the car doors, and I could practically feel the house vibrating with loud music.

"This isn't really my usual scene," Camille said as we climbed the steps. "The kid who lives here is a friend of a friend. You know what I mean?"

I nodded as if I did. I had two friends, Delia and Theo.

Camille pushed the front door open.

Wow. It was ten times louder inside. Most of the lights were off, and kids our age were crammed into every nook and cranny. They all spoke loudly, stumbling around in some sort of drunken bacchanalia. And it smelled like an apple-cinnamon candle.

Apple-cinnamon candle and alcohol.

A shirtless dude sprawled on a coffee table. He poured tequila into a shot glass and balanced it on his belly button. Another guy bent, closing his mouth around the shot glass, then tipped back his head. A triumphant roar passed around the room.

"You okay?" Camille asked me. "Wait. You've been to a party before, right?"

I shifted and raised my chin, trying and failing to own the room. I may have gone to an art school where most kids shared similar passions, but there was still a hierarchy. Ezra French had been at the top, moving in and out of social groups like an animal capable of living on both wet and dry land. Delia and I were at the bottom, essentially remoras, suckerfish incapable of surviving on their own. My stomach threatened to curl into a knot.

"Actually, this is my first. High school one, I mean." Which did not sound better. I kept myself from telling her about the last party I'd been to, at Shelby Wilkin's house. I'd spent the whole time helping her mom in the kitchen. My natural default was to find the oldest person in the room and see if they needed assistance.

"Just trust your gut," Camille advised.

"I don't know about that. My gut can't even handle grilled cheese." I'd had the flu bad when I was twelve and puked one up. Ever since I'd had an aversion to yellow melted foods.

Camille smiled. "Stay close, okay? Let's find the bathroom. I have to pee."

We waded in farther, and keeping true to my remora nature, I stuck close to Camille, the bigger, stronger fish. A line had formed for the bathroom on the main floor, and Camille reversed course to head upstairs. We found more people, but no line for the toilet. "I'll be one second. Then we'll go find Cody. He just texted. He's out back."

I assumed Cody was her friend who told her about the party. She flicked the light on in the bathroom and closed the door. A lava lamp lit a bedroom across the way, and inside, a few dudes smoked from a bong. I accidentally caught the eye of one. He was good looking in a nonthreatening way, with sable-colored hair that brushed his shoulders. He smiled. Stood, moseyed toward me.

"Hey. Casper." He held out a hand, introducing himself.

"Emma," I replied, feeling happy, dazzled by all this. Like making friends was easy. Why hadn't I done it before? And this new friend was cute, to boot. A cute *male* friend. I was totally the life of the party. Maybe all this—friendship, love, being social—wasn't so hard. Maybe I needed to stop overanalyzing everything and trust the world more.

"Have you met my friend Kevin? Kevin!" he yelled over his shoulder.

From the dark recesses of the lava lamp room emerged a lanky Asian kid.

"Kevin, meet Emma." He thrust his hands out. "I'm sure you two have lots in common." Casper's booming laugh filled the hallway before he ducked back into the room.

This happened sometimes. Twice to me, to be exact. Once in kindergarten, when I was paired with a Chinese kid for a cultural project, and then again in middle school in social studies for a geography project on Asia. So yes, I'd been a victim before of being the only other Asian in a room.

"Casper is an idiot." Kevin positioned himself against the wall close to me. "And he drinks bong water."

"Yep," I agreed. "The Venn diagram of the guy who drinks bong water, microaggresses people, and wonders why girls don't want to date him is a circle."

Kevin grinned, but then his face clouded. He rubbed his stomach. "Oh no. I think I'm going to be sick."

I didn't have a chance to jump back. He doubled over, opened his mouth, and threw up on the carpet. Vomit splashed on my shoes and a little on my bare knees. So gross.

Ugh, the smell.

Kevin groaned, still bent over. "I'm so sorry . . ."

I backed away. "It's cool." Really, it wasn't. I stifled a wince, and my vision swam, socially devastated and out of my element. The party, Casper, and the puke were all too much, messy and painful. Not a straw breaking the camel's back, but a two-ton weight. The bathroom door opened then, but it was too late. I beelined to the stairs. Camille shouted at my back, and I kind of jerkily waved and said, "I forgot, I have something."

I was done. Sensing my desperation to vacate the area, kids darted out of my way. Five seconds later I was out the door and around the block. The party muted to distant music and laughter, everyone but me having a good time. I leaned over to brace my hands on my knees but remembered Kevin's vomit. Flecks of orange speckled my legs.

I couldn't even.

My phone pinged with a text.

Are you okay? from Camille.

I don't feel good.

Slightly true. My sympathetic gag reflex had been activated. I swallowed against the urge to throw up.

Camille asked if I wanted a ride home. I reassured her I didn't. I already had one. A lie. But I wanted someone I knew to pick me up, someone who wouldn't judge me and who would come right away.

I found the number on my phone and hit the green Call button.

"Go for Theo."

"Oh my God, what a stupid way to answer the phone."

I scraped my shoes on someone's grass, just next to their Kindly Keep Dogs Off Our Lawn sign.

"What's wrong?" His voice bent with concern. Theo could always sense when I was on the verge.

A sprinkler turned on, dousing my legs. I ducked for cover and said, "I need a ride."

CHAPTER EIGHT

By the time Theo pulled up, my legs and part of my back were drenched. He'd barely come to a complete stop before I was swinging open the door to his Honda Civic. I'd dubbed it his *2 Fast 2 Furious* car. He'd installed RGB lighting around the interior that changed colors every couple of minutes—blue melting to purple to red to orange to yellow.

"Thanks for coming." I sat in his car, and he idled for a moment. I leaned my head back against the seat and closed my eyes.

"What's the matter? Is your mouth bleeding?"

He was wearing his glasses. Like when he first wakes up. He looked adorable, and I realized it was easier for me to talk to him when he was disguised like this—as a modern-day Clark Kent.

I opened my eyes and screwed up my face. "No." I flipped his mirror down. Camille's dark maroon gloss had gathered into the creases of my lips. "It's lip gloss." I swiped my mouth with the back of my hand and wiped it against my skirt. A pause. "Why aren't we moving?" This was not the fast getaway I had been hoping for.

"Seat belt." A streetlight reflected in his glasses.

I pulled the seat belt over my chest and clicked it in, then shot Theo a *Happy now?* look.

He frowned at me, sighed at length, then shifted gears to pull away. "What happened?"

"I went to a party—"

"Wait," Theo cut in. "Doesn't that violate the violin honor club code?"

"Hardy har har." Technically, it did. "I was humiliated by a guy who drinks bong water."

Theo scowled. "More context, please."

I turned my cheek and stared out the window, recounting the evening—who Camille was, how she'd oh so casually mentioned her mom might still be in love with her dad, then Casper introducing me to Kevin: *I'm sure you two have lots in common.*

Theo didn't say anything for a long time. So long that I finally had to look at him to make sure he was listening. He gripped the wheel, knuckles white. "Are you kidding me?"

I palmed my head. "I've been microaggressed twice this year so far." At Tanabata, on what should have been home turf, then at a party. "You know what? I shouldn't have run out of the party. I let some obnoxious guy and a little barf chase me away."

His face screwed up after noodling on that for a moment. "Wait. You didn't say anything about puke."

"Kevin threw up on my shoes."

"You're wearing vomit shoes *in my car*?"

"I scraped them off on the grass." Plus, there had been the sprinkler. I decided not to tell Theo my back was most likely soaking his fabric seat. Best not to push him. "They're clean now. And that's not the point." My anger was growing, and I wasn't sure whom it was aimed at. Although I did know what was at the heart of it—helpless frustration. "Clearly, I don't know how to handle myself in public. Clearly, I should stay inside." Maybe it was me. Maybe *I* was the problem. Maybe I attracted bongwater-drinking a-holes, induced vomiting in other Asian Americans, and repelled whom I *really* wanted. Speaking of . . . "This morning I saw Ezra French."

"Who's Ezra French?" A ferocious WTF dent appeared between Theo's eyebrows, the same expression he wore while gaming when he was losing a battle or confused by a riddle.

"He's a guy from my school. He was a senior last year. He got into every major music school with full-ride scholarships to play the cello. But didn't go. Nobody knows why," I said wistfully.

The dent between his eyebrows deepened. "So?"

"So. He was super popular. Girls wanted to date him. Guys wanted to be him."

He puffed out a laugh and relaxed into his seat more. We were cruising on the highway now. "You're telling me that the most popular guy at your school played the cello?" He clucked his tongue, flicked on a blinker, and changed lanes. "Art school kids."

Theo went to South Seattle, the public school down the road.

I frowned. "I ran into him, and you know what I said?" I told Theo the whole story, ending with "I cut the meat."

Theo inhaled and was silent for a beat, which I interpreted as appropriate horror-struck quiet. But then his shoulders started shaking. He let out a chuckle that turned to outright laughter. He placed his hand on his chest, which was firmer than I remembered, visibly trying to calm himself. We were going over a bridge, and he swerved slightly.

I poked him in the side. "Pay attention to the road."

"'I cut the meat'!" He whooped, wiping his eyes under his glasses, and righted the car. Then his arm snaked over, fingers poking my side in my most ticklish spot. "C'mon. It's funny. Laugh."

A flash of heat exploded over my skin at the touch, and I reluctantly laughed. I swatted him away and scrunched against the door, out of his arm's reach. When the spark faded, I sent him a grouchy look. "I should have walked home."

He sobered a little, both hands back on the wheel, exiting the highway. "Sorry."

But he wasn't. A decade-ish of friendship plus one year of being sworn enemies, when we'd endlessly pranked each other in seventh grade, equaled me being able to tell when Theo was genuinely remorseful. He still thought it was funny.

I sighed miserably and played with the hem of my skirt. "I'm going to have to tell my dad about Madison."

Theo scrubbed his face in frustration. We were in our neighborhood, passing the abandoned house where Jiji and I used to pick wild blackberries. "What? Why?"

Wasn't it obvious? Clearly not. "Because he's going to get his heart broken."

I'd spent a lot of time at Theo's house during the divorce, seeking refuge in the corduroy beanbag chair in his room, crying my eyes out. Theo, a fixer at heart, tried to make me feel better. He showed me a game where you build towns. Because he thought it might help to create something new.

"I don't want him to get hurt," I said quietly, projecting all those bad memories into my tone. Loving someone, then losing them, seeing someone you loved get hurt—all of it seemed intolerable. As Theo said the other day, hard pass.

He parked in his driveway and turned to me. "Can I give you some advice?"

"I feel like you're going to whether I say yes or not."

A ghost of a smile. "You know me well." He searched my eyes. "Don't let your damage sour their love story. Try to believe a little more in it."

I folded my arms across my chest and dropped my gaze to my lap. As much as I didn't want him to be, Theo was correct. My first impulse was always to protect my dad, Mom, Jiji, myself, those I cared about most.

"Fine. I won't say anything." I pretended to be exasperated, hoping to lighten my mood. I looked up at him. "Thanks again for coming to get me."

With a half smile, he tugged on a lock of my hair. All motion inside me stilled. "Anytime," he said.

The quiet seemed to grow, lassoing us in electricity. I suddenly felt very, very naked. Danger. Danger.

Abruptly I remembered Theo was my best friend.

The electricity shorted and fizzled out.

"Thanks again," I said.

Then I scrambled from the car and inside my house.

In the dark of my living room, my heartbeat thudded in my ears. I heard Theo's car door shut, followed by a beep as he set the alarm.

What had just happened? Did Theo know I was having less than innocent thoughts about him? The only reason I made it through my parents' divorce was because of him.

I was afraid of things changing between us. Or worse, me thinking things were changing, that something was happening, but it wasn't. He was probably just being reliable, lovable Theo. Kind, the ultimate boy next door. And that's where he needed to stay. Everything should continue as it was, as it had always been. Whatever fuse that had been lit had to be permanently capped.

Shelving my ruminations, I slipped off my shoes, put them outside, then padded up the stairs.

Mom's and Jiji's doors were closed, no light seeping through the cracks. Both were sleeping. I twisted the knob on Jiji's to check on him and silently tsked, seeing the half-eaten plate of senbei crackers on his nightstand. He lay face up, covers tucked underneath his armpits, mouth slightly open, face lax, deathly quiet, his pose funereal.

It may sound morbid, but a part of me was waiting for Jiji to die. Mom was there when my grandmother passed away. "It was beautiful," Mom said. "She was completely at peace. I'm so glad my dad is here. I want him to have the same experience." Thus, whenever Jiji fell into one of his vampire-like slumbers, I worried he might be dead.

Gently I laid a hand on his chest. He was warm. So maybe not dead. Or . . . freshly dead.

His arm whipped up, hand closing around my wrist. "Emma-chan." He opened his ancient eyes, old and beautiful like the Jomonsugi, a giant cedar tree.

I drew back. "Just making sure you're not dead."

He released me. "Sorry that I am not more dead for you."

I paused and frowned. "That's not what I meant. You know I like you best alive." His hearing aids were still in his ears. "Give me your hearing aids and go back to sleep."

He handed them off to me and closed his eyes. Within seconds he was lightly snoring again.

I took care of business, setting his hearing aids in the charger and clearing the plate, and left the room.

"Emma?" Mom's sleepy voice called out.

I peeked in her room, plate in my hand. "I'm home. Jiji was eating crackers in bed again. You okay?"

Mom was a lump in the dark. She shifted under the covers. Sometimes her hands hurt so bad, they kept her awake.

"I'm fine. I'll wash his sheets in the morning. Make sure you lock up."

"I will. Sorry I woke you." I began to retreat.

"It's okay. Oh," she said. "You got some mail. I put it on your dresser."

Mail.

That caught my interest, and I headed to my room. Plate held against my chest, I flicked on my light and saw it. A plain white envelope propped on my music stand, my name scrawled on the front in a vaguely familiar script. I slid the plate onto my dresser, took up the envelope, and peeled it open.

> Emma,
> I wish I'd had a better line to open with. I mean, I thought I had one. You don't know how many times I started to write you. How many crumpled pieces of paper are in my garbage can. Then I dashed out that one line and sent it: If I'm being honest, I loved you from the beginning.

> Since, I've realized my error. Correction, errors. Like not addressing you. Or clarifying who I am. Or what I'm doing.
>
> Nowhere to go from here but up, I suppose. All right. Here goes.
>
> I am from the future.
>
> You're laughing. I'm sure you're laughing. How could you not be? I laughed writing this.
>
> Though I'm sure for a different reason. Yours is probably in rueful doubt. Mine is to say, She's never going to believe you—you are a fool. Maybe acknowledging the pure fantasy, the whole impossibility of this entire scenario, will make it feel more real?
>
> Honestly, I'm not really sure what I'm doing here. What repercussions I might be reaping, communicating with someone in the past. It has occurred to me I might be making a deal with the devil. Or, at the very least, crossing the Rubicon.
>
> Yet here I am. Against the odds. Against time. I've come back for you, Emma. And if you let me, I'm going to change your life.

I wasn't laughing. But I was smiling, quizzical and confused. What in the world? A letter from the future? Change my life?

This had to be some awful practical joke. Like the time I had a crush on Henry Easton, and Molly Beetle pretended to be his sister, prank-called me, and said he'd written my name all over his journal. My stomach still bottomed out remembering it.

I flipped the piece of paper over, searching for a signature. No name to be found anywhere.

But it was the same handwriting, the same blue ink that bled into the fibers of the paper, as in the note from the St. Jameses' house, where Colin, Sebastian, Jennifer, and the spandex-wearing father lived.

> If I'm being honest, I loved you from the beginning.

Absurdity. I rejected the idea outright.
Note in hand, I hovered it over my trash can and dropped it in.
It would take a lot more than this to make me a believer.

CHAPTER NINE

Six days had slid by since I read the note, and real curiosity had begun to set in. I'd wasted last period, Special Projects, all week, Googling on my phone. The internet told me time travel was possible but unlikely. Things snowballed from there. I fell down a Reddit-thread rabbit hole about multiverses and branching timelines.

At the final bell I shot to attention. Crud. The Sherwood Institute was starting this afternoon. I rushed to downtown Seattle, parked in a garage that ate up of the rest of my tip from the St. Jameses' house, and raced to the entrance, violin case in hand.

Other music students filled the lobby. A girl with flaxen hair played the harp. Two guys stood near each other and rolled their lips, warming up for vocals. I hated being late and felt anxious standing there, trying to figure out who was in charge. I narrowed in on a floss-skinny guy with a ponytail, holding a clipboard. He appeared to be in charge.

"Hey." I shifted my violin case. "Emma Nakamura-Thatcher."

"You're late," he murmured. No eye contact.

I chewed my lip. Mom had forwarded me the information on

Sherwood. There was a clause that students must arrive on time or risk elimination from the program.

Did I want to be there? No.

Did I want to be kicked out? Bigger no.

Mom would kill me. Forget serial killers, spiders, downed electrical lines—the thing I feared most was my mother.

"Traffic was bad." A lie. But better than *I received a weird note over the weekend from a guy stating he was from the future, and I spent way too many minutes, who am I kidding, hours researching timeline splits*. Totally sounded reasonable and normal. "I'm here for—"

"Classical instrumental, voice, jazz, or composition?" Thick-rimmed glasses slid down his nose as he peered at the sheet.

"Classical instrumental. Violin." I held up my case.

He flipped to the back of the clipboard and used his pen to search the page. "Studio five."

"Can you just point me—"

He flung a hand toward a hall and called, "Next!"

I wandered in the direction he'd indicated. This place was nice. Modern, with walls that were solid pieces of wood, giving off a serene vibe. Plus, I bet the acoustics were fantastic. The doorways were numbered. Studio 5 was at the end.

I entered and started to talk, head still down. "Sorry I'm a few minutes late. Traffic was terrible." Might as well lean into the lie. "I have to drive across town to get here. Do you know where Seattle Arts and Music Academy is? That's where I go. Anyway, there was an accident. No one was hurt. Nothing tragic. Just a fender bender—" I looked up and stopped short, words dying on my tongue.

Oh, for crying out loud. I blinked once. Twice. Maybe I was in the early stages of some terminal disease where hallucinations, like letters from the future and secret crushes materializing in malls and music studios, were the first symptoms.

"Hey." Ezra French came toward me, hands jammed in his pockets, shoulders hunched like he was steeling himself against the world. He was wearing that same motorcycle jacket. I could practically smell the leather.

With that, with his melodic voice and solid shape, my worries about delusions disintegrated. A whole new problem arose—sweat beading on my hairline. What was worse? Let it go and pretend it wasn't happening and risk droplets cascading down my forehead like a waterfall, or wipe it away so fast that he might not notice?

"Hi." I cast my gaze around and landed on a stack of chairs. "So you're, uh, my mentor?" I swiped my forehead and tucked some hair behind my ear in what I hoped looked like a natural move. Not hiding sweat at all.

"Yep. I'm all yours, four hours a week." Suddenly the number four didn't seem so bad. "The acoustics in this room aren't great. It's multipurpose and also used for theater and dancing. We'll find somewhere better, but it will work for today." He found a chair, sat down, and rubbed his hands together. "So. Tell me. What's the dream here? Let me guess, Juilliard? Everyone always wants to go to Juilliard."

I needed a second. Maybe five. An hour tops. Unfortunately, Ezra was waiting for me to answer, his stare relentlessly gentle.

"No." I moved more into the room, closer to him. My stomach compressed, and I gave him a slight smile. "I'm actually not applying to any music schools."

He looked me up and down, and I remembered I was wearing shorts and it had been two days since I shaved my legs. "Not applying to music schools?"

I sat in the chair across from him, violin case in my lap like a shield. "I've got my application in at University of Washington." It was just a thirty-minute commute from my house.

He cupped the back of his neck. "Not many people's first choice for music programs. But okay."

I pressed my knees together. "I didn't apply for their school of music."

It took a beat for understanding to dawn. "Why are you here, then?"

"My mom signed me up."

I was here under duress. To reiterate, I was more afraid of her than a late-night stroll through the woods with Hansel and Gretel.

Ezra leaned forward, rested his elbows on his knees, and clasped his hands together. "Come again?"

More explanation was warranted. "I need to stay close to home, pursue a career that pays more than music . . . something with a better track, like nursing or tech. Plus, I prefer small, realizable dreams. Sure things. You know?"

He nodded. "Got it. Let me hear you play."

"Sorry?"

I thought I'd been clear. No need to practice, perform, or prepare a piece for the big recital, since I wouldn't be applying to Juilliard. Actually, Berklee College of Music would have been my top choice. But whatever. We could spend this time on other things, such as my new interest in time travel.

"I want to hear you play." He shrugged off his jacket, leaned back in his chair, and crossed his arms, biceps slightly bulging. Arms, my weakness. "If you're terrible, it shouldn't be a problem. You can forgo the program. I'll wish you happy trails as you trot off to whatever boring, soul-sucking career you've chosen. And I'll write your mom and tell her you're a talentless hack. That it's best to keep your violin playing to a padded room or basement so the neighbors don't hear."

My brain screeched to a halt. Anger surfaced. "One, ouch. Two, many people find working in the healthcare industry very rewarding. And three, I don't suck."

A shrug. "So you say."

I skirted my hands over my violin case, the cool black plastic grounding me. "I see what you're doing."

He blinked at me. "What am I doing?"

"If I play and I'm good, you're going to say I'm wasting my talent, then rope me into applying for music schools."

"You're one hundred percent right. Now that we've cleared that up . . ." He rubbed his hands together. "Let's go." When I didn't move, he shooed me along. "Come on. You're here for two hours regardless. You came all this way. What's the harm?"

I stood, called him an asshat in my head while I removed my violin from its case. After shuffling to the center of the room, I turned and faced Ezra. The full weight of his amber eyes fell on me.

Violin in hand, I positioned it on my shoulder. I could have played poorly, but all that pride I'd inherited from Jiji wouldn't allow it. I set my bow across the strings and drew out Pachelbel's Canon in D Major. Closing my eyes, I let the music carry me, giving myself over to the notes, which always expressed what I couldn't—sadness, happiness, fear, and anger. My voice was louder on the violin, bolder and demanding, even reckless sometimes.

By the time I finished, I was winded. My chest rose hard and fast, and Ezra was staring at me. His mouth opened and closed. "You don't suck."

The bow dangled at my side. Playing like that always drained me, but in a good way. Wrung out like I'd exorcised something.

"You're really good." He dug into his pocket and produced two cherry suckers, offering me one.

I stepped forward and took the sucker. "Thank you."

"You really feel it, don't you?" He unwrapped the sucker and twirled it inside his cheek.

"What?" I licked my lips, a little lightheaded and dizzy, high from playing, from being in a room with Ezra.

"The music."

I nodded. "I do. Ever since I was little." I motioned to my ear. "Most days I hear theme music playing in the back of my head. Like, I see people fighting and hear 'Flight of the Bumblebee.'" Music made me feel significant. A part of something. Connected.

"Same. It would be a shame to let all that talent go to waste." He stretched out his legs and crossed his ankles. "Play me something else."

I swallowed. My chest tightened. I'd played for teachers, for crowds, Delia, Theo, and my parents, but somehow this moment with Ezra felt ten times more intimate. He seemed to understand what others didn't: the effect of playing, how deep inside you reached to touch the music, that it came from light and dark places. I didn't like the vulnerability of it.

I shifted uncomfortably. "I don't know . . ."

"Come on." He'd said the same earlier as a dare and command, but this was a croon. A gentle plea.

I inhaled and shoved the sucker into my pocket. "Yeah, okay." I threw my shoulders back and repositioned my violin under my chin. Ezra crossed his arms, hung his head, body loose and relaxed, ready to receive.

I decided on Niel Gow's "Lament for the Death of His Second Wife." The first time I heard it, I was in the ninth grade, and Jiji had taken me to the symphony. We'd gotten all dolled up and sat in the nosebleeds at Benaroya Hall. But it didn't matter. I could hear perfectly. Those few simple notes. How gorgeous they were. How devastating. I wept. After, I'd practiced the solo until I was breathless, memorizing it and able to play it by rote.

Ezra adjusted in his seat, relaxing to lean his head against the mirrored wall, and closed his eyes. His chest rose and fell with heavy breaths. I thought he might be sleeping. That I had put him to sleep. But then he asked me to play again, and it sounded reverent. Like what he desired most in the world was my music.

So I did.

I played for him.

I left Sherwood floating on air and sucking the cherry lollipop on the way to the parking garage. Opening my car door, I sat behind the wheel and dropped my bag on the passenger seat. Random stuff fell out: a lip gloss, extra strings for my violin, my wallet, a crisp white envelope.

Cold pause.

I picked up the envelope. Time moved slow and thick, like molasses.

Emma.

I saw my name scrawled on the front in the same handwriting as the other notes—chaotic, distinctly boyish. My heart pounded a percussion against my ribs as I opened the letter and read.

> Dear Emma,
> What can I say that will convince you? You want proof? Irrefutable evidence that I know you? That I know you now, in the past? That I know you in the future? That I have loved you through the years? You'll only believe me if I tell you something no one else can possibly know. I'll do you one better. How about three?
>
> One: You had a horrible perspiration problem when you were nine. Medical intervention was necessary, and every year before school starts, your mother spirits you away to see Dr. Peterson for shots in your armpits.
>
> Two: Sometimes, you think about how you might be stuck in one long dream. That you might be living an entire life in the span of a single night, a few seconds of sleep. You're terrified of what happens when you wake up.

Three: You believe instruments have souls, and when played, it is how they speak.

Last—I know, I know, I said three things, but I've thought of something else, and I don't want to start this letter again. Honestly, I haven't handwritten this much in a long time. My hand hurts. I might lose a digit.

Where was I? Oh yeah. A few weeks ago you went to the Japanese garden. You were missing your grandmother and thinking there wasn't a language for heartbreak. No vernacular. It's an unspeakable thing. On a piece of paper you made a wish and tied it to a stalk of bamboo. Hoping the words might come true. Hoping for proof that love is real, that it can last a lifetime.

I'm here to tell you: It can.

CHAPTER TEN

The letter fell from my hands and into my lap. He knew my secrets—things I'd never told anyone.

Except for the first. My mom knew about my armpits. When I had sworn her to secrecy, she'd rolled her eyes. "Who am I going to tell?" she said. "Nobody I know is interested in your armpits."

But everything else I'd kept inside. Deep inside.

Unease skittered up my spine.

Breathe, Emma, just breathe.

I shuddered, needed to sit down, then remembered I was already sitting. Maybe a full recline would be good.

Someone had spray-painted a sunset on the garage wall—an ombre of oranges and reds. Words had been graffitied below: "It's a new day."

Was I convinced? Had he persuaded me?

The answer came in a rush. Yes. Yes, he had. These notes were real. No one in the world could know these things about me.

Unless I had told them. In the future.

He'd have to be someone I trusted . . . maybe even the love of my life. And I knew him. Now. In his past, in my present. That's what he'd said.

I drove to Delia's with the windows down, dimly registering the day and temperature. Friday. End of August. Right after the Sherwood Institute. Cool but humid. Dull gray sky, a thunderstorm on the horizon. I should probably close the windows, but I was flush with excitement, hot with confusion. Someone was writing to me from the future. But who? The question echoed in my head. *Who? Who? Who?*

A rattling noise came from my engine that I should probably get checked, but who had the time? Certainly not me, the girl receiving notes from the future. Ha!

I sped up. Foot heavy on the pedal, I cruised through a yellow light and swerved into the left lane, narrowly missing a semi turning into the right. A screaming horn followed, and I slowed, heart racing and head woozy.

That was close.

Too close.

I needed to get a hold of myself. "I am warm. I am dry." I chanted the words until my pulse slowed. Nerves steadier, I addressed the letter now sitting on the passenger seat. "You almost made me have an accident."

Super. I was talking to a piece of paper.

Hands trembling and foot much lighter on the gas, I arrived at Delia's. She lived with her dads in a nineteenth-century converted schoolhouse. I let myself in through the yellow-painted door.

"Delia?" I called.

The vibe in the house was *American Gothic* meets Wes Anderson. There was a flaking vegan-leather couch, a portrait of the family all wearing monster masks, and a giant replica of Polyclitus's *Canon*, the Greek statue that inspired Michelangelo's *David*. One of Delia's dads was an artist and worked as a landscape architect. Her other dad was an anesthesiologist. His favorite joke, and one I'd heard often, was that he put people to sleep for a living.

"It's me. Emma!" I called, maybe a little too loud and shrill. But I was desperate to see Delia. She'd help me make sense of the situation. "Delia, are you home?"

"In the kitchen," one of her dads yelled.

I found Delia and her dads in a Norman Rockwell–esque scene. The three were gathered around the kitchen island, a box of Top Pot doughnuts open between them. All smiling. Being adorable. The smell of sugar, as light as cotton candy, was suspended in the air.

Delia really hit the jackpot in terms of happy parents. I mean, they *oozed* affection. Even her grandmother kissed everyone on the lips. Which was startling the first time I met her.

"Hey, hungry?" one of her dads greeted me.

My stomach churned at the thought of anything inside it. "No thanks. I'm good."

Delia ripped a bite from a pink frosted doughnut.

"You sure? These are celebration doughnuts." He jiggled the box. "At work today we removed a fibroid, and it was the size of a cantaloupe. Biggest one I've ever seen."

Delia grimaced and dropped her doughnut, sprinkles falling onto the concrete countertop. "I feel like our family needs an HR person."

Her other dad smiled. "Says the girl who made her American Girl doll into someone who survived the Donner party."

Delia shrugged. "There was so much backstory to work with."

"Delia," I squeaked out. "Sidebar?"

She rose from the counter and followed me out of the room, away from her dads. Pink frosting clung to the corner of her lips and she licked it away. "What's up? Whoa. You look totally freaked."

I nodded, because I was. "Look." I shoved the note into her hands.

Delia read the letter while we slowly climbed the stairs to her room. She stopped at the top.

"What do you—"

"Shush," she cut me off. "Almost finished. You know I'm a slow reader." Two minutes later Delia looked up at me. "What is this?"

It took all of ten minutes to explain the situation, including the contents of the two previous notes—"If I'm being honest, I loved you from the beginning" and "I am from the future."

"What is going on?" I asked. "Who is sending these? I mean, this is real, right? This is a real thing? This is happening?"

Delia's smushed-face cat, Leslie, slipped through the doorway and wound around her owner's legs. "I don't know. You tell me. Do you really get shots in your armpits for excessive sweating?"

"Everything in that letter, and that's what you focus on?"

She picked up Leslie, dropped her chin between the cat's triangle ears, and faux-pouted. "I can't believe you never told me you have a sweating problem. I've told you everything. Even about the time I thought hair grew on boys' penises and had to have a very uncomfortable conversation with my dads, which included drawings, a quiz, and the word 'shaft.'"

"Delia. Focus."

Delia sighed dejectedly. "You think you know someone . . ."

"Fine," I snapped out. "I have the Niagara Falls of armpits. I'm sorry I never told you. May we move on now?"

A magnanimous nod. "I accept your apology." Delia let Leslie drop from her arms. "And yes, we can move on now. I know exactly what we should do."

I perked up. Delia had been the right person to come to. Her love language was supporting best friends and anything cats.

"Tell me," I said hastily, because you could not Google "Who is writing me love letters from the future?"

I had to know. That door I'd shut so many years ago, standing in my dad's apartment, had been cracked open. Light spilling in, pooling at my feet, I was wading in the promise of love always staying. I wanted it so bad, and here, this future boy, whom I knew now, was handing forever to me.

I just needed to figure out who he was.

She flipped up her pointer finger. "Murder," she said in her signature wispy voice. Her middle finger followed suit. "Board."

CHAPTER ELEVEN

"Done," Delia said, pinning the last photograph onto a giant corkboard.

We were in her art studio, right across from her bedroom. She occupied the whole second floor. The last two hours had been spent on creation. Delia had swept aside bits of glass used for mosaics, eight different kinds of scissors, X-Acto knives, and paper cutters to clear an area. Briefly I wondered if my friend might be keeping too many sharp objects, but I didn't let it distract me from the issue at hand. While Delia successfully converted the space into a crime scene investigation hub, minus the "crime" and "scene," I filled her in on Ezra and Sherwood. Which had made her pause at length and raise her eyebrows before moving again.

"So." Delia stepped back, proud of her work. On a nearby table she snapped her laptop shut. "What do you think?"

I stared at the board, vision partially obscured by silicone under-eye patches. Delia had a set on too. Because why not address the circles under our eyes while trying to solve a mystery? A classic two-birds-one-stone situation.

I peeled the eye patches off and tossed them into the trash.

Dead center of the corkboard was an eight-by-ten photograph of me at thirteen, surrounded by clues we'd collected from the letters. Clues such as *Loved Emma at first sight*, *Knows Emma's secrets*, *Knows Emma now* . . .

I circled back to my eighth-grade school picture and winced. The photograph had been snapped right after I seemed to have sprouted a mustache and unibrow overnight, then been forced to run a mile by a gym teacher with a dark side. My oily skin reflected the light. This picture had made me highly self-conscious, and that self-consciousness had followed me into high school. Most of this uneasiness revolved around my body and face. They weren't too bad, especially after waxing and blotting paper, but I had always believed they could be better.

Long story short, I will always spiritually have bad facial hair.

I pulled my legs in to my chest, a box cutter hanging loose in my hands because I needed something to hold on to. The sun was close to setting, gray light waning. The sky was a bleak contrast to all the screaming colors in Delia's art studio. "I still can't believe this is happening."

"You and me both." Delia sighed, hearts in her eyes. "But I do so love a murder board." She crossed her arms. "Now, on to suspects. Who do you think the letter writer might be?"

Delia had helped me pull candidates from my most distant memories—nearly every crush or boy I'd ever interacted with.

Like Liam Huxley, my first kiss, from middle school. Had he been carrying a torch all these years?

And Brandon with no last name from Long Beach.

"Bad news." Delia's nose was back in her laptop. "The only Brandon I could find in Long Beach is in jail."

"What? Let me see." She turned the screen my way. I scanned the mug shot of a scary dude with bloodshot eyes. "That guy is forty-two. My Brandon had floppy hair and skateboarded everywhere."

Delia wrote Liam's and Brandon's names on index cards using a sparkly gel pen and pinned both to the board.

"Obviously, we should put Theo on the list." Delia picked up a yardstick and slapped the corkboard, the end landing on the clue *Able to travel back in time*. "He makes the *most* sense right now. He knows you the best and also has the potential technical and scientific savvy to figure out sending letters from the future one day."

Theo.

A thrill shot through me at the thought.

It could be possible. Theo and I were close. We knew a lot about each other. Like the time he got strep throat from his turtle. Or the time I wore body glitter to Christmas and got a rash from the lotion.

A memory floated up. When I'd been sick with flu and delirious, Theo had made me smoothies and insisted on hanging around outside my door so I wouldn't be alone.

Jeez. He was pathologically good.

We had spent hours and hours together. Could I have confided in him in the future? Had we held hands, and I'd whispered my secrets to him? Bared my soul, telling him I'd once wished for love to always stay?

More importantly, did I *want* it to be Theo? There was something comfortable, something easy, about him. Sometimes friendship grew into love, and I had definitely thought about kissing him.

My throat felt dry as I said, "Next, please."

She pinned Theo's name to the board, then turned to face me again. "I think we should also add Ezra French."

Involuntarily my thumb pushed on the button of the box cutter, the blade rising up.

Over the years I'd done some low-key stalking. To my great disappointment, Ezra didn't have much of an online presence. The only picture of him I could find online was from Getty Images. No joke. It had been snapped when he'd filled in for a famous musician performing at Carnegie Hall. The caption called Ezra a savant, a musical wunderkind. His gaze was downcast, shoulders slumped in an *Aw, shucks* kind of way. Thick lashes fanned his cheeks. He looked like a fallen angel sometimes.

Delia printed this image with a watermarked copyright and stuck it to the board.

Self-preservation reared; I dared not get my hopes up. "Delia. Impossible." Ezra was too cool, too awesome, too out of my league.

"I dunno." Delia bent down and removed the box cutter from my grip. "I'm just going to take this." She set it on a table and went on. "It's very suspicious these letters started right after seeing him again."

"You think Ezra French took one look at my purple underwear, heard me say 'I cut the meat,' and fell immediately in love?"

"Yes," she said. "That's exactly what I think. I think he was smitten. He saw you in your knee-length shorts and orthopedic socks and was swept away. He had to have you."

I could only laugh.

"What about those boys? From the house you clean?"

It took a beat for her question to land. "Colin and Sebastian?" The brothers from Yarrow Point hadn't been in my thoughts, well, at all.

"Their house is where the first note showed up." Delia gestured to the murder board, where the locations of the notes had all been pinned—Yarrow Point, my house, the parking garage outside Sherwood. Her fingers perched on the keyboard. "What's their last name?"

I told her, and she found them in a few keystrokes. Sebastian and Colin were the twin sons of Jennifer and James (no joke) St. James. Further digging produced yearbook photos of the twins on their crew and basketball teams. The whir of the printer sounded, and Colin and Sebastian, wearing navy blazers with red-and-gold ties, sidled up next to Ezra, Theo, and the other boys from my past on the board.

Exhausted, I allowed myself to fall backward into a pile of one-inch multicolored pieces of paper.

"Wait, stay there." Delia hopped off and rummaged around in a corner. She came back with a Polaroid camera.

Click.

The picture was spit out. Undeveloped photo in one hand and camera in the other, she squatted next to me. "Who do you want it to be?"

I stared at the ceiling, unseeing, and processed her question. At the thought of love, a familiar scary feeling surfaced. It was hard to shake the notion that love wasn't a good thing, wasn't something that existed just to lift you above its head, only to body-slam you back down.

But now . . .

Now there was a *guarantee*. A chance to have love with none of the risk, none of the pain. The letter writer loved me now and loved me in the future. If I could find him in the present, we could be together. Always. No heartache ever. Honey-thick hope spread through my veins, pushing aside the fear. "I can't answer that."

She shook the picture and handed it to me. I was looking at the camera, my gaze soft and unfocused, a halo of confetti around me.

I sat up. "Pretty picture."

"Pretty girl," Delia volleyed back.

One hundred percent disagreed. Delia was a phenomenal photographer. With the proper lighting, she could make a naked mole rat the spokesanimal for an antiaging skin care line.

I groaned and rubbed my eyes. "Why won't the sender just tell me his name?"

Delia scoffed. "Haven't you ever read any time-travel novels?" At my confused expression, she threw up her hands. "The butterfly effect. Change one thing in the past, and a million things change in the future."

"That is very inconvenient."

Delia smiled, overzealous. "I am insanely jealous. Ezra French is your mentor, and you're receiving love letters from the future." She hugged me, squeezing me breathless.

"If our situations were reversed, you wouldn't be able to talk to Ezra anyway." My voice was muffled by her shoulder.

We could dig on each other with no offense. Banter was part of our friendship currency. She made fun of my clothes. I made fun of her aversion to direct eye contact.

She sighed, but her voice stayed sweet and warm. "I hate you so much right now."

• • •

I came home to Mom prepping dinner, moving around the kitchen—pulling tortillas from the fridge, placing shredded chicken inside, then rolling them for enchiladas. Jiji sat at the kitchen table, a plate of senbei in front of him. She pulled a can opener from the drawer and clipped it to a can of red sauce, trying to grip but letting go with a wince.

"Here. Let me." I hip-bumped her out of the way and cranked the opener. The scent of umami-rich tomato paste filled the air.

"Thanks," she said. "How was school? Today was your first day at Sherwood, right? How'd that go?"

"Fine," I said, unable to elaborate.

My brain hyperfocused on everything that had happened in the last few hours. Ezra my mentor. Letters from the future. A boy who loved me now, who always would.

"Fine? That's all?" She shifted to Jiji. "Dad," Mom said in Japanese. "I'm making dinner right now. Please don't eat. You'll ruin your appetite."

Jiji kept eating the crackers. "Your enchiladas are too spicy. Gives me heartburn. I will be up all night." He rubbed his chest.

Lightning streaked across the sky and light rain began, splattering against the thin glass of our kitchen window. Theo's car was parked in his driveway. The lights were on in his house, and I searched for the silhouette of him.

"I made them mild." Mom opened the oven and shoved the enchiladas in. She paused at the table and pushed the crackers from Jiji's reach. "Dinner will be ready in twenty. I'm going to take a quick shower." She skipped off, saloon doors swinging behind her.

Jiji leaned forward and plucked a cracker from the plate.

"Don't tell your mother," he said. As usual, he looked as if he had stepped from an AARP catalog—bland-colored cardigan and pleated pants.

"She's going to know if you don't eat dinner."

"Eh," he said, and reached for another one.

"Jiji?" The oven fan clicked on and whirred. "Can I ask you a hypothetical question?"

"Hypothetical questions are rarely hypothetical."

"But this one is."

He stared at me overlong. "Go ahead."

Where to start? "I need to figure out who someone is. Someone who has been writing me letters but not signing their name." I paused. "Hypothetically."

Jiji pursed his lips, thinking. "Is someone threatening you?"

"No, nothing like that."

Unlike Dad or Mom, Jiji wouldn't press for more. "Reconnaissance." His milky eyes came alive, and his smile curved with the one word.

Relief flooded my limbs. "Yes," I said. "Recon. How does one do that?"

He looked meaningfully at the empty cracker plate. I popped up, grabbed the box from the cabinet, and handed it to him. He fished out a cracker and chewed. "You survey, gather information. Find out as much as you can about the enemy. Determine their whereabouts, their activities, make them reveal their weak spots."

I rolled my lips between my teeth, straightened, and dipped my chin at Jiji. Thunder clapped in the distance. Recon might be difficult, but there *was* something I could do.

I could go straight to the source.

LOVE ME TOMORROW

Okay, Letter Writer.

You got me. I'm a believer.

So, questions.

I have them. Who are you? Why are you contacting me now? How old are you? What's your name? Is Jiji still alive? Is my mom? My dad? Am I crazy for believing you? What's the future like? What's the future me like? How did you know my wish? I never told anyone about it.

Who are you? I know I already asked that. But fair is fair. You know so much about me—how do you know so much about me?!—and I don't know anything about you. Other than you're prone to hyperbole. Lose a finger from writing 276 words? Please. (Yes, I counted.)

Change my life how?

I hope you get this. I'm not sure what the rules are, how any of it works. Can I write back to you? I suppose I'll find out if this is a one-way thing. But just in case this works, answer my questions. I'm listening now.

P.S. If this is some elaborate prank, I will tear a hole through space and time and find you. There isn't a galaxy you'd be safe in. You cannot imagine the things I would do to you.

P.P.S. I hope I can trust you.

Emma,

The future is pretty much the same. Except for the whole time travel development and rich people carrying around hooded falcons? (In case you can't tell, I'm kidding about the falcons. They don't really wear hoods.)

Re: your questions. How did I know about the wish? And the secret rendezvous with Dr. Peterson, the fact that you believe instruments have souls (and you've named your violin Esther), and the dream life you fear waking from? Because you've told me these things in my time, in the future.

And last, who am I? I can't tell you. I'm sorry. I don't want to mess with the space-time continuum. Say the wrong thing, we've colonized the moon and a corgi is our president. That wouldn't be so bad, I guess. I do love corgis, really any animal that resembles a sausage. I can't tell you anything about your family, either. I'm sorry about that, too. Please see the aforementioned space-time continuum.

That said, I don't want an unequal power dynamic between us either. I'm up for some Q + A. Here are a few facts about me.

1. My most treasured possession is an album.
2. I make a mean queso dip.
3. My first childhood crush (i.e., unhealthy obsession) was Miss Piggy, and it probably lasted about a year beyond the healthy age range.
4. I think we should bring back yearning. As in "I yearn for you."

I'm going to go out on a limb here and tell you I saw future Emma the other day. You are well, and healthy. You live by yourself in a one-bedroom apartment. You like your living room the best, how it faces west, the way the light comes in in the afternoon, when it hits the hardwood floors.

We got coffee and went for a walk. There was a bench, and we sat for a while watching a turtle try to climb onto a log. Your smile was soft. A little sad.

"Did you know I made a wish once for proof that love can last?" you told me.

"Emma," I said. "Are you happy?"

"Enough," you replied.

We left it at that. But I didn't sleep the whole night. I was kept up, an ache in my gut. I went home. The whole five-hour flight to Boston, I couldn't stop thinking of you, of turning back the clock, of do-overs, of second chances . . .

Do you believe in other lives? Like there are versions of ourselves that are just particles of light waiting to materialize if only we take another path, step left instead of right? Because I do.

I believe there is another version of Emma out there, floating in the ether, unrealized. One who, when I ask if she is happy, says "yes" instead of "enough." I want you to have that life, and to have the love you deserve. And it's for a somewhat selfish reason on my part: Because I'm not whole if you're not happy.

P.S. Hunt me through space and time? Now who's prone to hyperbole? But I am interested in the things you would do to me. Would this be a clothing-optional thing? I'm sorry, you kind of walked into that.

P.P.S. You can trust me. I swear. If you were here, you'd see my hand over my heart. I [name redacted] hereby promise to do you no harm. I come in peace.

P.P.P.S. I've created an email: thechronosproject1@gmail.com. Seriously. I can't keep up with the handwritten notes. My fingers hurt.

CHAPTER TWELVE

I laughed to myself, struck giddy.

Holy eff, it had worked. He'd written me back. I'd woken up to the letter on my pillow. I'd been groggy-eyed when I sat up and opened the envelope to scan the contents. Now I read more slowly, heart thumping in my chest.

Done, I snapped a picture and sent it to Delia. She replied while I was in the shower. Towel wrapped around my body, hair dripping wet, I cleared the phone screen of fog and saw her texts.

> Forensically analyzing this, prepare for incoming.

> Sausage-shaped dogs, swoon! Adding corgis to the board.

> Queso dip?

> Miss Piggy?

> Weird.

> But okay.

> It's probably not Theo

I knew his childhood crush was Wonder Woman, and he was lactose intolerant.

> He lives in Boston.

> Who do we know that might live in Boston one day?

I paused, half dressed and hair brushed. My mood dampened, thinking through her question. How many people lived in Boston? A lot. I frowned and tapped out a response.

> There are like hundreds of thousands of people in Boston.

> He could have gone there for college.

> Or maybe he went to school there and stuck around.

> Heading to breakfast with my dad.

> Talk after.

Her last texts came through just as I arrived at the restaurant in Bellevue to meet up with Dad, Madison, and Camille:

> I'm not whole if you're not happy. Stop it. He really loves you, double swoon!!!

> Have you written him back yet?

> Call me when you're done with breakfast.

> LYB!

The hostess showed me to a table set with white linens. Camille was already sitting next to the window and texting. "Mom and Adrian are running late," she said, head still bent. "They told us to order an appetizer if we want."

I slid into a chair, wishing I were with Delia, in front of the murder board, pinning up new clues. The window overlooked the summer patio, cleared for the rainy season. Yellow umbrellas had been bunched and huddled together under a black-striped awning.

"You okay?" She dropped her phone onto the table. "You still not feeling well? You look a little pale."

Right. We hadn't texted since the party. The night when she'd handed me the information grenade that her family still went on vacations together, despite her parents being divorced. And I'd fled the party after Kevin threw up on my shoes, shooting off a text to Camille that I was under the weather.

"I'm fine." Just hopelessly distracted by a certain letter I'd brought in my bag. I'd reread it at a long red light, analyzing and reanalyzing the words.

"Wet toilet seats," Camille suddenly announced.

"What?" I startled from my thoughts.

"Things I hate."

Oh, she was picking that up again. "Yeah." I smiled. Boston and the letter writer dissolved in my mind. "We as a nation don't speak about wet toilet seats enough."

Camille grinned.

A waiter moseyed up to our table. "Can I get you something other than water to drink?"

"Two Bloody Marys." Camille spoke with the confidence of someone twenty-one.

"Got it." He dashed our order off on a tiny notepad. "Two *virgin* Bloody Marys."

Dad and Madison showed up just as he was unloading our drinks onto the table. They were holding hands, smiling. Clearly happy with each other, at the sight of Camille and me, at the possibilities of our blended family.

Dad gave me a side hug and settled in next to me. "Hitting the hard stuff?"

"I raged last night, just trying to reverse course," I deadpanned. I'd never had any practical experience with the hair of the dog. Still, I'd seen enough to know Bloody Marys were used as a popular hangover remedy. Usually I wouldn't tease my dad, evidenced by his raised eyebrows and momentary stunned silence. But I was ripping a page from Camille's notebook. I was pretty sure Camille was having a good influence on me.

"I think you've forgotten I'm your dad, and you're seventeen."

He pulled my drink over and sipped it. "Yum. Electrolytes. And alcohol-free." He set it down near my plate.

"What's everyone having?" Madison beamed at me.

I shot her a smile back, then slid my attention to the menu.

"They always seem to come back to each other," Camille had said about her parents. I told Theo I'd let it go, but it seemed the idea was still hanging on. A fingernail of worry pressed into my skin. Was my dad being played for a fool? Did he know how much Madison and her ex hung out?

All at once the waiter was by me, pad opened expectantly. I pointed to something on the menu. "I'll have this."

"The pork nachos?" He hesitated, scratching his hair with the end of his pencil. "We don't serve lunch until eleven. But I'm sure they'll make an exception." He jotted my order down and moved on to Camille.

Besides being practical, I didn't like the thought of inconveniencing anyone. Stopping the waiter to say I'd changed my mind seemed too much of a bother, so when Dad turned a brow at me, I doubled down and shrugged. "Sounded good."

Everyone else ordered breakfast, and once the food was delivered, Dad said, "Did I ever tell you about when I was nearly arrested at a park with Emma?" His fork hovered above his poached eggs.

My mind spun, trying to remember what he was talking about.

"You were probably too young to remember," he told me.

I picked up a tortilla chip and nibbled. Not bad. Nachos should be introduced into the canon of breakfast foods.

"Emma was in first grade. No wait, kindergarten." Dad's voice was gruff but warm. "She only wanted to hang out with the teachers in the classroom during recess. She even asked to eat lunch with them." Not unusual, at least for me. Vaguely I remembered feeling safe with Mrs. Hannah. I liked the way she smiled at me, as if I was her best friend. And how she'd give me stickers and share her sandwiches. Ham and Swiss cheese on a croissant would always taste like first grade. "Her teacher suggested we support"—Dad air-quoted the word "support"—"Emma in making more friends her age."

"Oh. I think I do remember this."

It was fall. The trees still had some of their leaves. The sky was overcast, and there was no rain that day. It was when Mom and Dad were still in sync. She washed the dishes and he dried them. He'd spin her around the living room while they listened to Aretha Franklin. And every birthday, she'd make his favorite carrot cake.

I didn't like remembering those days. The memories were more bitter than sweet. But for the first time, while Dad was telling this story, that usual sting of loss was all but absent. In fact, I was downright near happy.

"I took you to a park," Dad said.

Madison's smile widened. Camille perched her chin on her palm. Dad had always been a gifted storyteller, always wove a pretty tale. No wonder he was a writer.

"To practice picking up kids," I chimed in. That's what he'd told me in the car. I'd sat in the backseat of our old Volvo.

He lightly slapped his thigh. "Yes."

At the edge of the park, he'd placed his hands on my shoulders and addressed me earnestly. "You said, 'Come on, go make some friends for Daddy. Ask them if they want to play. Maybe come over.'"

Madison made a face and so did Camille.

Dad winced. "One of the other parents overheard and was concerned."

"Naturally," Camille interjected.

Dad winked at her. "The police were called."

"I was so excited to sit in their cruiser." I bounced a little in my seat, free-falling into the memory.

Dad bobbed his head. "They let Emma sit in the front seat."

"They showed me how to use the sirens!" I had tipped my chin to the lights, marveling at the spinning blue and red.

"Then what happened?" Madison urged Dad on as soon as a waiter moved out of earshot.

"They let me go with a warning about word choice and a strong suggestion to shave my mustache," said Dad.

Madison hooted. Shared laughter pinged around the table.

Later we ordered the cinnamon doughnuts served with warm caramel and chocolate.

"Well, should we tell them?" Madison looked meaningfully at my dad.

He wiped his mouth with a napkin. "As good as any time, I suppose."

Madison's hands curled in. "We're engaged." She paused, smiled, and held up both hands, wiggling her fingers. "Surprise!"

Hold up. Record scratch. *Engaged?* The word hit my stomach like a mallet. Doughnut fell from my mouth, landing in a very unfortunate brown blob on the plate.

Dad wore a half unsure smile, and I dodged it in favor of looking at Camille staring with heat at her mom.

"Engaged? As in married?" she asked. "What's the rush? You just moved in together. I mean, it's not like you're a couple of virgins rushing to the altar." Camille gestured wildly at herself. "I mean, the jig is up."

"Please, Camille." Madison's face strained.

Same, Madison. Same, I thought. I did not need to think of Madison and my dad that way. As far as I was concerned, they had one of those twin-bed 1950s situations happening upstairs in his townhouse.

Dad coughed out a laugh.

Madison swiveled to him. "Don't encourage her."

"Sorry," Camille said. "This is so fast, that's all."

"Emma," Dad said, sobering. "You're quiet."

My lips pressed tight to keep from blurting, *Madison goes on vacation with her ex-husband and might still be in love with him.* The idea of Dad marrying and having his heart broken again was a hot knife sliding through my ribs.

Silence thick, Madison and Dad found each other's hands on top of the table, watching me intensely.

What a minefield.

I eased into a smile and met my dad's eyes. "This is what you want?"

"I'm happy," he said. "We've been thinking of marriage for a while, but we wanted you and Camille to meet first. To make sure we all got along."

I twisted my napkin in my lap and steeled myself to lie. "Don't let your damage sour their love story," Theo had said. Heart in my windpipe, I forced my smile to spread, pushing my reservations to the periphery.

"Great," I said, and Dad relaxed. "Good. Congratulations."

Then I raised my glass in a toast to Madison and Dad.

From: Emma Nakamura-Thatcher
(ethatch121@gmail.com)
To: Letter Writer
(thechronosproject1@gmail.com)
Subject: Does this make you the arbiter of my soul?

Email is infinitely more convenient—why didn't you do this from the beginning?

I have so many more questions now.

First and most important—Miss Piggy. Super intrigued. What was it about her exactly? The pink skin? The hair? Don't tell me the nose!

Future Emma sounds lonely. So you've come back to change the course of my life. What's your plan, then?

Do you really love me? I don't understand why we're not together right now or in the future.

Last question. Since you seem to be pretty wise, Miss Piggy excluded . . . if you knew something about someone that would potentially hurt someone you loved, would you tell them?

I feel safe writing to you. But I'm still not sure if I should.

From: Letter Writer (thechronosproject1@gmail.com)
To: Emma Nakamura-Thatcher (ethatch121@gmail.com)
Subject: Arbiter of your soul? Nah.

Answering in order here.

Why no email from the start? I thought I'd end up in a junk folder somewhere. Plus, there is a certain timelessness to handwritten letters, don't you think?

Why Miss Piggy? Satin dresses all the way. She went to the opera with Kermit once. Wore this red off-the-shoulder number . . . made me shiver.

Future Emma? Lonely, maybe. Stuck, definitely. The plan is for me to help you live your life. Thus, I issue you a challenge. Say yes to something you'd usually say no to. Take a chance, Emma. Don't play it so safe for once. It's time to shed your reserved skin.

I do really love you. I can't tell you why we're not together. Again, I reference the space-time continuum. There has never been anyone but you for me, though. What can I say? I couldn't leave you if I tried.

As for your last question . . . It's a little hard to say without knowing all the details, but I think you keep it to yourself. William Penn said: "It is wise not to seek a Secret, and honest not to reveal one." At the risk of being called a hypocrite, I wouldn't mess with someone else's future too much. These things tend to reveal themselves in time.

CHAPTER THIRTEEN

Next session at the Sherwood Institute, Ezra was waiting for me outside studio 5. "Follow me. You won't need your violin."

His hair was damp, his leather jacket beaded with water, and his jeans were rolled up slightly, showing his socks. The duct tape on his shoe flapped against the low carpet as he walked. Operatic notes, acoustic guitar, and a harp emanated from the spaces below the closed doors.

I opened the studio door, placed my violin inside, and hurried after him. "Where are we going?"

He stopped short and turned to me, eyes holding mine. At the end of the hall, light filtered through a large art deco stained-glass window, casting Ezra in a green haze. I wondered if I could take a picture of him and send it to Delia, but that would be weird. Right?

"You're a phenomenal musician, Emma." He grabbed my hands and pulled me along, backing into a set of heavy double doors, opening one. The room was dim, but he seemed to know the way. We moved along a black curtain, stepping over cords and winding around lights. We were backstage at the Sherwood

Auditorium. He dropped my hands, and I rubbed the places he'd touched, wanting to trap the warmth.

I had been waiting for Ezra to notice me for three years. Three. Years. I'd watched him from afar, wondering if others saw him like I did. The way he seemed sad sometimes, like he was carrying the weight of the world. Now I wondered if he'd thought about me too. For the first time I really considered if he could be the letter writer. If I wasn't crazy for thinking it, trying to morph a fantasy into reality.

Lights flared to life, then powered down to one-third of their brightness. The ambience of intimate evenings illuminated by thousands of candles.

"You really are talented," Ezra said again. He crossed the stage and sat on a piano bench draped with a cloth. He patted the space beside him. "This is where you belong."

My steps were unsure as I went to meet him. Rather than sit next to him on the bench, I knelt on the floor, sitting on my knees in seiza, like I used to with Jiji when I was a little girl and we made blueberry muffins. I'd loved to stir and drop the thick batter into the paper liners.

"What is this? Some sort of Sherwood Institute rite of passage?"

He leaned forward, completely serious. "No, that involves a mannequin and a lot of duct tape."

I let my eyes travel the veins snaking up his arms. "Shoot. I'm more of a Skull and Bones secret-society type of girl."

He cracked a faint smile. "Noted. Emma likes the violin, T-shirts with puns, hooded capes, and blood-based rituals."

I swallowed and remembered Delia's words. *He had to have you.*

I shook her voice away. Silly. I was being silly. Then again, on second thought, it wouldn't hurt to do some fact-finding, see if Ezra's tastes and background were a fit for the letter writer's. Now, how to float Miss Piggy into the conversation?

"Tell me what else Emma likes," he said in a velvet tone. "Tell me what you don't like. Or better yet, tell me a secret. Do you chew gum and swallow it? Is your first love close-up magic, and your second Dungeons and Dragons?"

I stiffened, feeling oddly protective. Theo loved that game. "D and D has some redeeming qualities."

He dipped his chin. "Got it. Defensive of Dungeons and Dragons. I'll add it to the list. What else?"

"Despite my affinity for blood-based rituals, I'm rather squeamish." I paused and lowered my voice to a serious decibel. "What are we doing here?"

"We'll get to that part. Right now I want to talk about what's holding you back. I don't understand. I see your potential. Why don't you want to live up to it? Why don't you want to apply to Juilliard?"

I rubbed my chest, feeling the secret dream slip between the bars behind which I'd imprisoned it. "Not Juilliard. Berklee. That's where I'd go."

He nodded slowly. "Berklee, then."

"Pfft," was the sound I made. A cross between *No* and *This is unbelievable* and *Nice try, buddy*. I was not buying into this whole *Dead Poets Society* unconventional thing Ezra had going on.

He eased back, elbows on the closed piano. "You know, I've been living with my aunt since I was eleven. She still takes care of my brothers. They're six and nine. My aunt works a lot and needs help with them, especially during the school year. That's why I'm still here. My brothers."

I absorbed his statement with an inhale. So that's why he didn't go to Manhattan School of Music, Columbia University, Thornton, or any of the other elite programs he'd been accepted to.

He pulled a face, scratched his jaw. "They're no walk in the park. Last night I caught them on the porch of our apartment, trying to feed a Band-Aid to a squirrel. It's like they've never heard of rabies. Somewhere there's a couple of tetanus shots with their names on them."

I bit my lip, trying not to smile, but finding permission when Ezra gave me a faint grin. "It's always funny after," he said. "I stuck around this year to help my aunt out."

I shifted, curling my legs and hugging them. "Can I ask? What happened to your parents?"

"Any guess where my mom is. My dad is in the army. Stationed at Fort Lewis but deployed in Germany." His whiskey eyes glinted in the low lights, and he looked away. "My relationship with him is complicated. As in, we don't talk." A muscle in his jaw pulsed. "He asked me the other day how the guitar was going."

"Ouch," I murmured.

"Yeah." He chuckled, the sound half amused, half pained. "My dad is a good guy. I believe he loves me. He connects more with my brothers, though. Maybe it's me. But I guess it's fine, right? The stuff with my dad. I get it. He's serving the country, protecting us, and I play music."

"I don't think that's true," I ventured. "Music isn't just music. It's how we say all the things we can't otherwise. It's how I make sense of the world. But I get what you're saying about your dad. I really do. After my parents announced they were getting divorced . . ." I stopped short.

"What is it?" I had his full attention.

"I've never told anyone this." Staring at Ezra, heart in my throat, I told him about riding my bike in the rain, crying in the middle of my dad's new apartment, and begging him to come home. If I'd had a hood, I would have put it on, pulled the drawstrings closed, and stared at my lap. But I wanted him to know that I understood about fractured families, living inside the wreck.

Once I was done, he stared at me, sharing an intense, silent exchange.

"Why won't you try for Berklee?" he asked, slicing into the quiet. "Is it a money thing? Their scholarships are competitive, but you're good enough to get one."

I wiped my clammy palms on my leggings. "My mom and grandpa need me."

"Go on," he said.

I stared out at the auditorium's red upholstered seats for the length of a few breaths. "I clean houses to help make ends meet. And my grandpa is old. He used to take care of me when I was younger." I shrugged as if it were a simple matter, no big thing. "He forgets to take his hearing aids out. Sometimes his memory isn't so good." Like when he thought my mom was my grandmother. An episode that lasted less than five seconds but shook my mom and me. The doctor said he didn't have dementia. But I still worried he might wander off or get confused and agitated. He was a bit more short-tempered these days. It was easy to be, I thought, when the world moved faster and faster around you.

Ezra's expression softened. "This all makes sense. I can't tell you what to do about the family stuff. That's a heavy decision. But think about Berklee?" He paused, smiled as if offering meager comfort. "We could be neighbors. I'm heading to New England Conservatory next fall."

Struck dumb, I stared at him, shifting from the intensity of the conversation to this new revelation. "New England Conservatory, as in Boston?"

"One and the same. They're holding a spot for me. My dad is retiring at the end of this year and I'll be free."

My heart roared to life. I tried hard to modulate my tone. "That's exciting."

He hummed and said, "Could be exciting for you, too. Think about it? Berklee."

My resting place had always been close to home. How would it feel to leave my mom and Jiji? Move somewhere far away? Like Boston? Where the letter writer lived in the future? *Impossible, not going to happen* was my instant reflex. But the desire for Berklee, to play music forever, grew into a new life, a second heartbeat in my chest.

CHAPTER FOURTEEN

I walked out of the Sherwood Institute on cloud nine, only to be slammed back to earth when my car wouldn't start.

"No, no, no," I ground out, punctuating each denial by banging my head against the steering wheel.

I'd give it one more try. Fourteenth time was the charm. *Here goes.* I gripped my keys and turned. The car spluttered to life. My heart leaped out of my chest. Yes!

But then—

The car made a grinding sound, metal against metal, and abruptly died. My heart hit the brown-stained carpeted floor.

I finally gave up and texted my mom: Hello. I've just leveled down to a newer, more vicious circle of hell.

Mom replied: I don't have time for this.

My car won't start, I thumbed back. I am in the middle of downtown Seattle. I dropped the pin with the address. I'd parked on the street instead of in the more expensive garage.

On my way, she said.

I hopped out of my busted vehicle and leaned back against the door. The rain had stopped, and the sun was peeking through the gray clouds.

Forty minutes later a black Honda Civic rolled up. Theo's car.

I sprung open the passenger door. "What are you doing here? I called my mom."

Theo flicked on his hazards and climbed from his car, leaving it running. "Grateful much? You aren't aware of it, but I will leave you to die here."

"Sorry," I said genuinely. "I'm hungry and grumpy."

Theo sighed and rounded his car. "Your mom is at a doctor's appointment. She asked me to grab you and look at your car." Mom was at doctor's appointment? Why didn't she tell me that? He held out a hand. "Keys."

I deposited them in his open fist, my fingers grazing his. Theo opened the driver's side door and sat down.

Covertly, I studied him. This was my first time seeing Theo since accepting the idea that the letter writer might be real. I'd crossed him off the list because of the queso dip and his childhood crush, Wonder Woman. Also, he was dead set on Caltech.

But what if Theo changed his mind and decided to go to a different school after all? Transferred from Caltech to a college in Boston after a year or two? Maybe he'd go to graduate school in Massachusetts. Or drop out to found a startup. Get a job in the Hub and move there. What if Future Theo was less strict about his lactose intolerance? What if he'd lied about Wonder Woman?

"Emma?"

I snapped to. "What?"

"You're acting weirder than usual. I asked what was going on with your car."

"No idea." I looked at my nails. "It won't start."

He stuck the keys in the ignition and turned. The same gasp

emitted from the engine. My poor Buick LeSabre. Theo cranked the ignition again, eyes darkening from moss to juniper as he focused. The hair at the nape of his neck curled. I wondered what it would be like to touch one of the strands, pull down on it and watch it spring back up.

"I think it's your starter. I can fix it, but we'll need to tow the car back to the house."

Of course Theo could fix it. He was a whiz at mechanics—science and engineering stuff came naturally to him. So naturally, he might be really into time travel. Was that too much of a leap? No pun intended.

We climbed into Theo's car and pulled into Seattle early-evening traffic. I turned and placed my violin case in the backseat.

"There's granola bars in the glove box," he said.

I popped it open and unwrapped a bar, biting into it and moaning. "So good. Have I mentioned how much I love oats and chocolate?"

Theo shot me a weird look and adjusted in his seat. "What were you doing out here, anyway?"

"Practicing with Ezra at the Sherwood Institute."

"The cello guy from your school?" Heat entered his tone.

"One and the same."

He pursed his lips. "Why didn't he help you?"

"I didn't ask him to help me."

"How come he didn't at least walk you to your car?"

"I don't know."

"Did he even offer?" Theo stopped at a crosswalk and agitatedly waved a woman with a stroller across.

"Why does it matter?"

"It's almost dark. That isn't the best neighborhood." His voice was terse.

"It's six thirty, and if it got too late, I was going to wait in the Burger King across the street."

He mumbled something that I missed and kept frowning, his forehead lined. Minutes passed. Theo continued to stew.

I sighed loudly and rolled my eyes.

Nothing.

An idea formed. I plugged my phone into his car, scrolled through, and hit Play. A pop song started. Excuse me, *the* pop song. The one Theo and I listened to nonstop in the fifth grade and made up our own choreography to.

I shimmied in my seat.

Theo steered out of downtown. One corner of his mouth turned up before slamming back down. "I'm still upset. This isn't going to work."

I shimmied again. "Are you sure? Because I think it's working."

He swiped a hand down his face, trying and failing to contain his smile. "You're the worst dancer I've ever seen."

I used my hand as a phone and placed it to my ear, mouthing along with the song. Most of our choreography was literal body interpretations of the lyrics. "Or am I the best dancer you've ever seen?"

Theo's grin hit me full force. "You're ridiculous and I hate you."

I laughed too and settled down. The song faded, and I let the rest of the album play.

We drove for a while, and I chewed on my thoughts.

Could Theo be the letter writer? He planned on Caltech. A

full-ride scholarship. But that didn't mean his future was set. He could deviate from his course. Or be rerouted. Maybe he wouldn't get into Caltech.

How would I *feel* if Theo was the letter writer? My stomach flipped, thrilled and anxious.

I cared for Theo so much. Sometimes it felt like we operated on the same emotional frequency. I felt what he felt. When he got headgear in middle school and could only drink from a straw, I woke with a phantom ache in my jaw. Then I made him smoothies, sat on the end of his bed, and played sad music on my violin—a soundtrack to match his mood.

He turned down the volume. "You're very serious all of a sudden, and it makes me suspicious."

I pursed my lips. "You're still set on Caltech next year, right?"

He checked his blind spot and crossed to the middle lane. "I'm working on my application right now."

Yes. Of course he was. Theo had had a vision board since he was thirteen. Excluding the pictures of dragons, it was all about manifesting his next twenty years. Advanced Placement classes in high school. Early college admission. Undergraduate double major in physics and mathematics, and graduate studies with an undetermined PhD track, but most likely in mechanics. I had a flash of him sitting in an H. G. Wells sled-like time machine. The image made me sort of buzzy. "What are your thoughts about time travel?"

He considered it. "That's a complicated question, and I'm glad you asked."

"Don't respond if the answer involves fishing."

How many times had I heard the story? Too many to count.

Mostly when he was playing games, one of his endless quests. He'd talk about fishing with his dad. How it wasn't about the catch, but the time spent together.

"And risk my nuts being torn clean from my body? No, thank you." He shot me a side grin. I'd put a hard stop to the fishing stories. Two dozen retellings would do in anyone. "Einstein's calculations show that time travel is theoretically possible, but it's never been proven."

"So you believe in it? Think it could happen? Like you might study it?"

Did Future Theo *invent* time travel? My palms began to sweat, and I wiped them against the seat.

He scoffed quietly. "No. Absolutely not. That stuff is fringe science. I'd be laughed from Caltech at the mention of it. Belly buttons will grow mouths and speak before time travel exists."

Okay. So maybe it was far-fetched, the idea of Theo inventing time travel.

"What's with the interest in time travel all of a sudden?" he asked, looking at me.

"I don't know." I forced the lie out and lightness into my voice. "I guess I'm just thinking of the future. If you could go back in time, what would you do?"

If Theo had the chance, would he reach back to someone he loved to help them, like the letter writer had with me?

"I don't know. Maybe I'd go back and meet one of my heroes?"

"Einstein?"

"Him or Isaac Newton," he said.

"What about to change someone's life?"

His eyes narrowed in skepticism. "I restate, weirder than

usual. Did you drink more than one Frappuccino today?"

The Frappuccino incident—when Delia and I had walked to the Starbucks down the street and gotten Frappuccinos but didn't know they had caffeine. We were three deep and so hyped before we realized it. Theo ran laps with us around the block.

Best to leave that alone, since I'd had a couple today. My first sip of coffee had been a point of no return.

"If I could go back in time, I'd make myself rich, like find out the lottery numbers or buy stock in Apple," I said.

Mom wouldn't have to work so hard, then. I could afford a full-time nurse for Jiji. Hire a chef. Someone to clean *our* house. Apply to Berklee and play my heart out at the Sherwood Institute finale recital with scouts.

My skin tingled at the possibilities. At what I would do, who I could be, whom I'd love.

If the world weren't such a thorny place, I'd be limitless.

From: Emma Nakamura-Thatcher
(ethatch121@gmail.com)
To: Letter Writer
(thechronosproject1@gmail.com)
Subject: Quoting William Penn? Does that mean you majored in philosophy? History?

So. The tricky scenario I mentioned . . . My dad is getting married, and I'm pretty sure the woman he's engaged to is still hung up on her ex. I decided not to say anything to him for now.

I wish you could tell me if he's with her in the future. If he's happy. Or if he's unhappy. In which case, I should really say something now. Your advice was a little hypocritical (you said it).

What's so wrong with wanting him not to get hurt? What's wrong with wanting him to take the path of least resistance?

From: Letter Writer (thechronosproject1@gmail.com)
To: Emma Nakamura-Thatcher (ethatch121@gmail.com)
Subject: I took philosophy as an elective. Next question, please.

Ah, got it. Your question was about your dad. I understand. I really do.

Of course you don't want your dad to get hurt. There would be something seriously wrong with you if you enjoyed that sort of thing. Taking the path of least resistance may keep a person safe, but it also keeps their life small too. And maybe that hurts more in the long run?

CHAPTER FIFTEEN

A writer, a musician, and an artist were in the same room...

It sounds like the beginning of a bad joke, but really, it was the start of the best idea ever. My smile widened at the sight of Delia and Camille in my bedroom.

In elementary and middle school, I'd had Theo. But then we'd gone to different high schools. The first day I ate lunch alone at a table in the farthest corner of the cafeteria. I almost took my tray to the bathroom but couldn't bring myself to eat in a stall, sitting on a toilet. I watched groups of kids with their heads tilted together, sharing secrets and having fun already. Theo's absence loomed large.

Soon after, I met Delia in fifth period, and instead of playing the icebreaker game of two truths and a lie, she asked me the same question she was asking Camille now:

"Do you like cats?" Delia lay across my bed, chin in her hand, and stared at Camille.

Camille sat at my desk, swiveling back and forth in the chair. She paused, tilted her head, considering. "Who doesn't?"

"That makes me instantly like you."

The conversation flowed naturally after that, running the gamut from what we liked to read—horror, romance, and everything in between—to our favorite movies. *Paddington 2* topped all our lists. We finished on "If you got a tattoo, what would you get?" I said I'd get an E string on the inside of my wrist, a mi, the first note I ever learned to play.

"May I ask"—Delia switched her focus to me—"what you are doing?"

"Nothing."

Actually, I was looking at Ezra's photograph from Getty Images on my phone. Maybe I was imagining the veins in his arms, how his muscles flexed when he held his bow and inched it slowly across his cello. Delia had freaked when I told her Ezra was going to New England Conservatory next year. In Boston. The same city the letter writer lived in. For my part, I was trying to stay calm about the whole thing. To keep from getting too excited and crashing through a window like the Johnsons' trash-eating golden retriever did after seeing a squirrel.

Camille lunged forward and plucked the phone from my hands. "Who's the guy?"

Delia crawled over, shot me a knowing smile, and answered. "His name is Ezra French," she said. "We went to high school with him. He enjoys the cello and cherry lollipops and has deep-set hooded eyes that stare into your soul. He is also Emma's mentor right now." My brow lowered at Delia. Undaunted, she continued. "She wants him to teach her *all* sorts of things."

I frowned even harder at Delia. But inside, my stomach was doing flip-flops. I'd replayed our afternoon on the stage over and over again in my head. Focusing on the way he'd leaned forward into me. The way he'd smiled. The softness in his tortured poet's eyes. Basically, analyzing every single second we'd been together and what signals, if any, he'd been sending.

Could he be writing to me from the future? Could he have fallen in love with me at first sight? Could he be the letter writer?

There I went again, chasing that squirrel.

Camille pursed her lips and threw my phone on the bed. "Good luck. That guy has heartbreaker written all over him."

"Ha!" I laughed at Camille's comment.

Camille drilled a finger on top of the phone, right over Ezra's face. "Trust me. I know a dangerous boy when I see one. And this one has red lights blinking all over him. And you"—she turned to Delia—"said he's a musician?"

Delia nodded once. "The best."

"That's even worse." Camille swiveled back to me. "He'll never love you more than his music."

I huffed out a laugh. Tight defensiveness rose up. "Come on."

"I mean it." She dipped her chin to the phone. "Ezra, that's his name?" Delia nodded in affirmation. "Ezra is a crying-on-the-floor, sage-your-house, change-your-hair, have-sex-with-someone-questionable, move-to-another-country, wreck-your-life type of guy. Trust me. I lost my third virginity to a guy like that, and I'm still not over it."

Delia piped in before I could ask what a third virginity was. "This conversation is making me realize I've never hugged anyone male except my dads, and that makes me deeply sad." She wilted a little.

I let out a shaky breath. "I don't want Ezra to be my boyfriend," I insisted, though it wasn't true. "I'd just like him to . . ." I stopped short.

What *did* I want from Ezra? What did I want for myself?

I zeroed in on the My Little Pony throw pillow on my bed. I'd had it since I was in second grade. My clothing was in the same arena. Old. Ill fitting, too big. From some bygone era. A perfect metaphor for the foot I still had stuck in the past. New underwear had been a good first step.

"It's not about Ezra. Well, maybe a little. I would like to be, to look like, someone he'd date. But what I really want . . ." I paused and waved a hand around, on the cusp of something. "None of this feels like me anymore, is what I mean."

"Well," said Camille on a pensive hum. "In that case, I can help you." She got to her feet, marched to my closet, and opened the door.

"What are you doing?" I asked.

She searched through the rack, stripping clothes from their hangers and tossing them on the bed. "Breaking your ancient curse of khaki pants and punny shirts." Staring down at the pile, Camille pressed her fingertips to her temples. She massaged as if rubbing away a tension headache. "Do you have anything outside the category of machine washable and made with comfort in mind?"

I dug through and pulled out a plain white T-shirt. "What about this? It's a V-neck."

Delia gave me two enthusiastic thumbs-ups.

"No." Camille snapped the shirt from my hands. "Just no." She scrunched her nose and perched her hands on her hips. "To be honest, all these clothes kind of make me want to say sorry and tell you everything is going to be okay." Flicking away a couple of Jiji's sweaters and two of my violin shirts, she unearthed a Hawaiian-print button-up and set it aside. Then did the same with my favorite pair of jeans, light blue denim and broken in. "These have potential. You got a pair of scissors?"

Delia shimmied off the bed. She dived into her bag and produced a pair of gleaming metal scissors. "Like these?"

Camille turned on some music, and it began.

Sixty minutes later I had reached my final form.

Maybe.

Delia and Camille hadn't let me see myself in the mirror yet.

"Hang on." Camille crouched in front of me, eyes focused as she snipped a thread from my jeans, which had turned into shorts. Very short shorts. "Okay." She rose from her crouching position. "Done. Take a peek."

Slowly I turned to the full-length mirror. My hand pressed to my tummy at the punch of excitement. My eyes traveled the length of my body.

Was it my body? I wasn't sure. A vague impression of me stared back from the mirror. My legs were showing. A lot more legs than I was used to showing. On top, I wore the Hawaiian-print shirt, but Camille had left the last three buttons undone and tied the flaps into a bow, my belly button playing peekaboo under the knot. I twirled to look at my butt.

"Wait." Delia appeared at my side and flicked open the top two buttons of the shirt so the shadow of my lacy bra showed.

"I don't know." I skirted my hands against the jean shorts. "Are these too short? You can practically see my vagina."

Delia frowned. "I'd say they're vagina suggestive at best."

I gestured downward toward my bare legs. "I'm so cold." Most days the weather topped out at fifty-five degrees.

"Here." Camille grabbed Jiji's cardigan and threw it at me.

I slipped it on, new and old Emma merging. The best of both worlds. I tried to picture myself wearing these clothes in a different place, in a different life . . . striding across campus at Berklee maybe. Since being onstage with Ezra, I'd been scrolling through the college's website, entertaining the idea of applying after all. I stroked the arm of the well-worn cardigan. But how could I leave Jiji? He needed me, and I needed him, too.

Delia gripped my waist and laid her head on my shoulder. "This is the outfit," she said. "Be one with your inner cat. Lick."

I smiled shakily. Delia's head still on my shoulder, I half turned. From the back, you couldn't tell I was wearing shorts. The sweater was too long. "Yeah. Okay. I feel good."

All of that had worked up an appetite. I spilled down the stairs with my newly anointed supergroup and into the kitchen for food.

Theo was at the sink, washing grease from his hands. "Hey," he said, back to us. "I think I fixed your car. It was the starter . . ." He turned, stopped short, towel hanging loose in his grip. "You look different." His voice was a little deeper than before. "And you smell . . ." He sniffed. "Like fruit?"

"It's strawberries," Camille offered. She'd had some lotion in her purse, and I'd smoothed it over my legs.

My newfound confidence fled. I suddenly felt unsure, awkward. My left hand moved to cover the thin strip of skin between my shirt and shorts.

"Strawberries." Theo kept his eyes on me, working the towel over his hands.

"It's for Emma's sex quest," Camille so helpfully announced.

Theo's smile died. "Sex quest?"

"She's joking," I cut in. "I wanted to look nice for my life. That's all."

A beat of recognition flashed on Theo's face, followed by . . . irritation? Jealousy? I wasn't sure. He hung his head and gripped the back of his neck. He huffed out a laugh. "Good. Then I don't have to tell you how breathtakingly dumb it is to change for a guy."

My cheeks prickled with the sting of his insult. "Ouch," I said tartly.

"Hi. I'm Camille." Camille stepped between us, hand out, cutting the tension.

Theo stared at me, then turned to Camille. "Hey. Theo." He placed his palm in hers.

"I like your shirt." Camille popped a hip against the counter.

Theo glanced down like he'd forgotten what he was wearing. On his tee was an animal with the head of an owl and the body of a bear, the words "Monstrous Creature" below it. "You play?"

"Some." She tilted her head. "You ever check out Chainmail?"

Theo's eyes flashed. "You know Chainmail, and you just play some?"

Camille grinned. "More than some." She put a hand on her chest. "Elektra the Bard."

"Griffin. Level-eight Paladin."

My eyes bounced back and forth between Camille and Theo.

"Are you witnessing this?" Delia whispered beside me, a box of graham crackers open in her hands.

"What is this?" I stage-whispered back to her.

Theo and Camille were lost in a conversation. Words such as "Volo" and "Xanathar" floated past my uncomprehending ears.

"I'm pretty sure this is an early mating ritual of Dungeons and Dragons. Very rarely seen in the wild," Delia said.

I snickered, though my thoughts were more serious. *Was* there a spark between Theo and Camille? I couldn't tell for sure. I once saw Theo chat up a middle-aged white dude at a train shop for forty minutes about tabletop games. After, he was all jittery like he'd mainlined Mountain Dew. When we got in the car, he hit the steering wheel and said, "I am so hyped. Do you have any idea who that guy was?" I did not.

Camille was speaking to Theo, whole body animated while she explained something. He smiled and glanced at me, tilted his head in such a way. We would do this often—catch each other's eyes across a room and know, without speaking, what the other was thinking.

Like right now I knew what he was doing, apologizing for calling me breathtakingly dumb.

I sent him a look back that meant *No worries. No worries at all.*

CHAPTER SIXTEEN

Sunday morning I slipped on ratty sweats and an old T-shirt, then headed to the St. Jameses' house in Yarrow Point. Wind whipped at my cheeks going up the drive. Hefting my buckets and vacuum, I nodded at Mrs. St. James. She stood parked in the dirt, wearing a pair of Gucci loafers, chatting with a landscaper. She waved me on inside. I pushed through the front door and got started. I tried to imagine wearing $1,200 shoes in bark chips, and honestly, I could not.

An hour later I was upstairs in the primary bedroom, picking up Mrs. St. James's clothes from the closet floor to vacuum. A hotel key card and receipt tumbled from the pocket of a pair of crepe pants.

I picked them up, peering at the key card in the low light of the closet. It was from a five-star hotel in downtown Seattle, a glass and metal building overlooking Elliott Bay. And the receipt was from the Michelin Starred restaurant inside. Multiple drinks. Two entrees. Signed by Colin and Sebastian's mom, dated last night.

Well. This didn't look too good. Mr. St. James was gone on a business trip. I knew because I'd folded his clothing for his suitcase last week. Was Mrs. St. James having an affair?

A dark cloud settled over me. I wished I had never seen the key card or receipt.

The sound of a throat clearing came from behind me, and I jumped.

Swinging around, I saw Sebastian. No, not Sebastian. Colin. The more sensitive, earnest, I-keep-old-Winnie-the-Pooh-books-on-my-shelf brother.

I hid the key card and receipt behind my back. "Hi," I squeaked out. My lungs had momentarily stopped working. "I didn't know you were home. Did you need something?" I managed an even voice.

I'd already tidied up his room, dusted all his shelves, and then vacuumed, starting at the farthermost corner so there wouldn't be any of my tracks in the carpet.

"I was, um . . ." He shifted from foot to foot, lurking like a too-tall, too-broad-shouldered dark omen. "You left this in my room." In his hand hung one of my microfiber towels. We bought them in bulk at Costco, along with Jiji's pants.

Shoving the receipt and key card into the waistband of my sweats, I stepped forward and took the towel. "Thanks."

"Sure," he murmured.

Silence descended, and my stomach growled, making the most unfortunate noise.

First, telling both brothers I found them equally unappealing during my initial clean, then word-vomiting "I cut the meat" at Ezra, and now this. Was it genetic? My susceptibility to embarrassing moments? "Probably should have eaten more than a banana this morning."

His eyes tracked me. "You've only eaten a banana today?"

"Technically, three-quarters of a banana." The last bite had had a bruise. I'd left it along with the peel on the passenger seat of my car. I shifted. The key card and receipt dug into my back.

My parents had had some pretty tense conversations during the divorce. Dad would be on his way. Mom would usher me next door to Theo's house so they could talk alone. Theo's mom sat me down in the living room, turned on *Mary Poppins*, and gave us leftover Cadbury Creme Eggs from Easter. She'd been trying so hard to make me happy because she felt sad for me.

I didn't want Colin, anyone, to have that type of memory. My throat clogged just fearing the possibility. This was how families eroded. Someone like me removed a tiny rock, and everything tumbled down. Plus, I didn't even know if she was cheating. She could have had dinner with a girlfriend, had too many drinks and crashed at a five-star hotel to sleep it off. Very plausible. Still. I would like it very much if Colin left, so I could dispose of the evidence.

"Was there something else you needed?"

"No," he said slowly, making a meal of the word. Another beat passed. My stomach stayed mercifully silent. He rocked back on his heels. "I guess I'll leave you to it, then." He shuffled off, and the tension eased from my body.

I buried the key card and receipt in the trash. Then stuffed Mrs. St. James's clothes in the dry-cleaning basket, men's cologne pluming. Sebastian's dad wore another scent, a bottle with a cowboy on it.

I cleaned the bathtub and glass canisters next to it, scrubbed the toilet, and forgot all about Colin. Easy, since he seemed to have disappeared.

Downstairs, I headed into the kitchen and stopped short.

That's where Colin had gone.

He was at the marble island, a towel slung over his shoulder. In front of him was a loaf of bread that smelled divine. There was also a bag of artisanal chips, which I did not know existed until that moment. Bold letters stated that each potato was hand-cut and fried in small batches. And there was more: thick-sliced turkey, ripe avocado, some type of aioli, whipped cream cheese, and red onion. He'd put it all into a mammoth sandwich.

"Here." He pushed the sandwich and plate in my direction. I glanced behind me to make sure he wasn't speaking to anyone else. Nope. Just us two. "I made you lunch. You said you hadn't eaten."

Again I glanced behind me. This was unheard of. Aside from my cups of tea with Mrs. Sydney, I'd never sat at a client's house and eaten their food. Would that be considered stealing? I mean, he was offering it. Maybe he was tricking me. But to what end? I didn't know the games rich people played. Maybe he was trying to fatten me up so he could hunt me.

"It's okay," he said. "Nobody else is here, if that's what you're worried about. Sebastian is out, my dad is in Thailand, and my mom went to the store—something about rabbits eating her bushes." He dipped his chin. "Sit. Eat."

I was hungry. The sandwich *did* look good, and it seemed to mean a lot to him. "Okay," I said, still leery.

His shoulders relaxed. A tiny smile. "Okay," he repeated back at me.

I placed my bucket under the island and carefully sat on one of the upholstered linen stools. Colin scooted the plate until it was square in front of me. The bread smelled even better up close.

"Something to drink?" he asked. They had one of those glass-door refrigerators. On the top shelf were cans of soda and bottles of carbonated water.

"Water." I picked up one half of the sandwich. "Please." He popped the cap off a bottle of Perrier and placed it in front of me. "Thank you." I watched him. "This is really unexpected and nice."

"You should make time for lunch," he said.

Well. There really was no way to process that statement, so instead I took a bite of the sandwich, and flavors exploded in my mouth. I stifled a groan.

The dent between Colin's eyebrows smoothed. "You like it? I've spent the last few years perfecting the turkey sandwich."

He was serious, and I was reminded, not in a bad way, that we were worlds apart. Mom and Dad shared the expenses where I was concerned. I always had clothes and food. But we shopped at Grocery Outlet and searched the sale racks at stores. Anything beyond that, like hand-carved deli turkey, was considered a luxury. It wasn't his fault, but Colin didn't understand the privilege of food. I put that aside, finished chewing, and swallowed. "It was worth it. Even if you had to quit school and pursue sandwich making full-time."

He put his elbows on the island and leaned toward me, as if readying to confess a dark secret. "I use whipped cream cheese, minced marjoram, and cranberry bread."

A funny image of Colin at an herb farm popped into my mind. Walking the fields, threading his way through the plants to find the perfect stalk of marjoram, and throwing an absolute fit when none of it was right.

"Try the other one."

I did. This half was better than the first. Toasted bread, bacon, turkey, ripe smashed avocado, garlic mayo, and red onion. "You have stolen fire from the gods," I said, taking another bite.

"I'm glad you like it."

His earnestness chipped away at my resistant shell. I took a sip of water, then said, "I do. So much."

He drew a finger across his lower lip. "I was thinking . . ."

The front door slammed shut and Sebastian strode in, wearing basketball shorts and a red T-shirt with a collegiate-looking *H* ringed with sweat. He didn't see me at first, only Colin. "That was a complete waste of time."

Colin straightened. "Sebastian, I thought you were going to play basketball."

I froze, sandwich in hand.

"That was the plan, but then all these kids showed up. So annoying," said Sebastian.

Colin scratched his jaw. "Yes. When did it become socially acceptable to bring children to a park?"

"Exactly. I . . ." Sebastian's eyes snapped to me. Silence stretched, dipping into uncomfortable territory. "Hello," he said, amused curiosity in his tone.

The smell of bleach wafted up from my bucket on the floor. Right. It reminded me I shouldn't be here, sitting at the counter, eating their food, complimenting my boss's sandwich-making skills. I was the house cleaner.

I pushed away from the island and stood abruptly, nearly knocking over my chair. "Oh, God. Sorry!" I smiled weakly as I righted the chair, frantically reaching for words. "Thanks for lunch. Super delicious. I should go. I mean, get back to work. Those toilets aren't going to clean themselves," I rushed out. "Thanks again, and don't worry about the dishes. I'll wash them when I do the kitchen."

Then I picked up my bucket and fled to the guest bathroom, shutting myself in.

CHAPTER SEVENTEEN

Next session at the Sherwood Institute, Ezra surprised me again.

He was waiting for me outside the building, rocking back on his heels by the glass doors. "Field trip," he announced, seeing me.

He didn't give me time to speak but breezed past me and started walking. I followed him down the block, eyes wide, air cool against my legs. I was wearing the outfit Camille and Delia had helped me put together.

"A couple of warnings before you see my car." Ezra was in front of me, keys twirling on his pointer finger. He had a bounce to his step. Like he was keeping a private rhythm. "The seat belts stick. And it came with a weird smell. Like it might need an exorcism."

"Got it," I said, trying to keep up. "It's a bring-your-own-airbags type of situation."

He scratched the top of his head. "Ejection seat might be better. This particular car has a habit of bursting into flames if rear-ended."

We rounded a corner.

Sandwiched between a minivan and a Mini Cooper was the ugliest car I'd ever seen. The bumper was crooked, and that was the nicest thing I could say about it. The body was rusted and sharp angled. The headlights were small and beady eyed. The back looked as if it had been hacked off by a rusty ax. Someone had tried to cover the original puke-green paint with matte black, but the color still shone through.

Ezra indeed had a demon car.

"I tried to fix the paint myself."

"You can't tell," I whispered, shocked.

He shook his head, shoulders slumped. "You're a terrible liar."

The heavy door creaked when I opened it. I settled in the passenger seat, while Ezra climbed into the driver's side. "It doesn't smell that bad."

He stuck the key into the ignition and turned, cranked the wheel, and cruised into traffic. "I sprayed some off-brand cologne from the dollar store in here a few weeks ago. It cost me two whole bucks. I splurged."

"Yeah, sometimes you have to treat yourself."

He fought a smile. "Amen."

Ten or so blocks down, he slowed and parked near an alley with an iron gate that looked as if it might be the entrance to a magical fantasyland.

"Here. You might need this." He popped open the glove box, elbow brushing my bare knee. The leather of his motorcycle jacket was soft against my skin. A sudden spark of heat rushed through me. He fisted a flashlight and handed it to me.

The sky was dim, the color of newspaper, but it was still day. What did we need a flashlight for? I wasn't sure I wanted to find out. "Maybe we should go back to Sherwood. Where flashlights aren't required."

"Trust me," he said, getting out of the car.

"Said the serial killer to the girl," I muttered, climbing out of the passenger seat, nerves and excitement tangled inside me.

He pushed open the gate. "After you."

I crept into the dark alley. "Now I am more and more sure I am about to become the star of a *Dateline* episode."

At the end was a metal trapdoor, and Ezra lifted it to reveal a rickety wooden staircase. "There a reason you reference murder so much?"

"What can I say? You inspire me."

He coughed a laugh into his fist. "In you go." He shone the flashlight down the stairs.

"I'm good." Self-preservation reared. Theo and I had watched *The Sixth Sense* when we were eleven. We'd snuck in an iPad and watched it on his bed. Remember that scene when Haley Joel Osment gets stuck in the dark room? I was staring into the face of that. "I actually feel better staying aboveground. Like my life has more meaning up here."

"I'll go first." Down he went, footsteps gently thumping against the wood. "Come on, fraidy-cat," he hollered, paused at the bottom, hands cupped around his mouth.

How did Ezra use a term like "fraidy-cat" and still sound cool? I peered at him, holding the flashlight, beam pointed down at his duct-taped shoes, and waiting.

Future Emma? Lonely, maybe. Stuck, definitely. The plan is for me to help you live your life. Thus, I issue you a challenge. Say yes to something you'd usually say no to. Take a chance, Emma. Don't play it so safe for once. It's time to shed your reserved skin. The letter writer's words flashed on the inside of my eyelids.

Okay. I got it.

I crept down after him. The stairs were definitely not up to code. Gooseflesh rose on my arms.

"Where are we?" I hopped down from the last step. The tunnel smelled musty and like burning wax.

"Seattle's underground. C'mon." He thrust out a hand.

I stared and remembered watching that same hand as it slid a bow across his cello while at SAMA. I had been in total awe of his strength and precision, of how we mere mortals could make such divine sounds.

I drew forward, hypnotized by the dark, the mystery, being with him, and I took Ezra's hand. To my abject disappointment, he did not lace his fingers through mine. Instead he held my hand like Jiji used to, fingers clamped over my palm.

We walked the line of a brick wall, and I startled when I saw cloaked, hooded figures lining the path ahead of us. Their hands were cupped and outstretched, cradling battery-lit votive candles. Sparkly beaded necklaces were draped around their wrists like rosaries.

Ezra squeezed my fingers.

The figures were still. Eerily still. Not real. My heart calmed down. "Papier-mâché?" One of the figures had a sign safety-pinned to its front: *This way madness lies.*

"Plaster," he said. "Ashley Peters made them a few years ago."

Right, she'd been a SAMA student. A sculptor. She was a senior when I was a freshman. After graduation she'd gone to the School of the Art Institute of Chicago. I understood I was in some sacred place where kids from SAMA gathered. Cool kids. Like Ezra and Ashley. Not like me or Delia.

There were a dozen or more hooded figures before the tunnel widened into a bustling room full of people. I recognized some of the kids from SAMA. Some I didn't know at all. But they all carried the same hip aura.

A makeshift stage had been built out of pallets. On top was a microphone. An assortment of instruments lay behind it. Orange extension cords ran along the floor, snaked down the tunnel, and disappeared. Mismatched lamps illuminated the space.

"Ezra!" a girl shouted across the way. She was manning a keg, pumping beer into plastic cups.

Ezra dropped my hand and gave her a salute.

Disappointment stabbed at my insides. Someone had dragged a chenille couch and matching armchair with yellow and blue chrysanthemums down here. Ezra told me to sit, and he'd get us something to drink. I followed his instructions, but I should have considered what would happen to my shorts when I did. In that they seemed to shrink to one-third their size. My legs were in bathing suit territory now. I watched him drop a few bills into a jar in exchange for two red Solo cups.

I whipped out my phone and texted Delia.

I'm out with Ezra and he just paid for my drink.

You're on a date, she replied with a burst of celebratory confetti.

Ezra came back, girl in tow. I stuffed my phone away. He flopped onto the couch and deposited a drink in my hand. Our thighs were touching, knee to hip. My heart thudded.

"Too much foam," the girl said. "I can fix that for you." She licked her finger and stuck it into my beer, swirling it around.

"Tenny. Gross," said Ezra. "Nobody wants your finger beer."

Tenny frowned hard at Ezra and swapped out my beer with hers. "I didn't drink from it yet," she explained with a wink.

A guy with bright green hair tapped the microphone. "This is kind of hard for me, but here goes. This poem is called 'Ode to Muffy.'" He began to read from a crumpled piece of paper.

"Are we poets now?" I leaned over and whispered to Ezra, throat dry, and confused about what we were doing here. How was this related to the violin or the Sherwood Institute?

"Yep," he said. "You're reading next."

I looked at him with wide, terrified eyes.

He cupped my knee. More fire erupted across my skin. "Kidding. We're here to listen. Plus, you must be this tall to be onstage." He held his hand up as if measuring me.

"Ha." I blinked at him, composed myself. "You're adorable." I sipped my beer. It was sour and room temperature.

He stared at me, a new look in his eyes.

"What?" I wondered if I had something stuck in my teeth. Note to self: Don't have a spinach salad with poppy-seed dressing before going out with a hot guy.

"I was just thinking. How come we never hung out when I was at SAMA?"

I didn't want to respond defensively, but the words came out anyway. "Is that a real question?"

Ezra slumped back against the couch and turned his cup in his hands. "Yes."

I shrugged, blood rushing to my cheeks. Having to explain was embarrassing.

I got it. Where Ezra was coming from, he had this whole couldn't-be-bothered, high-school-was-beneath-him vibe, but surely he understood who he'd been at school, the pedestal he'd stood on, how revered he'd been.

"I sat in the corner of the lunchroom."

Ezra listened, brow pinching, confused. "Okaaay." He drew the word out.

"You sat in the middle of the lunchroom. Under the halo of lights with all the other stars of SAMA, like Ashley Peters. I'm not . . . I wasn't one of the special ones. You were . . . are," I spluttered out.

He stared at me, unfazed. "Just because we never hung out doesn't mean I didn't see you, Emma."

I snorted, couldn't take the intensity. "Please."

"I'm serious." His voice deepened. "I saw you."

Well. I didn't know what to say to that. How to answer. Or handle the truth, that I had wanted Ezra to see me. Maybe even to love me. It was embarrassing even thinking it.

Could I trust him?

If he was the letter writer, I could. I could let go. I could say out loud what I hoped for.

I suppressed my smile and turned back toward the speaker. Green Hair continued to wax poetic into the microphone about playing in the park with Muffy. How time slowly changed things, how Muffy couldn't walk anymore and had to sit on a bench while he ran ahead. It made me think of Jiji, and tears sprung to my eyes. But then I straightened. "Wait a minute, is he talking about his hamster? I thought Muffy was his grandmother."

"Did you miss the part about him kissing Muffy's pink nose and comparing her teeth to ripe summer corn?"

My shoulders began to shake, and a peal of laughter burst forth. Ezra fought a smile.

When Green Hair finished, he hopped off the stage and crammed himself next to Tenny in the armchair.

"Nice poem, babe," she said to him.

He smacked her on the lips. "Thanks. Muffy was the best. You never really get over your first hamster, or your second or third or twenty-fifth." He sipped Tenny's beer and lifted his chin to me. "I'm Blue." Then he pointed to his green hair. "It's ironic."

"Emma," I said.

He leaned forward, addressing Ezra. "I thought of another name."

Ezra swiped a hand down his face. "Yeah? Do I want to know?"

Tenny grinned at me. "Did Ezra tell you we're starting a band?"

"Tenny and Blue are starting a band," Ezra qualified.

"For which Ezra would be our lead singer," Blue grumbled. He patted along his pant pocket and pulled out rolling papers plus a little baggie of weed.

"But I wouldn't go to school," Ezra interjected. "I'd trade in my full-ride scholarship for months of sleepless nights on a bus, eating shitty food at truck stops, and playing for nobody in crappy bars."

Blue spread a rolling paper on his knee, sprinkled in some dried, curled leaves, rolled the paper up, and licked it closed.

Tenny sighed, clasping her hands over her heart. "Sounds like a dream to me."

"It's a risk versus reward scenario, man," Blue said, then sparked the joint and took a drag.

The air smelled like a skunk mating with grass. I'd never smoked anything before, and I sank deeper into the couch, wondering if I would get high off the smoke too. Blue coughed and pounded his chest. He offered the joint around, and to my great relief, Ezra and Tenny passed. I did too.

Blue rolled on. "Sure, you're on the fast track right now. Maybe you'll even land in the Berlin Philharmonic. But you won't make much." Orchestra jobs were more about prestige than paychecks. "Plus, you haven't even heard my latest name." He drumrolled on his thighs. "Exploding Uteruses." He made ta-da hands. At the collective silence, he said, "Not a winner?"

"I think you should keep workshopping names," Tenny said.

Blue slumped forward. "Yeah, okay. I will." He leaned more into Ezra's space. "Think of it, man. I believe in us," he said. "Plus, if you sold some of your albums, we'd be set. Could fund the whole tour."

My thoughts stalled on that single word: "albums." As in *My most treasured possession is an album.* That's what the letter writer had said. I knew for certain, had stared at the words until my vision swam.

Ezra nudged me. "You're quiet all of a sudden."

"I'm fine. Good." I plastered a smile onto my face, hoping he couldn't see past it or hear the twist in my voice. "What's this about an album?"

"Album*s*," Blue corrected.

"Sorry, albums?"

Ezra examined his hands. "My mom left me some vinyl

records. They're the only things I have of hers." He shrugged, drank a little more beer. "She was into music too. Guess that's where I get it from."

Tenny bobbed her head. "The notes are in your genes."

"Three words." Blue zeroed in on me. "Beatles butcher cover." I wasn't familiar with it, and my face must have said so. "It's super rare," he explained. "*Yesterday and Today*—issued June 1966 and shot by Robert Whitaker."

"Iconic," Tenny singsonged.

Blue grinned at her before swiveling back to me, hands fanning out. "Totally. Picture it: A white background. The Beatles in lab coats, slabs of meat slung over their bodies, and decapitated doll heads. It was pulled from the market. You can see why."

I screwed up my face at the image.

Ezra was listening, half amused.

With the joint, Blue gestured at Ezra. "That album our friend here has is worth about ten-K, maybe more at auction."

"Already told you, I'm not selling it. It's all I've got of my mom," said Ezra.

His most treasured possession, I thought, my heart circling around a dizzying conclusion.

Ezra could be the letter writer.

CHAPTER EIGHTEEN

My ears buzzed with the revelation, and I lost track of the conversation. I didn't come to until Blue, Tenny, and Ezra were standing around me.

"You ready?" Ezra set his cup on the dusty floor and stared at me expectantly. "We're up."

My jaw hung open. I looked at him dead in the eye. "You said I wasn't performing."

"Not poetry," he said.

"I meant at all," I replied.

"Semantics." He canted his head. "I'm showing you what's possible. You've never played a venue or this kind of music before."

Exactly. I played in a chamber orchestra, had been trained in classical violin. The thought of doing anything else was ridiculous. Hell would freeze over twice before I got on that pallet stage. I crossed my arms and laughed awkwardly. "I'm good. I'll listen."

"Get on the stage, Emma." He said it with a faint half smile.

Tenny was already on the pallets, putting together a drum set. Blue was onstage too, looping a bass around his neck.

"*You* get on the stage," I said to Ezra.

"I'm going to. But not without you." He tilted his head at me. "I could pick you up and put you there."

I laughed, unbelieving. He wouldn't dare. "I'd like to see you try."

Too late, I realized I'd issued a challenge. He leaned down. "Hard way it is, then."

"No," I protested.

Then I found myself airborne, slung over Ezra's shoulder, stomach down, butt up.

"You're going to drop me," I hissed, clutching the back of his shirt.

Later I'd curse myself for not enjoying Ezra carrying me more. I'd relive it in bed later that night. The way his shoulder pressed into my stomach. How his arms wrapped around my thighs. How his hand cupped my hip.

"Hardly," he scoffed. "I carry around my brothers all the time. One on each shoulder. Like sacks of very wiggly potatoes."

Hoots and hollers followed us to the stage. Ezra put me down, and I smoothed back my hair.

He did not look winded. At all. Like hauling reluctant violinists to underground stages was his jam.

"You decided to join us." Tenny beamed at me.

"I don't have my violin." I set my jaw. Stars dotted my vision. I tugged down my shorts.

"Got you covered." Blue was holding the neck of an electric fiddle, which he gave to me.

"You planned this?" I accused Ezra. "And you play guitar?"

"Oh, Ezra can play anything with strings." Tenny hunkered down behind the drum set and winked at me.

"Of course I planned this." Ezra looped a guitar around his neck. "My dad made me do Boy Scouts for seven years. We were supposed to bond. I learned to tie knots and always be prepared. That, and drink milk or you'll have soft bones."

My hands grew clammy around the violin's neck; my stomach twirled into a hard knot. "I don't have any music."

"All good." Blue came from my right with a stand and set his phone on it. Notes to a popular song with a violin number floated in my vision. The tune was pretty simple. A few drawn-out chords right after the bridge.

Ezra sat on a stool. "Don't worry. I got you," he told me. He turned away and adjusted the microphone.

The crowd had gathered at the edge of the stage.

"Get ready to be part of history," Blue told me. "This will be one of those performances when people say they saw us first."

"Hey, everyone," Ezra said. His voice was low, raspy, seductive. Hoots and hollers, mainly of the female variety, followed. As for me, my throat was dry, and sweat was forming anywhere there was a crevice on my body. "This is my girl's first time playing with the band. She's a little nervous. Can we get a warm welcome?"

My girl. The words reverberated through me, clanging like a cymbal, as a lot of noise ensued, claps and whoops.

One guy cupped his hands over his mouth and called, "Play Chumbawamba."

Ezra strummed the guitar, tuned a string. Mouth close to the microphone, he started singing. And his voice. His. Voice. It wasn't perfect. But it was even and smooth, with the slightest rasp. It was easy and strong. Powerful. I believed Blue right then. They could be big.

Then the bridge came. The chorus was near starting. I dug in and drew out the notes.

There's something about playing with other people. What it brings out in you, being a part of something, sharing the same experience. It made the music feel bigger. Better. Less lonely.

I looked out into the crowd. There weren't a ton of people. Maybe twenty or so, but they were all smiling. All swaying, giving themselves over to the music and the heat.

I drew the bow across my violin. The note was too high for the song. I righted course. Hit the correct note, and the beat picked up.

The energy in the tunnel shifted, climbing higher and higher with the song. Ezra glanced back at me, tiger eyes glittering in the dim light. He bit his lip and smiled at me. I smiled back. It was like we were the only two people in the room.

The song ended, but the rush followed me offstage. It felt like my blood was somersaulting in my veins.

Ezra handed me a Solo cup full of beer. "You mad?"

I chugged it down. "No." How could I be angry? I felt like I could kick a door off its hinges. Amped. I was amped! My heart jackhammered under my ribs. "You should have been a voice major."

"Nah." He shoved his hands into his pockets and hung his head. "But that felt good, right?"

"Amazing." I bounced on my feet.

"This is what you'll be missing," he said. "Or some version of it if you skip music school."

That sobered me right up.

"Woo!" Blue hooked his arms around me and Ezra, pulling

us into headlocks and letting us go. "That was fucking awesome. I feel like we just all went to summer camp together. And you two . . ." He wagged a finger between Ezra and me. "Major chemistry. Emma, you are totally invited to join the band."

The rest of the evening unfurled slowly. Bad poetry and warm beer. Cherry suckers. Time slowed to a stop. I kind of understood then, when people said high school was the best years of their life.

Later, Ezra shuffled ahead of me down the tunnel and back up the stairs. I watched the glow of the faux candles against the back of his neck with quiet conviction. We climbed the stairs slowly. Evening had come. The stars were hidden behind clouds, but the moon was bright.

Ezra stopped, turned toward me. He caught my hands and scraped his thumbs against them. "Hey." His lips were stained red from the cherry sucker he'd just finished.

Ezra was moving to Boston next year. Ezra's most treasured possession was an album from his mom.

"Hi," I said back.

I liked the way his skin felt against mine. The smell of his leather jacket. I let my eyes linger on his chest, half afraid to look up. If he had let go of me, I might have floated away.

"Emma." He said my name so warmly, so assuringly, that I lifted my chin. Found him above me, a smile playing on his lips. He rubbed my bottom lip with his thumb before letting go.

Our mouths touched.

He tasted like beer and cherry suckers. One of his hands swept to my back and drew me closer to press against him. His tongue traced my lower lip.

The sound of the trapdoor slamming broke us apart. Caught, we pushed away from each other.

It was Tenny and Blue. "Night, guys," Tenny hollered, clinging to Blue as he carried her piggyback.

Somehow my shirt had hiked up, and I shoved it down. I leaned against the alley wall, hands behind my back, letting the brick cool me. My chest rose and fell with uneven breaths.

"We should go, I guess," Ezra said. Then he grabbed my hand again, but this time he interlaced our fingers, held on tight.

A series of flutters passed through my stomach and into my lungs.

I don't remember Ezra driving me back to the Sherwood Institute. All of it felt like a hazy dream. I sat in my car for a while, still wrapped in the night, in the music.

From: Emma Nakamura-Thatcher
(ethatch121@gmail.com)
To: Letter Writer
(thechronosproject1@gmail.com)
Subject: Intentionally left blank.

Well. I took your advice and did something I'd usually say no to. Drumroll, please. I went to a party and played onstage with the band.

Me.

Emma.

With the band.

I drank beer, too. Well, half a beer. In case you can see me. Can you see me? I'm in my car. Don't worry. I'm good to drive. Although someone was smoking weed. So just in case, after I'm done writing this, I am going to Google "contact high" and give myself a field sobriety test before heading home.

The bigger news is that . . . second drumroll, please.

I am going to apply to Berklee, as in the music school in Boston.

I wish I could see your reaction to this. But I am going to picture you as very pleased, impressed, and proud.

CHAPTER NINETEEN

The lights were on in my house when I got home. I sat in the driveway, car parked over an oil stain.

My phone chimed. Delia was texting.

> How was the beer?

> Warm but fine. But more importantly

>

> I kissed Ezra.

Within seconds Delia called.

"I think Ezra's the letter writer," I answered.

"Well, hello to you, too," said Delia, her voice a little breathier than usual.

"Are you okay? You sound winded."

"By your last message." I heard the patter of steps and then the click of a door shutting. "I was watching a movie with my dad and shrieked. He thought I might have appendicitis. I ran away before he could palpate my abdomen." Delia's dad had a bit of health anxiety. Which he'd passed on to Delia, and then me by osmosis. We spent a lot of time on WebMD, checking each other's moles. As all great friends do. "So." Delia's voice tremored with excitement. "Tell me everything."

"Ezra took me to this wild place. The Seattle underground. The space was very small and packed with SAMA students and other assorted randoms. You would have hated it."

"One hundred percent," she said. "Were there carbon monoxide detectors? I'm pretty sure harmful gases are heavier and accumulate in places like that. Do you feel okay? Woozy at all?"

"I feel fine."

"I'll check on you later to make sure." She paused. "How was the kiss?"

"World's greatest kiss. He did this thing where he rubbed my bottom lip with his thumb."

"Stop. I can't take it," she burst out, then followed with a bracing deep inhale. "Okay, go on."

"I'm pretty sure he's the letter writer."

"Yeah?" She fell quiet for a few seconds. "What makes you think that?"

"Well." I drew a hand across the wheel. "It all makes sense. He's going to Boston next year."

I didn't need to explain. Delia had read the letters except for the last two. I wasn't sure I'd show her those. They felt more personal.

"Then tonight he said his most treasured possessions are albums from his mom."

"He said that exactly?" Delia's tone was measured.

I frowned. "Not exactly, but come on, what are the odds? Boston and an album?"

"I don't know. Math isn't my strong suit." It wasn't mine, either. "But you know whose it is?"

Pitter-patter. More rain. I swiveled and squinted at Theo's darkened house. "The letter writer isn't Theo," I said, a little wistful. Theo might be a math and science genius. But the rest of the clues didn't point to him. At least, not like they did to Ezra.

"Maybe it's Theo. Maybe it's not," Delia said. "But what about the others?"

Colin, Sebastian, Brandon, or Liam, she meant. "What are you saying?"

"It's too early to tell, I think."

My thoughts stuttered, crashed. "You're such a party pooper."

"Not true. My dads assure me that I am very fun. And the prettiest."

I smiled. "I do think you are the most fun and prettiest."

"Same," she said. "Same."

We hung up, and I stepped from my car. The night was still young, and I was wide awake, energy still buzzing from the music, from Ezra's kiss. Theo's house was in my sight, Delia's hesitation at the forefront of my thoughts.

Was the next thing I did ill advised? Absolutely.

Was I still going to do it? One hundred percent.

Theo's room was on the bottom floor, his window on the opposite side of the house from ours, parallel to Mr. Arvid's shop. Because of its location, it was the hottest room in the summer and the coldest in the winter.

I circled around his house and jimmied open his window. If

he didn't want someone coming in, he should have locked it, I rationalized as I crawled through.

His room smelled the same as always, like Irish Spring soap and sheets left to dry in the sun. I clicked on his bedside lamp. Books were piled high on the nightstand. They were mostly science fiction. The novel on top had a giant clock on the cover, lightning piercing the center. A navy sheet and comforter were crumpled at the bottom of the bed, and the pillow still had a dent from where he'd slept.

There were also way too many collectible figurines.

I skirted around laundry and game controllers to his dresser, a solid piece of wood that had almost fallen on me when I was six and had tried to climb it.

On top was a photograph of him and me as kids. This was back when Theo's glasses magnified his eyes and made him look like a cartoon character sprung to life. I wasn't faring much better in the photo, my bangs an inch long after I'd given myself a haircut. Our mouths were red. Our smiles deranged. The photo had been snapped right after an elementary school art show. Theo and I had hidden under a table, mainlining fruit sherbet punch and sugar cookies. I thought about how there wasn't anyone else like Theo. How he was the only reason I'd made it through my parents' divorce. He was singular to me.

I slid open the top two drawers. Nothing but clothing. Below the television, I crouched and rifled through the cabinet. Only a console and games.

What was I looking for? Evidence he was the letter writer—a secret Miss Piggy stash, a plane ticket to Boston, a mystery album.

I crossed the room to his desk. On top was a computer with

two screens, a set of headphones, and books on coding. Theo wrote his own games. His current work in progress was something with zombie ponies set in the Bronze Age.

Sliding the middle drawer open, I saw a stack of blank paper. Stationery. My heart stopped. Then pounded heavy and intense. Could it be the same type of paper as the letter writer's? I brushed the tips of my fingers against the paper. Not the same as the letter writer's. His paper was rough, ink bleeding into the fibers. And this was smooth, well pressed. A heavy weight settled in my chest.

Sticky notes had been pasted around Theo's monitor. I plucked off a quote often attributed to Albert Einstein: "Imagination is everything."

The front door opened and shut quickly, and I jolted, eyes wide. Footsteps pounded. Lights flicked on in the hallway. I calculated the distance to the window. Too far. I slammed the drawer shut and dived into Theo's closet, situating myself behind the suit he'd worn to his great-grandfather's funeral, right as his bedroom door opened.

Through the slats I spied on Theo. He was breathing hard. Sweat matted his hair to his forehead and soaked the front of his T-shirt. He was wearing loose gym shorts. He ripped a pair of AirPods from his ears and threw them onto the bed.

This was bad. I did not want to be in Theo's room. I did not want to see what Theo did when he was alone.

What to do? I had to escape somehow. I silenced my phone and texted Delia. **Help. I'm stuck in Theo's room.**

Delia replied with a question mark.

I snuck in, I answered. **Trying to figure out if he's the letter writer.**

Because you made me doubt myself, I wanted to add, but my hands were shaking. I breathed in and out quietly, steadying myself. My whole body was one big jumble of nerves.

You really suck as a spy, she said.

I take it back, I said. You aren't the most fun or prettiest.

Hang on, I'll Google how to sneak out of a room. A moment passed, and Delia texted again. Do you, by chance, have a grappling hook with you?

Theo brought his shirt up, mopped his brow, and peeled it off over his head.

I should not have looked. Operative words being "should not have."

But my brain had lost control over my eyes. They stayed open, trained on Theo.

When had he gotten a six-pack? I'd seen him last summer without his shirt, and his body had not been nearly as defined as it was now.

He toed off his shoes and wandered to his bathroom, hands at the waistband of his shorts. I scrunched my eyes closed. The shower turned on. And that was my cue. I took a deep breath and began to crawl from the closet.

Halfway out, I heard my name.

"Emma?" Theo was at the threshold of his bathroom door. "What the hell are you doing?"

I slapped a hand over my eyes. "Please tell me you're not naked."

"I'm wearing shorts. What are you doing in my room?"

I let my hand fall away and peered up at Theo. A little trickle of sweat made its way down the hollow of his throat to his chest, then curved a shimmering path to his belly button. "It's a really funny story . . ." Then my brain stalled.

"Yeah? I can't wait to hear." His hands settled on his hips.

I got up and dusted myself off. "I needed to borrow some headphones. For my music." I pointed at my ears like a big dummy.

"And you thought they were in my closet?"

"It's where I'd keep mine." I paused. "If I had some." I said it all like it made perfect sense. Like he was the dummy for even questioning me.

Theo crossed the room to his desk. He unplugged the headphones from his computer and handed them to me. "Next time you need something, there's these wonderful inventions called phones. They're amazing."

"Ha!" I clutched the headphones to my chest. "Well, thanks for these. They're definitely going to come in handy . . ." I started toward the window, then remembered the door. People usually entered and exited rooms through doors.

"Hey, Em."

I stopped and turned back to Theo. His eyes were dark and intense, locked on me. "Yes?"

"Can you stay for a minute? I have something I wanted to talk to you about."

"Oh, yeah." I wanted to say no. But my brain wasn't working. I couldn't find a reasonable excuse. "Sure."

He sniffed under his armpit and made a face. "I'm just going to shower really quick." He gestured at his body, and I chewed my cheek. I definitely wasn't going to look at his abs again, or where that little drop of sweat had finally landed.

"Maybe I should wait out there." I jammed a thumb toward the living room.

"What? Why?" He said it like it was the most absurd idea he'd ever heard.

How many times had I hung out in Theo's room while he showered? Many times. It shouldn't have felt like a big deal, but suddenly it felt like a huge deal. Theo naked, and only a wall between us.

"I'll be right back. Hang tight." He shut the bathroom door.

Trapped, I flopped back on his bed and stared at the ceiling, listening to the sound of the water.

Theo didn't take long, but I was tired. The last bit of adrenaline from being onstage and Ezra's kiss dwindled. My eyelids felt heavy. I started to doze.

Theo's bed was so comfortable. It wasn't the first time I'd fallen asleep in it. Sometimes I'd zonk out watching him play video games.

Cold drops landed on my face. My eyes flew open. Theo was above me, fully dressed in pajama pants and a sweatshirt, water from his hair dripping onto my forehead. He laughed. I drew up my leg to kick him in the stomach, but he caught my ankle, shackling it with his hand.

"Easy," he said. "I was just making sure you were alive." His thumbs moved over my skin in soothing circles.

We stared at each other, an electrical charge flowing between us.

I thought about Theo. How good his touch felt.

Reality crashed in. Theo was my *friend*. I was 90 percent sure he wasn't the letter writer. We weren't meant for more. Why had I let Delia's doubts take root? Plus, there was Ezra. Whom I'd been kissing not two hours ago.

I scooted back and propped myself against his headboard. "You had something you wanted to talk to me about?"

"Right." He straightened and wouldn't make eye contact with me.

He was nervous. His tell was looking at the floor, which he always did when gathering his thoughts. Theo prided himself on his smarts and liked things within his control. When he couldn't figure something out, he'd get all agitated.

Like right then. Oh, Lord. Was he going to confess he loved me? Did I even want that? I held my breath and gripped his comforter. "I was wondering . . ."

My pulse raced. "Yes?"

His mouth was tense. He searched my face. "I was wondering what you thought about me asking Camille out?"

Okay. Not what I was expecting. At all. My mouth juddered open. "Asking Camille out?" I parroted back, dazed.

"Yeah." He stopped at the foot of the bed and placed his hands on his hips. "She seems cool. We have a ton in common. What do you think?"

What did I think?

Theo wants to ask Camille out. I said it a few more times in my head just to be clear. *Theo wants to ask Camille out. Theo wants to ask Camille out.*

Not me.

Which meant he couldn't be the letter writer, because the letter writer had said he'd loved me from the moment he saw me. If that were true, Theo wouldn't be asking out someone else.

I nodded slowly, then faster. "Yeah," I managed. "You should do that."

"Okay." He smiled, a jackpot grin.

I yanked out my phone. "Here's her number." My voice was tighter, higher, than I intended.

I batted off a jab of disappointment. Maybe I would lose Theo after all, but to another girl. This was something I'd never foreseen. I'd thought he'd always be mine. *Selfish,* I thought. I was being selfish.

I stood toe to toe with Theo. "Just don't tell her your favorite pair of pants used to be a pair of capris."

He shook his hair at me again. "Never. There are some things you take to the grave."

I darted back, hunched over, and hid, cold droplets landing on the back of my neck.

Ezra and me.

Camille and Theo.

It had been decided.

From: Letter Writer
(thechronosproject1@gmail.com)
To: Emma Nakamura-Thatcher
(ethatch121@gmail.com)
Subject: Re: Intentionally left blank.

Can I see you? No.

I don't have a crystal ball. I don't know what you're going to say. I don't know what you're going to do. Picture time as a loop rather than linear. When I contact you, I am sending this email to a specific place down to the nanosecond. I cannot see how your decisions might alter your course the next day, month, or year. I can only see you in the future. Where you are right now. Honestly? This isn't quite an exact science. I had to sign a thousand-page waiver to use this technology. Like, I had to initial a clause about risk of decapitation. But so far, so good.

Applying to Berklee? That's big news. I'd wish you luck, but I don't think you need it. Just remember us little people when you're playing with the philharmonic.

How did it feel? Taking a risk, I mean.

From: Emma Nakamura-Thatcher
(ethatch121@gmail.com)
To: Letter Writer
(thechronosproject1@gmail.com)
Subject: Keep your head on (sorry, I couldn't help myself)

Taking the risk felt good.

I think I've realized I've been a little numb. Or maybe not numb . . . but not living life to the fullest. Venturing forth hasn't ever really been my strong suit. Although I did play a lot of survival games with Jiji—you know, that whole thing where we pretended we were lost in the woods and had to forage for food. If you ever need to know how to collect rain for fresh water, I'm your gal. But it was fun because it was comfortable. Our house wasn't far away, a dozen steps, and then I'd be in front of my refrigerator, food within reach. Perhaps my imagination has always been preferable to real life.

Jeez. I'm babbling now.

What I'm saying is, those games made me feel alive, more than I felt in real life. And maybe there was something wrong with that. Maybe *life* should make you feel alive, ya know?

Why am I telling you all this? I wish I knew who you were. I wish you didn't have to answer my questions so carefully. Maybe it's better that I don't know. I say things to you I wouldn't say out loud. There's safety in anonymity. It makes me braver, I think. *You* make me feel braver.

MAYBE IT'S TIME TO POP THE BUBBLE.

BE BIG.

From: Letter Writer (thechronosproject1@gmail.com)
To: Emma Nakamura-Thatcher (ethatch121@gmail.com)
Subject: My head is attached but my heart belongs to you (too much?)

All caps, huh? You must mean business.

CHAPTER TWENTY

I had never been this girl. Light as air, heart on her sleeve, walking across a park to see a boy.

Ezra had texted on Monday during lunch and asked if I'd meet him at Marymoor that evening, outside of our usual sessions.

I arrived near dusk, when the sky was topaz bleeding into sapphire. The Space Needle glowed, backlit by the orange-and-red sunset. It was October, and the weather was still mercurial, with scattered showers and sunbursts. Forty-degree mornings and seventy-degree afternoons punctuated by blusters of leaves trapped in the wind.

A big screen had been set up, and people were sitting on plaid blankets or low folding chairs. Food tents dotted the periphery, selling three-dollar beers, macarons, and Philly cheesesteak sandwiches. The air smelled like wet grass and grilled onions.

Ezra spied me and came loping across the lawn, hands jammed in his pockets. "Hey, you found us."

"Us" was Blue and Tenny. Both had their instruments. Ezra had said to bring my violin. I noted his cello, and a guitar set up too.

"What are we doing?" I asked Ezra. Not an hour ago I'd finished my Berklee application. Hitting Send and sliding in a month ahead of the November deadline.

"We're playing," he said. "The soundtrack for the movie."

Hence the big screen in front of me.

"And for money," Tenny said as we reached her. She adjusted her drum kit. At her feet, Ezra's cello case was open. Already a few dollar bills had been thrown in. A sign was taped to the front that said Every Time You Don't Tip, a Child Gets a Mullet. A picture of a kid with a mullet who looked vaguely familiar was posted to it.

"Oh my God." I laughed, bringing my face closer to the photograph. "Is that you?"

Ezra rolled his eyes. "Nothing is sacred anymore."

"Can you believe he tried to hide this from me in his room?" Tenny said. "To not share such glory with the world."

"This is why I didn't have you come here first," Ezra told me. "Questionable adolescent haircuts are more second-date material."

Second date. The statement came at me like a parade, cornets trumpeting.

"Totally agree," Blue said. "I didn't tell Tenny about my vestigial tail until we were five dates in."

"It really is the cutest." Tenny leaned over to kiss the tip of Blue's nose.

"He's kidding about the tail." Ezra sat behind his cello. He paused. "I think."

More people gathered on the lawn. I flipped through the sheet music on a stand. The big screen flickered, and the opening credits rolled. Chin set on my violin, I set my bow across the strings and began to draw out the melody for the opening credits.

The film was a historical romance. Because of course it was. The story centered around a down-on-her-luck farm girl who loves the lord of the castle, who loves another girl, a lady. Or he thinks he does. The farm girl is funny and challenges him. She shows him things he's never seen before. Makes him come alive. She is a window, and he sees the world differently through her.

But then . . . but then things go missing around the castle. A tapestry. A gold vase. The farm girl is blamed and sold to another household (because you could do that back in those days).

Tenny picked up on the drums and I rested, my part done for now.

The movie took a turn. The lord decides to marry the lady, but on their wedding day, with the help of a plucky housekeeper, the lord learns the lady framed the farm girl. The farm girl didn't steal a thing, and he sent her away before hearing her out. He leaves the lady at the altar and rides on his stallion to rescue the farm girl.

But plot twist: She's doing just fine when he finds her. She's whipped the new household into shape, and the new lord is absolutely besotted with her. He knows a good thing when he sees it. He's given her jewels, dresses, a room full of books, and even this scraggly horse that can never be ridden again, so all it does is cost money to keep it.

The first lord leaves dejected, realizing he's lost his chance. He's walking through the rain—and here came the violin solo.

Tenny eased off the drums. Blue paused on the bass. Ezra stopped and rested his hands on the neck of his cello.

I dug in, playing the soft and sweet notes, letting them lift and catch in the breeze.

There's something special about sharing the same story with a group of strangers. Experiencing it together. You're not alone then.

"I've been a little numb," I'd told the letter writer. Numb *and* closed off, I realized now. My life had been emptier as a result.

I'd filled the blank space with classical music, Jiji, and old clothes—things from the past. What did that mean? I didn't know. But what I had been before didn't seem like enough anymore. It kind of brought tears to my eyes. What all had I been missing?

I felt emotional. Exposed. It was a state I couldn't stand myself in and had tried never to be in again since that day in the rain when I'd begged my dad to come home.

On the screen, lightning struck and branches cracked from the trees. A burst of light, and then the farm girl is there riding the scraggly horse, appearing just in time to save the first lord's life. I decided I'd hate the movie if the horse died. But it didn't. It was happily ever after all around. The farm girl realizes she can't live without the lord, even though he's completely flawed. The lord promises to spend the rest of his life making it up to the farm girl. The film ends with the plucky housekeeper feeding the old horse apples while the lord and farm girl look on, wedding bands on their ring fingers.

I finished on my violin and rested my bow at my side. Wind whipped at my cheeks. My heartbeat was steady and strong in my chest. Ezra was staring at me. He dipped his chin, a slow, approving motion. I swallowed audibly, feeling changed. As if I had found a new hidden room. And Ezra stood right in the middle.

CHAPTER TWENTY-ONE

Moviegoers trudged up the lawn, dropping change and crumpled dollar bills into the cello case. Then, slowly, they drifted off. Pickups drove onto the grass. Food tents were collapsed and loaded onto truck beds.

Park almost empty, the four of us sat around Ezra's cello case and counted the loot.

"Ahem." Blue cleared his throat. "I believe a toast is in order." From inside his jacket he drew a silver flask. He uncapped the bottle and raised it. "To Ezra making the best, wisest decision of his life vis-à-vis listening to me."

My attention darted to Ezra.

He plucked a piece of grass from the lawn and twirled it between his fingers. "I'm giving it a shot. Next summer," he began to explain, and I held my breath. "On the road with these maniacs. Before I head to Boston."

The tension inside me unwound.

He was still planning on going to Boston. Ezra was still the letter writer. Probably.

I patched together the timeline. Ezra would go on the road with Blue and Tenny. They'd have a great time, make bad decisions, make all the memories, but soon they'd run out of money, and he'd head to Boston as planned. Then, he'd stay there and begin writing to me years later.

"Unless we get a record deal," Blue said.

Ezra gusted out a laugh. "Sure, man."

Blue opened his mouth, and Tenny covered it with her hand. "It's just his fear talking." She looked meaningfully at Ezra. "You want this as bad as us."

"It would be pretty sweet," Ezra admitted begrudgingly.

Blue hollered, raised the flask, and toasted. "To the band."

The flask was passed around, and I sipped. I wasn't sure what kind of alcohol it was, but it was brown and full-bodied and left the taste of cereal on my tongue.

Flask back in his grip, Blue raised it again. "Another toast. This one for luck. May the music gods smile down upon us. Here's to the butcher album selling and making the difference between a shitty van and a shittier van."

Ice flooded my veins. "You're selling your mom's albums?" His most treasured possessions? Why would he do that? Unless . . . The thought stuck between the folds of my brain. I refused to release it yet.

Ezra took the flask from Blue and drank. He wiped his mouth with the back of his hand. "I figured she'd want me to. That's why she left them, right? So I could pursue something I loved."

Unless . . . the albums weren't his most treasured possessions. The thought shook free. Had I been wrong about Ezra being the letter writer? Perhaps so.

It also seemed like I couldn't trust my instincts.

"Cool." I managed an even tone.

Meanwhile, Tenny dug into the cello case, separating bills from pieces of paper.

"What's this?" I angled my body forward and plucked a folded paper from the case. I flattened it and began to read out loud: "'To the cute cello player . . .'" My voice trailed off. A phone number was scrawled on the bottom, along with a name: Courtney.

Tenny grabbed the phone number from my hand. "That's one," she said. "I've got less than ten."

"No way," Blue said. "Ezra's going to break a dozen tonight. I saw a couple of regulars in the crowd. They were *not* here for the movie."

I dimmed. "What are you talking about?"

Blue and Tenny were oblivious to my mood change. They were too wrapped up in each other and counting money.

"It's a dumb game they play." Ezra dragged a hand through his hair. "It doesn't mean anything."

"We bet on how many phone numbers Ezra will get. Winner gets to choose anything from the thrift store for the other to wear to any place," Blue explained.

"Like a fur coat to a vegetarian restaurant," Tenny deadpanned. "I almost got red paint thrown on me."

"Faux fur," Blue qualified. "Or a shirt with a leggy olive doing questionable things to a martini glass."

"Honestly, I feel like there were no losers with the olive martini stripper shirt," Tenny said.

"My mom would strongly disagree, since I wore it to my cousin's bar mitzvah," said Blue.

"Like I said, it's a dumb game," Ezra mumbled. He made a

show of balling up all the papers and numbers and throwing them over his shoulder.

Littering, but okay. As long as he was throwing the numbers away.

We continued counting the tips and then divided the money four ways. Blue won the bet—Ezra had received thirteen phone numbers in the case.

Tenny and Blue skipped off toward the water. Ezra stood, motioned with his head at the park. "Walk with me?"

I rose, dusting myself off. "Sure."

He bumped my shoulder and grabbed my hand. Goose bumps broke out across my skin. "You know, you inspired me to take a chance with the band. It's about the risk. Following your dreams."

I wondered about how my current actions were bending the future. Up until this point I'd considered this only when it came to myself, my own life and choices—not how my changes might be altering someone else's path. The weight of my decisions suddenly became much heavier.

I smiled even though I felt a little off.

He squeezed my palm. "You all right? You've got a faraway look."

My thoughts were all tangled. And at the hard, knotted center? The knowledge that I might have been terribly wrong. Ezra probably wasn't the letter writer.

My gaze skirted over the lawn while I searched for the right words, or any words, for that matter. A glimpse of brown hair by a park bench caught my attention.

Madison?

I recognized her gait, the set of her shoulders. But I did not recognize the man beside her. Not my dad, that was for sure. The world started to slip out from underneath me. My internal balance twisted and tilted.

I dropped Ezra's hand. Took a step in Madison's direction.

"Emma?" Ezra said.

"Hey! I thought you might be here." A voice coasted on top of his. A girl's. Lyrical. Pumped up with excitement.

I turned. Watched, as if in slow motion, as she darted, graceful as a gazelle, across the lawn to plant a kiss on Ezra's cheek. Watched as he captured her in a loose hug. Watched how his fingers dug into her hip before letting her go, easing her back to arm's length.

"Janey?" Ezra's mouth twisted uncomfortably. "What are you doing here?"

"It's a three-day weekend." She rolled her eyes.

I didn't miss how pretty she was. Her cheeks sprinkled with freckles, her hair naturally highlighted by the sun. She wore a New England Conservatory sweatshirt with the neck cut to expose a red bra strap and one delicate shoulder. "So I thought I'd come visit. Hey, I'm Janey." She turned to me, finally noticing my presence. She gave me a little wave. "Oh my God, I love your shorts and your hair."

I looked at her, too shocked to speak. To make matters worse, this beautiful woman (Ezra's girlfriend? His ex-girlfriend? His friend that was a girl?) was super nice.

"I'm starving." She rubbed her flat tummy. "I've been driving for hours. I know where we should go." She focused on Ezra. "To that place you told me about. That serves breakfast twenty-four hours a day, Biscuit something . . ." She snapped her fingers, searching for the name.

"Biscuit Bitch," I filled in, which was kind of a historic achievement—the ability to find words past all the pain. But I couldn't smile. My throat felt like it was going to close.

What had I been thinking? That Ezra loved *me*? He had girls driving across the country for him.

"Right!" She beamed. "You want to join us?" She slapped her forehead. "I didn't even ask your name. So rude."

"Uh, Emma." My heart dipped low in my chest, sitting there painfully. "Thanks for the offer, but I've got to head home."

I started off on a slow, steady walk, steps growing shorter and quicker the farther away I got.

In the distance I heard Ezra call my name, but I was already too far gone.

Back in my car, I sat for a moment, heart hammering under my ribs, and tracked Madison and the man as they walked and disappeared into a copse of trees.

While my sight was focused on Madison, my thoughts circled around Ezra and Janey. How dumb I'd been, forcing puzzle pieces together, pieces that so clearly did not fit. Plus, the letter writer had said "album." Not "*albums*."

My throat swelled and I wanted to cry, but I forced myself to wait until I'd pulled away and was several blocks from the park. At a safe distance, tears poured. I dashed away the wetness at a red stoplight.

"Stupid, stupid," I called myself.

I drove the rest of the way home in the same awful state. When I turned onto my street, I buttoned it up. I didn't want my mom or Jiji to see me crying. That would lead to questions. To pity. Or worse, that all-knowing look from my mom. The *I told you so* look. She didn't know about Ezra, and she'd never brimmed with love advice. But I'd categorize what she did say in the same vein as how she spoke about black widows, feral hogs, and exposed electrical wires—just stay away.

Yes, love was a dangerous game—the biggest risk of all. And I'd fallen for Ezra. For his half-lidded eyes and sexy slouch.

I had wanted him to be the letter writer.

I still *wished* he were.

I parked alongside the curb. Theo was outside his house, pacing the sidewalk on the phone, laughing. He saw me, mouthed "Camille," pointing at his cell.

Not trusting my voice, I gave him two thumbs-ups and dashed inside the house. Mom was watching television. Jiji was already in bed. I waved at her and beelined for my room.

Once inside, I sat on the floor, needing to feel something firm underneath me.

My phone pinged. A text from Ezra: **You ran away before I could explain.**

I didn't answer. Nothing he could say would make a difference.

Ezra was not my forever love, and Madison probably wasn't my dad's, either.

Maybe there was no such thing.

> From: Letter Writer
> (thechronosproject1@gmail.com)
> To: Emma Nakamura-Thatcher
> (ethatch121@gmail.com)
> Subject: C'mon, don't leave me hanging

You left me on a cliff-hanger. "Maybe it's time to pop the bubble." What does that mean? I assume it involves more risk. I am here for it.

> From: Emma Nakamura-Thatcher
> (ethatch121@gmail.com)
> To: Letter Writer
> (thechronosproject1@gmail.com)
> Subject: Fully deflated now

Today was a bad day.

> From: Letter Writer
> (thechronosproject1@gmail.com)
> To: Emma Nakamura-Thatcher
> (ethatch121@gmail.com)
> Subject: Re: Fully deflated now

?

From: Emma Nakamura Thatcher
(ethatch121@gmail.com)
To: Letter Writer
(thechronosproject1@gmail.com)
Subject: Re: Fully deflated now

I thought I knew who you were. I know, I know, we discussed this. But I couldn't help but search for you. Can you blame me? Turns out, he's not you. At least, I don't think. Ugh. I'm so confused. Everything feels so messed up right now.

To boot, I saw my dad's fiancée with another dude tonight. They weren't holding hands or anything salacious, but they did look awfully cozy. Now my head is spinning again.

I don't want him to get hurt.

I don't want to get hurt either.

The whole brokenhearted thing—there should be a lifetime cap on sad.

From: Letter Writer (thechronosproject1@gmail.com)
To: Emma Nakamura-Thatcher (ethatch121@gmail.com)
Subject: I wish I could hug you

I hear you. Like, how much can one human being be expected to feel in a lifetime? I think everyone out there can remember the day when they learned the terrible truth about the grown-up world, how impermanent it all is. Your pet runs away from home and gets hit by a car. Your grandfather dies. Your parents announce they're divorcing.

I'm going to quote another philosopher because I feel shit with words right now, and why say something when someone else has said it better?

"The wound is the place where the Light enters."—Rumi

CHAPTER TWENTY-TWO

Delia brought chocolate croissants to school the next morning. I ate my feelings in one of the private studios, then cried my eyes out.

Later that week I wasn't in much better shape. I was busted and brokenhearted, hiding in Jiji's old sweaters, warm and cozy and safe, cuffs unraveling. I generally avoided thinking about anything related to Ezra. I wanted to go back to my numb space, where my heart was callous but safe.

One boon: Mother Nature did me a solid, matching the weather to my mood. It was bleak and gray and rainy out, downright awful. It was coming down in sheets as I hurried into 900 Degrees, a wood-fired pizza place, to meet Dad, Madison, and Camille.

Another family dinner to induce bonding. The timing was uncanny, right after seeing Madison out with another man—her ex? Not her ex? I didn't know. Obviously, I was still stewing about it. But I couldn't cancel without invoking a full interrogation from my dad and Camille. My plan? To keep quiet and leave as soon as possible.

I was the last to arrive. They'd already settled in at a table under a window overlooking Lake Washington. Colin's house was a blurry white blob on the other side.

I offered the table a less-than-cheerful hi, then crumpled into a seat.

Dad tilted his head at me in unspoken disapproval. He made eye contact with Madison, and they shared the same expression. One I'd seen on both my parents' faces before, which said: *Teens, what are you going to do?*

A waiter came by and deposited a basket of garlic knots on the table. He was wearing Converse shoes. Same as Ezra. He was everywhere I looked.

I picked up a menu to hide my face. Nerves racked my insides. My thoughts turned to Ezra and that girl again. Janey. I conjured stomach-twisting images of them together: Ezra playing the cello, her dropping a kiss into his messy hair.

"Your hot neighbor called me." Camille bent close. The menu shielded us from Madison and Dad.

"Yeah." I surveyed the menu. "He asked for your number. I gave it to him. I hope you don't mind."

"Not at all." She popped a garlic knot into her mouth and licked her fingers.

Dad was telling Madison about a book he was starting to write: a survival story set in Alaska during the Gold Rush. Madison was bobbing her head, following along.

"What about you, kiddo?" Dad turned to me. "What have you been up to this week?"

"Not much." I pulled a napkin from the holder and began to shred it. Behind Madison and Dad was a mural of the Last Supper, the table piled high with pizza and calzones. "I went to

Marymoor Park Monday evening." I stared hard at Madison, watching her face, looking for any flicker of guilt. "Have you ever been there, Madison?" I kind of felt outside my body. Like I was a puppet, someone else controlling me. "Because I think I saw you."

"Emma," Dad gently chastised.

It was my tone, flat and accusatory.

Then Camille said, "You're being weird."

My eyes drifted down to Madison's hand folded around her own napkin. On her left ring finger was a gold band, a small opal set inside it. I was finding it hard to sit and rein myself in. In fact, it was impossible. I stood abruptly.

"Sorry," I said, my voice uneven. I pressed the heels of my palms into my eyes. "I'll go."

I grabbed my jacket and my bag and marched out of the restaurant. Rain plastered my hair to my head.

"Emma!" I heard Dad behind me. His footsteps pounded down the wet concrete. He caught up and placed a hand on my arm, spinning me around. "What was that?" He gestured inside, where I couldn't see Madison and Camille anymore, just the warm glow of the front windows and the blur of patrons nearest them. I felt terrible about the way I'd acted, but I was still confused and angry.

I crossed my arms. "How well do you know Madison?"

"We've been dating for almost a year now." He raised his voice over the rain. "I like to think I know her pretty well."

"Do you know she sees her ex-husband all the time? Do you know Camille thinks they're going to get back together, and they go on vacation together? Do you know what Madison was doing Monday night? Because I do. I saw her at Marymoor Park with some guy, probably her ex-husband."

Dad shook his head a little. "Listen." He stopped as a car drove into the parking lot. He pulled me to the side of the building under a black-and-white-striped awning. "You're having doubts about me getting married again," he started. "I get it. But that doesn't give you the right to go off and make accusations. You owe an apology to Madison."

My emotional fortitude was in shambles. I swallowed down my urge to cry. It felt like Dad wasn't taking my side. It was like he'd been hypnotized by Madison, her meat loaf, and her all-around good-gal aura. Same as I'd been with the letter writer, and Ezra, and music.

"I don't want you to get married. She's going to break your heart." I searched Dad's face, beseeching him to understand.

Dad took two deep breaths before speaking. "I'm sorry you feel that way." My posture deflated. This was Dad's way of saying, *You are wrong, and I am right.* "Can we go inside and talk about this?"

My chin wobbled. I was so tired. I wanted to go home, wrap myself in one of Jiji's sweaters, play sad music, let the notes coast over me in a soothing balm. "No. It's all right." My voice was rough with frustration. "I'm going to go home."

Dad breathed deep. "Okay. We'll talk tomorrow. We should probably both cool off."

"Sure," I said, barely audible, feeling myself shutting down.

"The weather is getting bad," Dad went on. "Text me when you get home safe."

"Yup."

I forced my legs to move and ducked my head, rain pummeling the back of my neck. Inside my car, I started the engine and cranked the heat. The interior smelled like wet wool. I turned on my headlights just as Dad disappeared into the restaurant. I pulled away, imagining him walking toward Madison and Camille, their open faces.

I'd never felt more alone.

Home, I closed the front door with a quiet snick. Mom and Jiji knew I was out to dinner with Dad and his fiancée—something he'd told Mom via text. I wasn't supposed to be home for another hour or two. Hopefully, I could sneak upstairs, get in the shower, and collect myself under a stream of water without having to talk to anyone.

I was on the landing when I heard a sniffle. Mom's door was cracked, and I padded toward it, then stood outside and listened for a beat. Another sniffle. Of all the sounds I disliked most in the world, Mom crying was top of the list. I crept closer. Mom was sitting on the edge of her bed, hunched, hands fumbling with a tube of Voltaren gel.

A memory surged forward. After the divorce there were days when Mom didn't get out of bed. I had stood in the doorway back then, too. Watching my mom, worried about her, unsure how she—how we—would go on.

Then I'd feel Jiji's hand on my shoulder, gently pulling me away. "Come," he'd say. "I made noodles. Your favorite."

Now Mom sensed my presence. "Oh, Emma." She startled, dropping the gel. "I didn't know you were home. Why are you back so early?"

I pushed the door open and swooped down, retrieving the tube. "Here. Let me." I sat beside her on the bed, squeezed some gel out, and took one of her hands in mine, gently massaging her knotted fingers. The fight with Dad was still fresh. But worry for Mom pierced the anger, diffused it. "I forgot I have a test tomorrow. I need to study."

As much as possible, I avoided bringing up Dad around Mom and vice versa. I did mental gymnastics where they were concerned, mapping out the consequences of mentioning one parent to the other. Like if I told Mom I'd fought with Dad, she'd be concerned, maybe upset with him. Then she'd call him. They'd for sure fight. It would snowball from there. So I kept mum on what had happened that evening. My emotional frequency was to placate, to keep the peace first and foremost. It was weird being a kid of divorced parents, feeling like I had to protect them from each other.

Mom inhaled deeply and closed her eyes. "That feels good."

I swallowed. "Theo said you were at the doctor when I called after my car wouldn't start."

She nodded, eyes still closed. I could see the veins in the paper-thin skin of her eyelids. "The doctor suggested we do a cortisone shot. I'm not sure how I'll manage. He said I need to consider lightening my workload." She opened her eyes. "Or else I'll need surgery down the line."

"Mom . . . ," I ventured, still massaging her hand, working my way up her knuckles. "Maybe it is time to slow down."

She scoffed. "And who will replace me?"

"I can help you." I placed her hand in her lap and stood. *But what about Berklee? What about next year?* I shushed the naysaying voice in my head. "You should do the cortisone shot. I can take on more."

"Emma..." She started to shake her head. "You just said you have a test. Plus, Sherwood—"

"I have lots of free time. I promise." I knelt before her, hands on her hands. "Let me help. Please."

The Sherwood Institute could go; it's not like I wanted to see Ezra ever again anyway. I was needed at home. I'd double up on my cleaning days.

It was a solution. For now.

"It would be nice not to be in so much pain all the time. I could take a few days off and start physical therapy." She hesitated. "Are you sure you can handle it?"

"Yes, of course I can."

"You sure?" she asked again.

I nodded eagerly. "So sure."

She cupped my cheek, and I felt my grandmother in that movement, the echo of her. "You're unstoppable."

I beamed at her, sending every single reassuring thought I had vibrating through that smile.

It would be all right. I *was* unstoppable. There was no question. I'd run myself ragged to take care of Mom and Jiji, my family.

CHAPTER TWENTY-THREE

The idea of seeing Ezra in person made my stomach churn, a mixture of fresh humiliation, sad and mad, so I skipped Sherwood that week, called in sick, and got to work.

Cue the cleaning montage.

Saturday, Mrs. Sydney's house was up first. She surprised me with apricot scones and English breakfast tea in her disco room. While I sipped, she opened up about her second marriage, to a foreman on a construction crew, Angus. They used to go to Studio 54, and there was a picture of a young Mrs. Sydney in a short, rainbow-colored sequined dress and platform heels with her legs wrapped around Angus's waist as he dipped her. She still had the dress in her closet and showed it to me.

Sunday was a frazzled stay-at-home mom of five kiddos. Mrs. Presley apologized profusely for the mess. Some type of gooey substance was stuck on the dining room ceiling, water-resistant crayons filled the bathtub, and stickers covered the dishwasher.

Monday, a couple with a detailed checklist of what they'd like done in their house. Use only streak-free glass cleaner, iron all sheets, then spray them with lavender (provided). As a tip, they left me cans of expired food and near-rotten fruit—they didn't want anything to go to waste and was sure I could use them or knew of somebody who could.

My new routine became school and work.

I sat through my core classes and art-track seminars, scribbling notes. I shoved sandwiches down my throat at lunch, doing my homework. Then I'd doze in last period, Special Projects, jolt awake at the final bell, and hurry to a client's house. Where I cleaned and dusted the blinds. Bleached bathtubs. Swept floors and cobwebs. Vacuumed corners and crawl spaces. Emptied trash cans. Changed bed linens. Lather. Rinse. Repeat.

By Thursday afternoon I was exhausted. So tired that I didn't have time to think of the letter writer or Ezra or the fight with my dad. The gut bomb of reality had settled in. Which was precisely where I needed to be: in reality, with my feet planted firmly on the ground.

The St. James family had hosted a party the night before. It took me so many hours to clean. To scrape the catering dishes and put them back into crates in the garage. To haul bags of trash to the curb. To scrub and restock the bathrooms. Last, I tackled a wine stain on the living room carpet. I spent an extra thirty minutes gently coaxing it from the wool until my arms felt like limp noodles.

Done for the day, I piled my cleaning supplies into my still-noisy but running car and went in search of Colin's mom. She'd forgotten to leave the usual lavender cash envelope. Mrs. St. James owed me five hundred bucks.

I searched downstairs, calling her name softly down hallways and into rooms. "Mrs. St. James, I'm all done." Underlying subtext: *Please pay me so I can get out of here and continue to ignore my problems and quietly self-destruct on my own.* Desolation required solitude and the violin.

I climbed the stairs. Her bedroom was empty. So was the rest of the house.

Except for one bedroom with the door closed. Colin's. He'd made himself scarce while I cleaned his room, then snuck back in while I was working downstairs.

I knocked softly.

He opened the door and almost smiled. Was he happy to see me? "Emma."

"Hey." I tilted my chin up to meet his smile. I had a flash of him making me a sandwich, sliding the plate toward me. I remembered how I'd run from the room and said, *Those toilets aren't going to clean themselves.* I rubbed my arm, hoping to erase the awkward memory. "Do you know where your mom is?"

He leaned against the doorframe, propping himself up by a shoulder. "I don't know. I haven't known where she was for most of my childhood. I always knew where my nannies were, though. I'd cry when they left."

He was joking. Or not joking. I couldn't tell.

"Well," I said. "That very, very sad story aside, your mom owes me for the cleaning today."

"I'll text her." He darted back into his room.

I watched from the doorway as he thumbed out a message. The back of Colin's hair was perfectly trimmed, cut close to the scalp, longer on top, and he was wearing loose track pants and a thick gray hoodie—casual but expensive. In contrast, my outfit was secondhand—ragged leggings and an oversized T-shirt with an unfortunate oil stain over the left boob. The phone pinged right away with a response. "She said she forgot and apologizes. She'll pay you double next time. That good?"

I stared at him. "Actually. It's not. I'd like to be paid today, please."

That money went toward my family's bills. Bills that were due soon.

He was in front of me again. "All right," he said slowly, stuffing his hands into the kangaroo pocket of his sweatshirt. "Come back in a little bit, then, when she's home. It's not a big deal."

"It is kind of a big deal," I explained just as slowly. I pressed my hands to my chest, feeling a curl of anger unravel. "Waiting means I have to hang out in your neighborhood until your mom gets home because I can't afford the gas to drive back and forth across town."

My tone was sharp, crisp. Because I was mad. At Ezra for having a girlfriend. At my dad for not listening. At clients like Colin's family. The whole lot made me feel disposable.

"Your mother's actions affect other people. I need that money. I need to deposit it in the bank today so the money posts tomorrow so I can help my mom pay bills." Typing was painful for my mom. We sat side by side and went through the accounts together. You don't know how much you use your hands until you can't anymore. I was my mom's hands and mine. Being two people was tough. "So yeah. It is a big deal. I am not here at your convenience," I finished, my voice low.

"Am I interrupting something?" I stiffened at Sebastian's voice behind me. I hadn't heard him come up the stairs. Damn the St. Jameses' plush carpeting.

"All good, brother," Colin said tightly. He scratched the back of his neck. "I didn't know you were here."

"Just got home." Sebastian glowered at me with a look that could peel wallpaper. "I was down the street. Mom called and asked if I had any cash on me to pay the cleaner."

Sebastian edged closer and handed me five crisp one-hundred-dollar bills.

I took them and hung my head. My hands were shaky, my cheeks on fire.

"You sure everything is okay?" he asked his brother.

Clearly, Sebastian had heard some or most of what I'd said to Colin. Despite it all, I stood by what I'd said. But the rush of anger was now on simmer. After this I knew I'd cry. That's how it usually worked with me. Mad, then tears.

"Never better," Colin said. His light eyes swept over my face. "Let's not hold Emma up."

"Yeah." My voice was slightly strangled. "Thanks for this."

I toed the carpet, held up the wad of bills, murmured something about next time, and scampered off.

Let the record show: I did not fall apart until I was in my car. I fumbled with the keys and finally got the door unlocked. Inside, it smelled like lemon cleaner. I stuffed the cash in my glove box and shoved it closed, but it fell open. I slammed it over and over until it finally clicked shut.

I huffed out a frustrated laugh and sent a text to Delia. **I went off on a client today. Not one of my prouder moments.**

Her reply came immediately: **She is beauty. She is grace. She'll throw a toilet wand in your face.**

I smiled. Then a few tears leaked. I dashed them away, but they only kept coming. All of it crashed down on me, the emotions I could only process through a good bawl fest. Those angry feelings again, toward Ezra and my dad. Toward the letter writer, who had swept into my life and made me throw everything around like a tornado, leaving destruction in my wake. On top of that, I was frustrated over the situation with my mom. What little I was doing didn't seem like enough. I was a mess and making a mess of things.

Sometimes you just need a good cry. That's what I told myself. Tomorrow would be better.

"I got an interesting phone call from Mrs. St. James today," Mom said.

I was at the sink, hands soapy and full of dishes.

Mom was at the table. She'd tried to help me dry, but I'd shooed her away. "Keep me company," I'd said.

"Did something happen at the house today?" she asked when I didn't say anything.

I felt her eyes on my back.

I set a dish on the drying rack, squirted more soap onto the sponge, and curved it around the edge of a chipped plate, gaze fixated on the little yellow daffodils along the rim. "Nope. All went well. I was my usual delightful self."

"Huh. She said she was sorry she didn't leave an envelope and promised to next time."

Colin had told on me. Twerp.

"I told her it was no problem," Mom said.

I bobbed my head.

"She was very apologetic," Mom continued. "Oddly so."

"Weird."

I drained the sink, watching the water twist into a whirlpool. I imagined what Colin might have said to his mom. Did he tell her how badly we needed the money? How poor we were?

I didn't want to be pitied.

Then again, they were only doing what I had not so delicately suggested, trying to be more considerate.

Gah. Now I kind of felt like shit. I hadn't been my best self. Maybe I'd gone too far. I needed to apologize to Colin. I decided to the next time I saw him.

"She said she was very sorry for any inconvenience. She said it three times. 'I'm sorry for any *inconvenience*.'" Mom stressed the last word.

It looked like I was definitely going to have to apologize to Colin. What a tangle.

Just then Jiji wandered in, distracting Mom.

My phone flashed with a calendar reminder: Sherwood Institute tomorrow. I hesitated a few breaths before opening my email.

A new email from the letter writer. I bypassed his note to write one of my own. One to the director of the Sherwood Institute, telling him I wouldn't be continuing with the program. Mom never needed to know any of it. I'd leave the house when I was supposed to be at the institute. I could cover for a few weeks, maybe take some extra shifts without her knowing. I'd say the extra income was from tips. The situation was a win-win. A good lie.

I could feel Jiji frowning at me.

I smiled at him. "You need something?"

His eyes flickered over me. "You look at your phone too much," Jiji said finally. "Makes your posture bad."

I straightened and tucked my phone away.

Mom rose from her chair, rubbing her hands absentmindedly. "That household is our biggest client," she said sternly. "Let's just make sure everything goes smoothly next time you're there. We can't afford to lose them."

"Sure thing," I said brightly. "I'll take care of it."

"I know you will," Mom said, all confidence in me. "Good night, then."

She drifted off through the saloon doors, Jiji following. I wiped down the counters, then hauled the trash outside and down to the curb. The whole neighborhood smelled like soggy dirt.

I climbed the porch, chewed on a thumbnail.

Sitting on the cold top step, I knew what I had to do.

From: Emma Nakamura-Thatcher
(ethatch121@gmail.com)
To: Letter Writer
(thechronosproject1@gmail.com)
Subject: Is it supposed to be helpful that the angst is universal?

I still remember the ride to my dad's apartment. How he looked when he opened the door. The way he cried, telling me he couldn't come home. I even remember the smell of that night, the rain and the wet leaves. The fall always makes me a little sad now.

It's funny how some memories stick. Become part of your DNA, alter you. I think I was—I think I could have been—a different person before that night. That unlived-lives thing you mentioned.

I get it. People fall in and out of love all the time. They survive. But I'd rather not go through it. Delia says I'm afraid of putting myself out there, and I think: Is there any wonder why?

From: Letter Writer
(thechronosproject1@gmail.com)
To: Emma Nakamura-Thatcher
(ethatch121@gmail.com)
Subject: Ruh-roh

I don't like the sound of this.

From: Emma Nakamura-Thatcher
(ethatch121@gmail.com)
To: Letter Writer
(thechronosproject1@gmail.com)
Subject: You're going to like this a lot less

I'm just saying, maybe I've mastered the hiding game. But there's a reason. I wish I could go back in time. Is that possible? I'd like a do-over, please.

Honestly? I wish I'd never listened to you. I wish I'd never gone underground and to the park and spent myself on a boy in a band—because now I'm even emptier than before.

Things were simple and easy before you barged in with all the talk about corgis and changing my life and *love*.

I'm waving my white flag. I'm done with all of this.

CHAPTER TWENTY-FOUR

Emma over and out.

CHAPTER TWENTY-FIVE

Next clean, Colin was waiting outside his house for me when I got there. I stopped short, seeing his big body hunched on the doorstep.

He stood and tilted his chin up in greeting.

A dark tide of foreboding washed over me. Was I about to be fired?

He jogged down the steps to meet me. He wore loose jeans and a sweatshirt from his rowing team at Clearview Prep. At the center was a stitched round emblem of a maroon-and-gold roaring lion. The Latin words "non sibi sed omnibus" arced around it. "Here. Let me help you."

He reached for the bucket and vacuum, and I jerked back. "I've got it."

"Okay." He sucked his bottom lip and shoved his hands into his pockets, shoulders pulled in from the cold. "Listen, I need to talk to you about something."

Okay, I was being fired. It was surprising that Colin was spearheading this, but whatever. I wasn't going to let it happen. I remembered Mom. Her hands curled in like the dried leaves I'd raked from our yard that morning. I had to do whatever it took to keep this job.

I set my vacuum and bucket down with a thunk. "Before you say anything, I want to apologize."

His face twisted. "What?"

"I'm sorry," I told him. "For going off on you. I was having a bad day and took it out on you. I apologize if I made you feel uncomfortable." I closed my eyes. "Please don't fire me."

Nothing.

I opened my eyes.

He was staring at me, unmoving. "You're apologizing to me?"

"Profusely." I'd get down on my hands and knees and beg. I wouldn't like it, but I'd do it. What was pride when you had to keep the lights on?

"You shouldn't be apologizing," he said. "Because you have nothing to be sorry for."

I sniffed, noting how good it smelled in Colin's neighborhood. Like the air was different, sweeter and cleaner. No hint of dead leaves. The streets were pristine, storm drains clear.

"I'm not getting fired?"

"No. Of course not." His eyebrows pulled together, serious. "Everything you said was true. I'm an asshole."

"I wouldn't say that exactly," I drawled, stunned by this turn of events, still processing that I wasn't getting fired. Maybe I'd use a little extra electricity tonight in celebration.

"Overprivileged," he stated.

I stared at the ground and didn't deny it. His driveway was flagstone with grass planted between each slab. A little patch of clovers had sprung up between the perfect blades.

"*I* am sorry," he said, voice deep and earnest. "You were right. I was insensitive when I blew you off about the money. I don't understand your life. It was presumptuous of me to pretend that I did." He inhaled and held up his hands, looked at me meaningfully. "Okay?"

I felt my eyes bugging out. "Okay."

He accepted this with a nod. I blinked and watched as Colin slipped back inside ahead of me. I hung out a moment, letting the cold air wrap around me and this new knowledge sink in: Colin was sorry. I wasn't fired.

Honestly, I wasn't sure how to feel. I shifted, noticing I was a bit lighter on my feet. Also, my mood had turned an inch up, the best it had been in days.

The cleaning went by fast, quick and quiet. The house suddenly like any other job, where I was invisible. Upstairs, I paused at Colin's door and listened.

No sound on the other side.

I pushed into his room, brows rising in surprise. His bed had been made. The pillows had been fluffed. The duvet had been smoothed. The carpet was vacuumed. Poorly. There were footprints all over it, and the dusting had been totally ignored.

But still.

"He watched videos on how to make a bed." I swung around to see Sebastian in the hall. "He spent at least an hour ironing the sheets. Weirdo."

"He did a good job," I puffed out.

Sebastian stepped closer to me. "My brother isn't that bad, you know." He paused. "I mean, he has a terrible sense of humor, eats too much sugar, and obsesses over turkey sandwiches." Sebastian was really selling me on him. "But his heart is good, and most of the time, so are his intentions." His smile was self-deprecating, a little jaded. "Not like me. Not like the rest of the family." He held up an envelope between two fingers. "My mom wanted me to make sure you saw this."

I took it and shoved it into my back pocket. "Thanks."

He dipped his chin at me and walked on, brushing my arm as he passed.

Theo was leaving his house right as I pulled up.

"Hey." He mock-saluted me, keys in his hand.

I'd parked behind him. Our cars were bumper to bumper, near kissing.

"Hey," I said, getting out and popping a hip against my car. I squinted against the sun and at Theo. Mid-October, and the evening air was crisp and cold. Theo wore a shirt I'd seen before. It was green and sporty and looked ready for the zombie apocalypse. He hadn't worn a jacket since the fourth grade, when most of the boys at our elementary school started ditching their winter coats for short sleeves. I didn't get it. "Where are you off to?" I crossed my arms against the chill.

"I'm hanging out with Camille today."

I dropped my eyes, hoping Theo wouldn't see my mood darken. I hadn't spoken with Camille or my dad since that dinner. I wasn't sure what to say to either of them.

"We're going to play D and D at the mall," he went on.

The mall nearby had become a hangout for gamers. Past the fabric and Daiso stores, around the corner from a Korean barbecue place, an atrium was now cluttered with tables and foldout chairs. Theo and his friends came, they drank boba, and they conquered. Sometimes I tagged along, mostly for the used bookstore and ramen bar.

"I'm going to introduce her to my Dungeon Master."

I whistled low. "You sure you're ready for that? It's a big step."

I'd met Theo's Dungeon Master before. He was a twenty-five-year-old University of Washington graduate student named Tim. He had made himself a robotic arm and used it to roll the dice.

Theo owl-eyed me. "You're hilarious." He held his arms out to his sides. "Seriously. What do you think?"

That's when I saw it. Theo was *nervous*.

How unexpected. What uncharted territory. I'd grown used to his nerdy confidence. He was always so sure of himself, and it was catching. He once convinced me miniature trains were cool and that it would be fun to attend an exhibition two hours away in a county that banned caffeinated soda.

"Hey." I stepped onto the curb, closer, and looked up at him. His jaw was clenched, and my heart ached for him. "Tim is questionable, but you're great."

He visibly relaxed. "I like her," he admitted.

"If she doesn't like you, too, she's a fool."

He met my eyes. "Maybe we'll go on a double date sometime. Me and Camille and you and the cello guy."

"Oh," I said. "Ezra and I aren't a thing anymore."

Last Friday, when I was supposed to be at the Sherwood Institute, I'd killed time at Delia's. We watched *Antiques Roadshow*, my favorite. I scrolled through the nonstop texts from Ezra. He'd been blowing up my phone since the concert with explanations of who Janey was, their history, wondering why I wasn't showing up for Sherwood. And the last, a baffled: **You quit?**

Theo's brow furrowed. "What? How come?"

Finally I'd blocked Ezra. A bit dramatic, but I didn't want to see his name on my screen.

I felt Theo's inspection as I looked at the ground. "Who knows? Sometimes these things don't work out. It just wasn't meant to be."

Love fades, then it ends. Nothing lasts forever. Lately I'd managed to sidestep direct answers like a pro. I was too embarrassed to admit the truth. Ezra could have anyone, so why would he choose me? He wasn't my future or forever love.

Theo frowned. "Did he do something? Because I'll—"

"You'll what? Take Tim's robotic arm and rip him a new one?"

"For someone who doesn't like Tim, you bring him up a lot," said Theo. "And no, I wouldn't beat up the banjo player—"

"His name is Ezra, and he plays the cello," I corrected.

Theo waved it off. "I wouldn't beat him up." He paused, thinking. "I'd hack his social media accounts and flood them with an uncomfortable amount of SpongeBob SquarePants memes."

"That is oddly specific," I said.

"Did he do something, Emma? Truth." Theo's mouth formed a serious line.

I looked away, taking a moment to collect my thoughts. "It just . . . didn't work out. But you know what? It's all for the best. I've got so much going on; he was a big distraction anyway. Plus, I don't think . . ." I pulled a face and dismissed it all with a wave of my hand. "I don't think I'm the lovable type. Love, it's just not for me is what I'm saying."

"Emma," he said, low.

"I'm going to be late getting dinner ready for Jiji." I smiled brightly. I wanted Theo to be with someone like Camille. I wanted him to be happy. Because I loved him. Like I loved Delia as a friend, I internally qualified. "And you don't want to be late meeting Camille. If she gets there before you, Tim will probably start in on her about which dice set is best."

Theo grunted. "That's not even a question. Gemini dice, no contest. Hands down."

"It's embarrassing you know that."

He grinned lazily at me. A lock of hair fell into his eyes. "Don't get me started on wooden dice versus metal."

On instinct, I stood on my toes and reached up, pushing the hair back. It was something I'd done before. This was our way. Theo rescued me from parties and downtown Seattle when my car wouldn't start. And I fixed him up. I let my arm drift back to my side. Theo had stilled, his lips parted. I searched his face. My stomach flip-flopped. The silence stretched and grew taut.

"I'm going now," I said, rocking back on my heels.

"Yep, me too."

One of us had to move first. So I walked to my house, opened the front door, and turned to see Theo standing there. "Bye." I waved to him.

"Hey, Emma?" he said.

"Yes?"

"How's your engine been running?"

"What?"

He nodded at my car. "The starter," he said.

"Oh," I said. "It's still a bit noisy but driving better. I think it's fine."

His brow dipped in concern. "I'll take another look at it this weekend."

"It's fine. Really," I promised.

Then I went inside, and through the front window I watched Theo get into his car. Watched as he pulled a U-turn and drove off.

Both of us heading in separate directions.

CHAPTER TWENTY-SIX

My breaths came fast and short as I hauled my buckets and vacuum down Colin's long driveway.

I'd just finished cleaning his house, and I wasn't focused on my feet, where I was stepping. Instead I'd been thinking about the next two houses I needed to clean today, and how I wasn't going to look at my phone. I wasn't interested in checking for new emails from the letter writer or answering calls from my dad. Out of sight, out of mind.

After these cleans I had forty-eight hours off and vowed to sleep every minute I wasn't in school. I was making big plans with my bed when the tip of my sneaker hooked on one of the driveway's cobblestones.

I fell hard.

Lysol, Pledge, and Scrubbing Bubbles spilled onto the ground. My vacuum landed with a clatter. For a moment I stayed face down, catching my breath, mentally assessing my body parts. Everything felt okay.

I tried to stand, but my ankle folded, screaming in protest. Crap.

I rolled to my back and sat up. The cold cobblestones pressed through my jeans and into my skin as I studied my legs. The flesh above my sock was mottled pink. I tested my ankle, rolling my foot in and out, and winced.

Oof, that was painful.

I flopped backward, hand on my stomach, and closed my eyes. I sighed. What to do?

The front door slammed. Footsteps stopped inches from my hip. "Emma?" I heard Colin ask above me.

I opened my eyes, feeling stupid. For, well, obvious reasons. "Oh, hey."

"What happened? Did you faint? Where are you hurt?" His words came out rapid-fire. "I'll call an ambulance."

I half rose, resting on my elbows. "No need. It's just a sprain."

I'd had one before, when I was seven. Theo and I had been racing on scooters—I'd been behind him, taken a curve too fast, and fallen, landing wrong and twisting my ankle. This pain was vaguely familiar—throbbing and tender to the touch.

Colin's frown deepened. "Then I'll take you to a doctor." He paused. "You could have broken your leg or your neck. Why were you carrying so much?" he asked in a tone like he was asking me why I was sitting in the middle of a vat of acid.

"I carry that much all the time. Wait." I screwed up my nose. "Are you angry with me for getting hurt?"

"No." He scowled at me, face tight. "I'm not sure. Maybe."

"That's deranged."

He shrugged helplessly. "Doctor or ambulance, your choice."

"I just need a few minutes to rest and an ice pack. The swelling will go down." I was hilariously optimistic.

"Okay. Let's get you inside." He crouched low and patted his shoulder. He was wearing the same Clearview Prep hoodie as the other day. "Hop on."

The thought of mounting Colin's back and wrapping my legs around his waist for a ride had me saying, "I'm good." I'd rather sleep in the driveway like I lived here now.

He stayed crouched. "You can't walk."

"There's a cane in my car, in my trunk. Will you grab it?"

He stood and started down the driveway, then turned back. "Wait. You carry a cane in your car?"

"For my grandfather," I said, then shooed him along with my hands.

Colin brought the cane back. He helped me stand, and I winced at the pain but stayed mute as he helped me hobble up the driveway.

Twenty minutes later the swelling had only increased. Obeying the law of physics and inflammation, my ankle looked as if a baseball had been lodged under the skin.

I was resting in the St. Jameses' living room on one of their couches, my foot elevated on three velvet cushions, an ice pack laid over it.

"It's not better," Colin pointed out the obvious. "We should go to the doctor. I don't like the color it's turning."

"I think the purple and blue kind of complement my complexion." I sent him a smile.

That made his eyes squint. "This isn't funny."

"It's kind of funny." I flexed my ankle. "It feels pretty good. I'm sure I'm fine to work the rest of the day. I just need to move a little, walk it off. I'll get started here." I swung my legs over the couch and reached for my shoe.

"Emma," Colin said, giving me a knowing look. "You can't work."

"Of course I can." To prove my point, I stood and ventured a few steps. Jiji's cane stayed on the couch. "See?"

My ankle gave way. I let out a muffled, painful cry and started to fall.

Colin bit out a curse and braced me, his hands on my hips. "Admit it. You can't work."

At his touch I sucked in a breath. He was taller than me. Which wasn't saying much. Most people were taller than me. But Colin, with his shoulder width and his height, was like a cypress tree, and me a fern. I pulled back sharply. "I'll see if someone else can take my shifts."

Colin inhaled, as if appeased. "Then I'll take you to the doctor."

"You have a weird obsession with taking me to the doctor," I murmured, whipping out my phone.

His lips tilted up, and he blasted me with a smile that would put the stars to shame. I wondered how my lungs hadn't suddenly stopped working.

I hobbled the few steps back to the couch and collapsed, a down cushion swallowing me up. I opened my text thread with Theo and thumbed a message for help. Colin sat on the coffee table across from me, legs splayed, watching me. I was pretty sure he'd tackle me if I tried to move again.

Theo responded quickly: Sorry. I'm four hours outside the city. Camille and I took a road trip to one of the vortexes here.

"My friend isn't available." I bit my lip. Panic began to set in. My stomach became a slab of concrete. "We can't afford to lose a day's pay."

Colin was quiet for a beat, rubbing his thumbs together. Then he said, "I'll help you."

It wasn't often that I was stunned into silence. Finally I landed on a single syllable. "Ha!" He had to be joking.

"I'm serious." He straightened up, eyes bright. "I'll help you. Take me to your next job, tell me what to do. You can be my boss." He held out his arms. "Mold me."

I shook my head. "I don't think this is a good idea."

"What other choice do you have?"

Turned out the best choice was my only choice. Cane in hand, I limped behind Colin into the garage.

"I'm afraid this is one of those all-confidence, no-skill situations," I said while he gathered my cleaning supplies and loaded them into the back of his SUV—the BMW I'd seen him drive that made my vehicle look sickly in comparison. "Maybe you should put a blanket down?" The interior was pristine dove-gray leather with matching carpet, and smelled fresh-from-the-lot new. What if the bleach spilled?

"It's fine." He slammed the trunk. "Do you need help getting in the car?"

I said no, then demonstrated that I most definitely did when I couldn't hop in. Colin circled the hood and hoisted me into the front passenger seat, and I emitted a little yelp.

"This car is too high."

I sounded like Jiji at the movie theater. *This popcorn is too buttery. This soda is too fizzy. The screen is too large. The seats are too soft.*

"I'll give BMW that feedback. They're friends of the family." He pushed a button and started the car. Heat blasted from the vents. A little screen in the dashboard lit up and said: *Welcome, Colin.*

"Let me guess, you vacation together in Aspen for the winter."

"Swiss Alps, actually." He backed out using a camera. "Stefan has a chalet we stay in. We wear matching pajamas and sing carols."

I studied him to see if he was joking. I couldn't tell. "I'm actually unbearably curious about the print of the pajamas," I whispered.

"Plaid one-pieces with bum flaps."

I let out a sound of disbelief. "I figured they'd have dollar bills printed on them."

"We only wear those on certain occasions, you know, when a family member is being coronated or has just entered the eight-digit club."

I laughed stiffly. "Seriously?"

A grin. "No. But we do have special attire for when we hunt bald eagles."

Sinking lower in the seat, I glared at him. "As a general rule, I find hunting endangered species to be in poor taste."

"Technically, bald eagles aren't endangered anymore. But with that in mind, I won't tell you about my family's secret history with the dodo bird, then."

I gaped at him.

He glanced at me. Grinned crookedly. "Kidding. Mostly."

Colin whistled low, eyes traveling the height of Mrs. Sydney's Dorothy Draper–inspired mansion. "You clean this whole thing by yourself?"

"Top to bottom," I replied, limping up the path lined with animal topiaries. I stopped at the giant paneled door and tapped gently with the brass knocker.

Mrs. Sydney answered with a smile that grew twice its size upon seeing Colin. "You brought a friend. And a handsome friend at that," she said to me out of the side of her mouth. "Come on in, I've got tea and pastries. I thought we'd try the new bakery that opened down the street. They're famous for their orange basil scones. Have you ever heard of such a thing?"

I'd explained about Mrs. Sydney to Colin in the car. We were paid to clean but also to listen. And there was never any charge for our time beyond what it took to dust and mop. Mrs. Sydney always offered to pay my hourly wage when we sat at her tea table, and I always declined.

The conversation was just as valuable.

"So." Mrs. Sydney poured Colin a cup of Earl Grey and handed it over. She had a ring on each one of her fingers, all precious gems—rubies, sapphires, emeralds. The tea set had a delicate floral pattern etched in gold. She'd also dragged over a little upholstered footstool, which I'd propped my ankle on. "You're here to help our Emma out?"

Colin opened a little canister and added a lump of sugar to his tea with a set of teal enameled tongs. It was surreal seeing him dip a toe into my world, his big body crammed into Mrs. Sydney's jewel box of a tearoom. "I'm helping Emma out. But she's helping me out too. More, actually." He cleared his throat, and his eyebrows pulled together, serious. "It has recently come to my attention that my worldview is rather small. This is me broadening my horizons."

"Well." Mrs. Sydney patted her chest. Her eyes were misty. "That is a beautiful sentiment. Isn't it, Emma?"

I watched him for a long beat, my heart winging at his statement. "Yeah," I said, fidgeting.

"I like your wallpaper," Colin said.

Mrs. Sydney half turned. Behind her was a bust of a Roman emperor set against leopard wallpaper. "Thank you. It's vintage. I found it in a little French village when I was on honeymoon with my second husband." She paused. "No, fourth husband. His name was Royce . . ."

Colin diligently nodded while Mrs. Sydney spoke, drinking in her every word, asking follow-up questions.

The utter warmth that rolled through me could have swept me under. I wanted Mrs. Sydney to be handled with care, respected. And I realized it was important to me that Mrs. Sydney liked Colin.

Despite Colin's comfort at Mrs. Sydney's tea table, I learned very quickly he was out of his element entirely washing dishes and mopping floors and folding laundry—he did this weird trifold, almost-origami thing with trousers that I'd never seen before. But he took each task so seriously. Like when he dusted the plantation shutters in Mrs. Sydney's aviary-themed dining room, running his finger along the slat of wood and raising it for me to inspect. No dust. I dipped my chin, approving. His eyes shimmered with pride.

Well, well, well. Colin St. James was full of surprises.

At the end of the day we stood outside the last house. It was the Presleys', with their five children, golden retriever, and bonus room that acted more like an anything-goes space. We'd cleaned the whole thing top to bottom in three hours—a new record.

"I'm going to be finding glitter everywhere for the next ten years." A fine sheen of sweat had formed on Colin's brow. He uncapped a plastic water bottle and chugged it, throat muscles working as he drank.

"Glitter is the herpes of the craft world."

"We should put that on a T-shirt. It's something everyone should know."

I grinned and thumbed through the envelope from the Presleys. "I feel like I should give you half of what we earned today."

Colin had done most of the heavy work. I'd hobbled around doing what I could at waist level, saving Colin from mistakes such as pouring dish soap into the dishwasher, cleaning the floors with Pledge, and not separating darks from lights.

He shook his head. "You don't owe me anything."

"I said that I feel like I should, not that I'm going to," I qualified, brushing a strand of hair from my face. "But seriously, thank you for your help."

"No problem." He dull-punched my arm awkwardly, and I found it to be just about the most charming thing ever.

"I have an idea."

Colin's gaze dipped to my mouth and then back up to meet my eyes. "I love ideas."

"The Presleys gave us a nice tip. Want to grab something to eat? My treat. Anything up to"—I flipped through the money, counting, calculating bills, what I had to spare—"twenty bucks."

He sucked on his lower lip a moment. "Honestly, there's

nothing more I'd rather do."

My heart thrummed.

Sometimes people say things they don't mean. *Your baby is so cute. You can't tell your haircut is crooked. That top is amazing on you. I promise I won't say anything. I'll love you forever.*

But for some reason I was near certain Colin really meant what he said.

CHAPTER TWENTY-SEVEN

Lo and behold, I was in Colin's car again. On our way to a small restaurant he swore had the best Mexican food this side of town. A turn of events that felt, at best, a little weird, and at worst, possibly unwise.

Cane in hand, I limped through the parking lot to the restaurant. Tomorrow I'd wrap my ankle tight and be ready to clean by myself next week. I decided to keep that to myself lest Colin start the doctor talk again.

A sleepy papier-mâché alligator leaned against the wall next to the door, sombrero tipped over its eyes. Inside was dim, lighting low and hot pink. Black velvet booths lined one wall, and a bar was on the other side. A sign invited us to seat ourselves.

We grabbed plastic menus, and Colin led us to a corner spot. A candle flickered in the middle of the table. It was all a little . . . romantic. Was this too cozy? Too intimate?

Colin perused the menu. "I could really murder a few tacos. Seeing how hard you worked today made me feel even more upset that you don't usually eat lunch."

"Not true. I eat a banana or a Slim Jim sometimes."

He kept his eyes on the menu. "You're not making it better."

I looked around. Ninety percent of the patrons were couples. "This isn't a date," I blurted.

Just then a waitress with mermaid hair arrived, balancing a carafe of water, cups, and a basket of chips with two dishes of salsa on a tray, and deposited everything onto the table. With a coffin-shaped nail, she pointed to the salsa on my right. "Mild." She swept her finger to the left. "Burn-your-tongue-off hot. Be back to take your order in five." A wink and she was gone.

Colin filled a cup with water and slid it to me. With his other hand, he reached up and scratched his eyebrow. "I didn't think this was a date."

I felt foolish and leaned in. "Okay. Good. I just want to be clear."

"Point taken." Colin slumped back in his seat and stretched his legs on either side of my feet. Amusement tilted his lips up. "Plus, I've decided you're too pretty for me. If we dated, it would make me look shallow."

I snorted and looked away; my cheeks flushed. "You're ridiculous."

The waitress returned. She flipped open her notepad, and Colin looked at me to go first. I skimmed the entrees, all of which far exceeded my twenty-dollar budget. "I'm just going to stick with the chips." I put the menu down.

Colin's face was etched with tension. He ordered two fajitas, beef and chicken, plus guacamole.

I added up the cost, upward of sixty dollars, and started to sweat. Did he still think I was paying?

Then he saved me by saying, "Will you put it on the St. James tab?"

Mermaid Hair brightened. "Absolutely! I'll just get this started for you. Holler if you want anything else."

I took a chip from the basket and stared at the grains of corn in it. "Your family owns this restaurant, don't they?"

"Is it going to make you hate me more if I say yes?"

I sucked in a breath. "I don't hate you."

"You just think I'm spoiled." He wore a defensive, tight smile.

I shook my head. "'Spoiled' means 'rotten.' I don't think that about you."

"What do you think of me, then?"

A loaded question, if there ever was one. "I don't know anymore. I thought I had you and your brother figured out . . ." I trailed off, immediately remorseful.

"Let me guess. A couple of rich latchkey kids. You aren't wrong." He dipped a chip in the burn-your-tongue-off salsa and chewed.

I took a moment to absorb this. "Your parents aren't around much. You're not close to them?"

By this I meant emotionally and physically. I hadn't seen Mr. St. James in weeks. And Mrs. St. James was nice, if a little distant. It was hard to picture her overflowing with affection for her sons. She'd been savage about parties and decorations, concerned with what Hermès hand towels to hang in each bathroom and what others might think about the gold stitching against the silver peony wallpaper. Their house was beautiful but sterile, as if designed to allow as little interaction with one another as possible. Colin's and Sebastian's rooms were together but in a different wing, far from their parents'.

By contrast, my house was a shoebox. We crowded into the bedrooms upstairs. Each of us had our own, but the walls were paper thin, and we shared a bathroom. There had been times when I'd begrudged our tiny space, but now I was thankful for it.

"Let's just say on Christmas and birthdays, my dad gives us a hearty handshake and says 'Well done' before heading off to golf or bike."

Sipping my water, I imagined my dad's look if I ever tried to shake his hand. "Your dad does own a lot of Lycra."

"That's something I don't like to think about."

"Tiny shorts," I said. "And shirts with pads built into the chest to avoid nipple chafing."

"Stop." He squinted his eyes shut.

The waitress returned, sliding a black earthenware dish of guacamole and two sizzling fajita plates onto the table. Carefully, Colin positioned everything in the middle and dropped a basket filled with warm tortillas square in front of me. Then he lifted his chin, as if to say, *Go on*.

I got to work spreading sour cream on a tortilla and sprinkling in chicken. A bubble of emotion for Colin ballooned beneath my ribs. "It must be hard, though, not having your parents available." I hadn't spoken to my dad in weeks, and honestly, it didn't feel right. Like a part of me was missing.

"It's not all bad," Colin said, piling a fajita so full that it barely closed. I imagined how many calories it took to keep his body running. "There are certain upsides. Eat what you want. Stay up late. Do whatever strikes you . . . clean houses, build boats." He took a giant bite, chewed, and swallowed. "There's a certain lawlessness to it."

I smiled. That kind of freedom did sound appealing. "Are you close with Sebastian?"

He nodded. "Despite Dad trying to pit us against each other." Already he was on to his second fajita. I was halfway through my first. "His core value is competition and being the best. That's how it was when he was growing up, with his brother. You should see us around the holidays. It's a constant one-upping between my dad and uncle. One morning I came out of my room, and they were arm wrestling. They'd been at it all night." He paused. Ate more. Seriously, where did he put it all? "What about you? Tell me why you keep a cane in your car."

I looked at Jiji's cane propped against the table. "It's for my grandfather. He's stubborn and cranky and doesn't like using a cane. But I always keep one nearby in case his knee starts acting up. Although, his knee probably wouldn't act up so much if he used the cane in the first place. One of those chicken-and-egg scenarios."

He nodded like he got it. "What about your mom and dad? Where are they?"

"I live with my mom. She has some health problems. Early arthritis in her hands." I stuck up my fingers and wiggled them. "It's hard for her to work now, which is why I'm helping out more. My dad is a writer. An author." I shifted my gaze to the basket of chips. "He's getting remarried soon, and uh, we're not currently speaking."

"Yeah?" He lifted his chin. Waited expectantly for me to continue.

I put down my food, appetite gone. "Next subject, please."

He also put his food down. "Same subject. No wonder you thought I was spoiled. You're working your ass off for your family, and here I am wiping mine with dollar bills."

"Again. I don't think you're spoiled." I stopped. "You've never done that though, right?" I motioned delicately to my backside.

"No. But there was that one time we lit a fire using a five-dollar bill because we wanted fondue." He balled up his napkin and threw it on his plate.

"Oh wow." I softened the comment with a smile. "I'm pretty sure that's a federal crime. Let's keep that between us, for a variety of reasons."

He crossed his heart. "In the vault."

Mermaid Hair brought a folio. "Just need a signature for the comped meal," she said.

Colin scribbled his name, and I decided I'd really hate him if he didn't leave a tip. But then he produced a twenty from his wallet. I offered mine, and he waved me off. "I just have one question before we leave," he said.

I was stuffing the money back in my purse. "Okay. Shoot."

"What's a Slim Jim?"

CHAPTER TWENTY-EIGHT

"My treat," I said, slapping the Slim Jims down on the hood of Colin's car outside the 7-Eleven. The metal was warm under my palm, but the air outside was cool, the sky threatening rain.

He picked up a package and read the label. His lips pressed together, and his brow furrowed as if he were about to attempt a Herculean feat. "Processed meat."

Based on Colin's refrigerator and pantry contents, I'd bet he was raised on organic, unprocessed, non-GMO everything.

"You pick first." I'd bought all three flavors: original, mild, and spicy. I'd also purchased a blue Slurpee.

"Who's the grinning man on the front with reflective sunglasses?"

"That's 'Macho Man' Randy Savage. Their spokesperson. He personally saved the Slim Jim brand. Without him, Slim Jims wouldn't be established in the snack pantheon."

"So we have him to thank for the immortality of meat sticks."

"Stop stalling." I sipped my Slurpee.

He swiped the original-flavored stick, ripped open the

package, and took a bite. He chewed slowly, savoring it. "It tastes like pepperoni."

I grinned crookedly. "That's the nitrates."

He jogged a little in place. "I can feel my blood pressure rising. I like it." He swallowed and took another bite.

"Imagine. You could have gone your entire life never having a Slim Jim if it weren't for me."

"How did I ever survive?" He opened the mild-flavored Slim Jim and took a large bite.

"Growing up, I never tried cheesecake. I thought it would be gross because cheese plus cake. But turns out I was wrong. I missed so many years of cheesecake," I said.

"Slim Jims are my cheesecake."

A maroon van with tinted windows pulled in. I watched as it parked. A lump lodged in my throat as the doors opened and Blue, Tenny, and Ezra climbed out. They hadn't seen me yet. I struggled with what to do, my brain short-circuiting. Run? Hide?

Too late.

"Emma?" Tenny hurried over, threw her arms my neck, and hugged me tight. "Where have you been?"

"Hey." Blue sidled up, and Tenny released her choke hold. "Check out our new van. Isn't she a beauty? We saved a seat for you. Don't mind the brown stain on it."

"Hey, guys." My wave was tiny, unsure.

Blue and Tenny wore awful shirts with each other's faces airbrushed on them. I was trying really hard not to be happy seeing the couple again, but Blue and Tenny were so easy to love, their energy and buoyant mood contagious.

"Hey, Emma." I couldn't look at him, but the deep timbre of Ezra's voice hit me square in the solar plexus. Mercy, please. I tunneled back in time. To Sherwood. To the underground. The music we played together. The magic we'd created. "I've been calling you."

"Yeah . . . ," I said, because I didn't know what to say. I only knew I didn't want to have this conversation right now.

Ezra looked past me at Colin, mouth curving down. "Who's your friend?"

"Oh, um . . . this is Colin," I said.

Colin stuck his hand out. "How you doing, mate?"

What? I gaped at Colin, suddenly bemused at his spontaneous accent.

"Good." Ezra shook Colin's hand.

I watched it in slow motion. Both of them rigid, intensity emanating.

Maybe I should have been thrilled. A little excited to show Ezra that he didn't mean anything to me anymore, that I had moved on. He didn't need to know Colin and I were just friends. But all I felt was uncomfortable.

"And this is Blue and Tenny." I waved at the pair, both of them smiling like a couple of Cheshire cats.

"How's it going?" Colin idly scratched the back of his neck.

"Oh, it's going, man. It's going," Blue said.

"Can I talk to you for a sec?" Ezra asked me then, eyes darting between Colin and me.

"I don't think so—" I started.

But Blue cut in. "Colin, my man, this your car?" He nodded at the BMW.

Colin looked behind him as if surprised it was there. "Yeah, it is."

"Mind if I check it out?" Already Blue was reaching for the backseat door, Tenny at his shoulder, encouraging him with a smile.

Colin hesitated, looking between me and Ezra.

"It's fine," I said. "Go on. I wouldn't leave Blue and Tenny alone in your car."

Blue and Tenny were, in fact, crawling into the back and shutting the door. Colin hopped into the driver's seat. A moment later the engine fired and the bass thumped.

Ezra stepped closer to me, and I stepped back. My ankle buckled, and I braced myself against the brick wall of the 7-Eleven.

"What happened to your foot?" he asked carefully.

"I twisted my ankle."

I was all tangled up inside. The whole moment was surreal. Tenny and Blue with Colin in his car. Ezra and I, feet away from each other, positioned between the 7-Eleven doors and a garbage can piled high with sour gummy worm wrappers.

"What's up?" I said, pushing past the lump in my throat.

Ezra made a sound of frustration. *"What's up?"* He moved his body, bending so he was at my level. "*What's up* is I've been calling you and texting you, and you quit Sherwood."

Same Ezra. Challenging me. Not letting me off the hook.

"I get it," he went on. "That was a really awkward run-in, but it's not what you think. Janey and I met when I toured the conservatory last year. We kept in touch and hooked up a few times."

I did not need to know that. My overactive imagination flooded with fresh images of Janey and Ezra. I squeezed my eyes shut and opened them. Ezra was still right there. Still talking.

"But we were never official. I didn't even know she was coming into town. I think she thought surprising me would somehow make it that way. I guess I should have been clearer with her from the beginning. I know you think I'm a dirtbag. Maybe I deserve it. But please come back to Sherwood," he pled. "The admissions officer from Berklee got in touch. They're excited to see you audition. Do you know how many times that happens? A college reaches out with enthusiasm like that? Never. You have to come back."

The doors to Colin's car slammed shut.

"Sweet ride," Blue announced. "But I'm going to stick with what I've got. My 1982 Ford Econoline van, you know?" He patted the hood, right above the crooked bumper. "They don't make them like this anymore."

Colin nodded like it all made perfect sense.

That surreal feeling returned again. It was as if I was watching two disparate worlds merge.

"I like the . . . what is that hanging from the mirror?" Colin said, tipping his chin at the windshield.

"Shrunken head," said Tenny.

"Well . . ." I trailed off and tugged on my ear.

"Guess we should get on with it," Blue said. "We've got places to be. Pop-Tarts to pop. You know how it goes." Bells chimed as he held the door open for Tenny and Ezra. Tenny slipped under his arm and into the store.

Ezra stayed put, commanding me to look at him with his silence. When I finally did, he said, "Give what I said some thought?"

"Okay." My voice sounded garbled.

The hard line of Ezra's mouth softened. The memory of

kissing him hit a tender spot, where a faint spark still remained. I struggled to keep my thoughts straight. I needed Ezra to move along and go into the 7-Eleven so my brain would start working again. So I could process it all, everything he'd said. If I'd overreacted seeing Janey, and if I had, what that meant. "I will."

Colin drove, and the car was silent. The air filled with questions, and my ears started to ring. I don't know why, but I felt like I owed him an explanation.

"I went to school with them. Well, not Blue and Tenny, but Ezra," I said. Discomfort scratched at my chest. "He plays the cello, and we—"

"It's none of my business," he said flatly. "You don't have to tell me."

"I want to." I smoothed my hands over my jeans. "I was in this program, the Sherwood Institute." I glanced at Colin to see if the name registered anything for him. His face was blank. "It's for music. I play the violin."

"You play the violin?" Wonder eased the frustration from his tone.

"I do. Anyway, Ezra and I were together." We'd kissed. I'd thought it was serious. He didn't. "Maybe. I'm not sure, but it's over." He visibly relaxed at the word "over." "It was good to see Tenny and Blue, though. Sorry they climbed in your car. They're a trip."

He hummed pensively, focusing on traffic and making a left turn. "Thanks for explaining."

"Of course," I told him. "But did you spontaneously develop an Australian accent back there?"

His cheeks dusted the lightest shade of pink. "Nah."

"Because it sounded like it."

"If I had done that—which I'm not saying I did—I wouldn't want to talk about it."

"Oi, mate," I said. "Let's put another shrimp on the barbie."

He smiled reluctantly. "You might have a future in voice work." We came to his street then, and he parked in front of my car. "You going to be okay to drive?"

"I only need my right foot." I wiggled it in proof, fit as a fiddle.

"I was thinking," he said, drawing a thumb around the steering wheel. Even his hands were big, twice the size of mine. "We should exchange phone numbers."

"You have my phone number."

"My mom has it," he pushed out, eyes widening meaningfully. "But I want you to give me your phone number." His jaw firmed. "What if I spill red wine on the carpet or have the sudden urge to use one-hundred-dollar bills as kindling for a fire?"

"Do you want my number for a cleaning or privilege emergency?"

He rested his head against the seat. "No. I want your number because we're friends. We are, aren't we?"

I studied him and nodded once, confirming. The moment seemed enormous. Momentous. "Yeah. We're friends."

CHAPTER TWENTY-NINE

Hours of time on my hands and forced to sit on the couch for a day waiting for my ankle to heal, I had gone back and perused Ezra's text messages. Pretty much a summary of what he'd told me outside the 7-Eleven. Janey and Ezra were never official. He'd made it clear to her. *Please text or call.*

Reading it all, I'd felt a cold shadow leave me. The kind that departs when you might have been wrong, when you're ready to see things in a new light. This was making me rethink a lot of my recent actions.

Hence the waffling over the letter writer's most recent email. To look or not to look?

In many ways I was more my mom's child than my dad's. I liked order, timeliness, a good sale—anything 50 percent off— and I was stubborn to a fault. After the divorce my mom adopted a we-don't-need-him attitude with my dad, which had been in effect for years. When we decided on a course of action, we committed. There was some comfort in living a restrained life. Did I want to let the letter writer back in? The Sherwood Institute? Ezra? My ankle was better, but the rest of me still had some healing to do.

"Come on. Open it. You know you want to." Delia was on the floor of the carpeted practice room. She sat crisscross, a pair of gleaming scissors in her hand and a pile of magenta and lime squares of paper in front of her.

We'd holed up in a soundproof booth for lunch.

My phone had dimmed. A tap of my fingers woke it up, and I read the new email subject line from the letter writer: *Warning: drinking and writing.*

Nope. Wouldn't do it.

I placed the phone face down and glanced at Delia. "What are you working on?"

She grinned at me. "Nice. You sidestepped that like a pro." She exhaled. "You're lucky I'm feeling very self-involved right now and am inclined to take the bait." She set the scissors down and flexed her hands. The price of her art was carpal tunnel and finger ice baths in the evenings. "I'm creating a series of paper mosaics based on famous past portraits of ladies posing with cats."

"That's brilliant. Tell me more." My attention drifted back down to my phone.

"Your self-denial is adorable." She tilted her head at me, clasped her hands together as if in fervent prayer. "Open the email. I beg you. Put us both out of our misery."

We were twenty minutes into lunch, and I'd been like this the whole time, distracted, half-heartedly present. Not to mention the morning. Three periods had passed, and I couldn't tell you what I'd learned. The email had appeared that morning while I was making Jiji a spinach smoothie I'd cajoled him into drinking by promising bacon after. Two fat pieces I'd sizzled in grease and plated, waving them under his nose.

I narrowed my eyes at her. "If I read it, I won't write back."

She suppressed a smile and returned to cutting. "Whatever you need to tell yourself to sleep at night."

I let out a laugh-slash-groan. "This is a terrible idea."

But the truth? I was unbearably curious. Even more, I missed the letter writer. He'd been my confidant. A friend. Why had I cut him off? Out of some misplaced sense of self-preservation?

"Said every person before something great happened."

"I'm going to open it now."

I promised myself to stay levelheaded. To not overthink it.

My heart thundered in my ears as I clicked.

From: Letter Writer
(thechronosproject1@gmail.com)
To: Emma Nakamura-Thatcher
(ethatch121@gmail.com)
Subject: Warning: drinking and writing.

You're right. This isn't fair. This whole situation is so imbalanced. I deserve your vehemence. Would you believe I've been doing what I think is best? But you know what they say about good intentions . . .

Actually, I can't remember.

Shit.

I'm a little drunk right now. Something big happened today. Huge. I've been waiting for it a long time. My friends dragged me out to a bar. They threatened they'd send me home if I said your name once.

Well, look at me now. Fresh out of a cab.

Apparently, I am poor company.

Someone even called me a party pooper. Which I haven't been called since the second grade, when I went to a birthday party and opened all the kid's presents while everyone was watching a clown named BJ. I feel like I deserve a pat on the back for not making the obvious joke here.

Please, Emma.

Hate me. Regret me. But please don't cast me aside. Want to talk about loneliness? When I think of you, I find I am free from solitude.

CHAPTER THIRTY

As sworn, I did not write him back. But I read the letter writer's email repeatedly, an embarrassing number of times over the course of the week.

It was damp and cool, and the pavement was wet from rain the night before, when I pulled up in front of Mrs. Sydney's house Saturday morning.

My phone alerted me to a text.

Question. My D&D group thinks I should make note cards of talking points for when I take Camille out to dinner tonight. That would be weird, right?

I thumbed a reply to Theo. So weird. Why would you take dating advice from them?

Theo's reply came right away. Are you assuming they don't date? That's a very harmful stereotype, Em.

I smiled and knocked on the door.

"Oh, hello, dear," Mrs. Sydney said when she answered, surprise fluttering in her expression. Didn't know why; it was our usual time for cleaning.

"Hi, Mrs. Sydney. How are you today?" I jostled my buckets and mop and began to step inside, expecting her to open the door wider, welcome me in like she always did.

She moved and blocked me. "I don't need you today."

Quietly, I scoffed. "Excuse me?"

She smiled, a mischievous glimmer in her warm brown eyes. She wore blue eye shadow, matching eyeliner, a fringed caftan, a turban, and chandelier earrings.

Fabulous all the way around. I coveted her life.

"Your friend came by last evening and cleaned."

"I'm not sure I understand."

"Colin," she said loudly, as if the problem was my hearing. "He cleaned my house. I'm all set for today. Bye now." The door shut in my face.

What the hell?

I marched from Mrs. Sydney's house. In my car I texted Colin. **Did you clean Mrs. Sydney's house?**

What was going on? Was he trying to steal my clients now? Colin didn't need the money. I did.

He answered. **Dusted all of her platform boots and washed some delicates that made the tips of my ears red. I did not know women that age still wore thongs.**

This isn't funny, I punched out angrily. **I need that money.**

And he knew I needed that money. What was his game?

Come over, he replied. **I'll explain.**

I sent back a series of question marks, devil faces, and middle fingers.

You're going to find a similar situation at the Presleys', too. The Presleys were my afternoon job. **Come over,** he said again. **I'll explain.**

How about explain right now, or I'll murder you? I volleyed back.

A gray bubble with three blinking dots appeared and then disappeared.

I pounded out a couple of bloody knives, then waited five whole minutes with no response from Colin. **On my way,** I wrote finally.

Great! he said. **I'll hide the knives.**

Thirty minutes later I was stomping up Colin's driveway and knocking.

Colin answered. "Emma," he said, my name rolling around in his mouth like a sweet treat. He leaned against the doorframe, wearing the rowing hoodie from his school again. It must be a favorite. He smirked. "What an unexpected surprise."

"Are your parents here?" I craned my neck, checking out the inside. I'd learned my lesson from last time. Check for an audience before laying into Colin.

"They're in Montreal for the week. Sebastian is around somewhere. Probably using an Excel spreadsheet to chart world domination."

"What are you up to, St. James?" I crossed my arms and tapped a toe, not in the mood.

"It's cold. Come in."

"Not happening. What's going on? If you're trying to steal my business . . ." I jammed a finger into his chest, and he wrapped his hand around it. For one searing beat, we both focused on where our bodies were connected. A strange, sudden electric buzz started at the base of my spine, then shorted out when he released me.

He cleared his throat. "I'm not stealing your business. Are you always so distrustful?"

Come to think of it, kind of.

Colin bent down, bracing his hands on his thighs so we were at eye level. "All your work is done for today and tomorrow, the whole weekend. I cleaned Mrs. Sydney's place and the Presleys'. I also cleaned my house."

I froze, staring at him. "I don't understand."

He straightened, beaming with pride. "Days off. I'm giving you two days off. Forty-eight hours of complete freedom." On the foyer table was an envelope, and he slid it toward me. I stepped inside and placed my hand on top of it. I could feel the shape of bills, a whole fat stack. "Payment from the houses and mine," he said.

"I don't know what to say. I probably should apologize for all the bad things I called you." I picked at some nonexistent lint on my shirt.

"You threatened to murder me, but you didn't call me any names."

"In my head I did." I tapped my temple with the corner of the envelope. "I may have brought your parents and family into it. Sorry." I paused. "Thank you." The words came out stiff. I hesitated. "I can't accept this, though." I tried giving the money back to him.

He held up his hands. "If you don't take it, I'll drive to every bank within a twenty-mile radius and try to deposit the money into your account."

I suppressed a smile. "I don't think banks give out information like that."

"You never know unless you try."

Fiddling with the envelope, I tried to remember the last time

I'd had a full day off. I couldn't. It was always work or school, school or work. And until very recently, work, school, or the Sherwood Institute.

"What should I do?" Regarding leisure time, I was out of practice.

"Anything you want."

I wanted to sleep more.

I wanted to do something fun, take a risk and not feel guilty about it.

I wanted to love without fear.

I also wanted to stop thinking about the letter writer's latest note: *Hate me. Regret me. But please don't cast me aside.*

I frowned, projecting my internal angst outward. "You could have told me this over the phone."

A simple nod. "I could have."

I was appeased by his immediate agreement. "What are you doing today?"

"Me?" He ran a hand over his head. "No big plans. I might take a walk around the block, maybe watch a movie. Mrs. Sydney was shocked when I told her I hadn't seen anything with Elizabeth Taylor in it. I was equally surprised she's never seen any of Gerard Butler's groundbreaking films."

A laugh slid from me. "A true crime."

"Well . . ." He trailed off.

"Well," I said slowly. "At the risk of interfering with your intentions to watch the entire Elizabeth Taylor catalog, would you want to hang out with me?"

He sucked in a deep breath. "I didn't do this to force you to keep me company."

"Of course not."

"But I did happen to put gas in the boat this morning." He paused. "Care for a swim?"

"It's fifty degrees out."

He eased out a smile. "I can help with that."

CHAPTER THIRTY-ONE

"This is not what I meant." I stepped onto Colin's dock.

"You look great," he hollered over his shoulder, eyeing me.

He'd taken me to the pool house, into the guest room where a row of wet suits hung in the closet. The closest fit had been neon yellow.

"Cool boat." I stopped and looked at the vessel. It was sleek, like something from a James Bond movie and way bigger than I had expected. From the house it had looked smaller. "You sure you can drive it?"

Colin leaped onto the stern. He wore a wet suit folded at the waist and kept his sweatshirt on. Why hadn't I thought of that? "It's a 2018 Mazu 52HT. One of the first models. And technically, it's not a boat. It's a mini yacht."

"Pfft," I said, taking Colin's hand as he helped me onto the boat. "A 2018. I've only been on yachts manufactured in 2020 or later, and all regular-sized. This is a big disappointment."

"Next time we'll take out the Odyssey, an actual yacht. But it's docked down south for the winter. Plus, we'd need a whole crew."

I puffed out a breath, feeling a new level of intimidation. I wasn't sure I was the water type. Like, I didn't fully submerge my head in a swimming pool until I was ten.

"Colin . . . I've actually never been on a boat before."

"A mini yacht. And you don't say?"

"It's true."

"Wait." Colin stopped; his eyes raked over me. "You can swim, right? I think I have a life vest somewhere in here." He opened a hatch built into the deck.

I laughed. "I know how to swim."

He stopped and studied me. "Maybe you should put one on anyway."

"I don't need to wear a life vest."

Colin pulled an orange life vest from the hatch and placed it on one of the plush red seats. "Just in case," he said.

I wandered around. The deck was hardwood, and below the hull was a door. "What's down there?"

Colin was untying ropes and flipping switches. Doing boat things. He stood at a wheel and fit a key into the ignition, and the engine started with a whir. "The cabin," he said. "Bathroom, kitchen, and bedroom."

I whistled low and found a seat toward the front of the boat.

We set off. The wind and the sound of the water were loud, and we didn't talk much. But when Colin sped up, I held my arms above my head as if on a roller coaster and let out a little yell. Then, embarrassed, I kept my arms down the rest of the ride but couldn't contain my smile. My cheeks were pink and cold when we stopped in the middle of Lake Washington and dropped anchor.

I moved to the stern and watched the gray waves gently lap against the wood. "How cold is the water?"

Colin was beside me. He handed off a set of water gloves and shoes. "This time of year, about fifty degrees."

"There's probably all sorts of bacteria in there," I said. Duck and fish poop, at least.

"You scared?" He said it like a challenge.

Ninety percent of me was my mother's child.

Then there was the 10 percent that belonged to my dad. The part that couldn't turn down a dare, that relished a challenge.

I slid on the gloves and shoes and jumped into the water. My whole body compressed with the cold, and my heart spiked. I surfaced on a gasp.

Colin was zipping his wet suit, his sweatshirt crumpled behind him.

Water lapped against my shoulders. "Colin, there's something I need to tell you."

"What?"

I drifted backward. "Promise you won't be mad?"

He leaned forward, face serious. "Promise."

"I'm not really that great of a swimmer." Then I slipped under the water and dived deep, paddling feet away.

Surfacing, I heard a splash and saw Colin swimming in neat, even strokes toward me.

"Got you!" I smiled.

He wiped water from his face and glared at me.

I stuck out my lower lip and laughed. "Was that a bridge too far?"

Colin emitted a warning grumble and lunged for me. I tried

to swim away, but he caught me by the ankles. I shrieked, arms flailing. He pulled me toward him. I slapped half-heartedly at his hands. Somehow he managed to turn me and hook me under the arms, and began pulling me toward the swim deck.

"What are you doing?" I asked, going limp.

"Rescuing you. Keep quiet. I used to be a junior lifeguard."

At the deck we hauled ourselves up and collapsed onto our backs. Boat rocking gently against the waves. Everything was so peaceful. So calm. Was that what money bought? Space and time?

"I've changed my mind about being rich. Money is the best. I'd do this every day."

Colin sniffled. He rose and walked to the hull, pulling out beach towels from some hidden cabinet. He handed one to me, and I wrapped it around my body, suppressing a groan at how soft the material was, how plush.

He used the towel to dry his hair, the blond locks falling in a disheveled mess. "There's clothes below." I followed him into the cabin. He rifled through another compartment and tossed white sweats, a sweatshirt, and thick socks onto the bed. "I'll change out here," he said.

I closed myself in the room and peeled the wet suit from my body, acutely conscious that only a thin wall separated naked me from naked Colin.

"Whose clothes are these?" I asked when I was dressed, opening the door.

I had rolled the pants eight times and bunched the sweatshirt sleeves past my wrists. If anything, I looked more ridiculous in this getup than in the wet suit. But I was warm.

Colin was stuffing his head into his crew sweatshirt and had on new sweats. A single drop of water slid down his chest. "Mine."

I touched the stenciled lettering on the front. "Harvard?"

"Dad's alma mater. He forced Sebastian and me to apply."

"Are you going?"

I shifted to the side as Colin passed me to the galley kitchen. He reached for a teakettle, filled it, then set it on a stand to boil. A blue light flashed on its base. "Had my interview last week."

His words settled around me. Harvard. As in, Cambridge. As in, basically Boston. Where the letter writer lived.

The first note had shown up at Colin's house.

If I'm being honest, I loved you from the beginning.

My reasonable voice beckoned through the fog. *Don't allow the idea to germinate.* I'd promised myself I wouldn't do this again—jump into the letter writer's orbit, spin around, trying to unravel the grand mystery.

"That's a big deal," I said finally.

"More like a foregone conclusion."

My eyebrows slanted down in confusion.

He continued. "Dad has our whole futures mapped out. Undergrad in economics, then on to Wharton, where we'll study business and then reach our final form as industry titans." He paused. "What about you? What's your plan for next year?"

"I'm going to stay home and commute to school." Compared with Colin's future, mine sounded significantly less shiny. *This is what you want,* I consoled myself. Jiji and Mom needed me. Berklee wasn't ever really an option. "Not nearly as impressive as you."

"Said the girl who's first-chair violin in her high school orchestra."

My mouth opened and closed. "Did you Google me?"

"No." He scoffed. "Of course not, that'd be weird. I happen to have a niche interest in young, up-and-coming, talented violinists in the Pacific Northwest. Purely a coincidence, that's all." He paused, his mood shifting to serious. "You should have told me you were so talented."

I reined in a smile, uncomfortable with accepting praise.

The teakettle whistled, and Colin pulled down two mugs from a cabinet. He dumped a packet of hot chocolate into each.

"From Belgium," he said, pouring and stirring.

I accepted one of the mugs and wrapped my hands around it, letting the warmth bleed into my palms. Rich notes of cinnamon, vanilla, and cocoa drifted to my nose. We cozied up on the couch on the deck, spreading thick plaid blankets over our legs.

"Can I ask you something?" Colin turned the mug in his hands. "Why did you decide to come out here with me today?"

I sipped the hot chocolate and waited for the sugar to melt on my tongue before answering. "I really don't know. I guess I like being with you."

A small smile curved his mouth, the warmth of which cascaded down to my toes. "I like being with you, too. You're different."

An internal wince.

I thought of our biggest difference—money. In that he had a lot and I had a little.

"Ah, I see. Am I not like anyone you've ever met?" I teased, hoping he wouldn't sense the underlying question. *Am I a novelty to you?* The mere idea of it hammered at my insides.

"You *are* different," he said, aquamarine eyes flashing with sincerity. "You're very sure of yourself but vulnerable, too. I like that you don't take shit from people." He stopped to catch his breath, and my hurt fell away, replaced by something far more pleasant. "I like knowing that when I'm with you, you're choosing me."

I scrunched up my nose. "Except for when we cleaned houses. I chose you under duress."

"I think that you don't have very many friends, maybe even family, but those that you do, you care for deeply," he said quietly.

I sobered instantly. Because he was right, of course. "I'd die for them."

"And then I think what it might feel like to be included in that select group." He downed the rest of his hot chocolate, his gaze unusually elusive. My pulse skittered and picked up as he finished, "I'm pretty sure I'd feel like I was the luckiest guy on the whole fucking planet."

From: Letter Writer (thechronosproject1@gmail.com)
To: Emma Nakamura-Thatcher (ethatch121@gmail.com)
Subject: I am sober now

Hello from the hangover from hell. I understand if you don't want to hear from me again. I will go away forever. But please just tell me you're okay.

From: Emma Nakamura-Thatcher (ethatch121@gmail.com)
To: Letter Writer (thechronosproject1@gmail.com)
Subject: Re: I am sober now

I'm okay.

CHAPTER THIRTY-TWO

My email made a whooshing sound as I sent the message to the letter writer.

I'd planned to delete his most recent note. Instead I'd tapped out the two words in response.

Because I didn't want him to go away forever.

He'd gotten under my skin, and I was finding it impossible to dig him out. When had the letter writer become such a fundamental part of me?

I shoved the question away and peeked out the living room window again, watching for Colin.

It was Sunday. Our earlier text exchange had gone like this:

Me: **Super random. There's a carnival in town. Want to go?**

Colin took forever to respond. I was picking up the phone to tell him never mind, forget it, when his response popped up. **Super random, but I was just telling Sebastian I had a hankering for stale popcorn and foldable rides with questionable safety ratings. Five? I'll pick you up. What's your address?**

I fired off my address and was immediately besieged by second thoughts. What would Colin think of my patchwork neighborhood, my house? All I could see were the flaws: the chipped exterior paint, the dented gutters, the wobbly outlets, the bald patches and brown grass in the lawn. I'd been fidgety for the last twenty minutes.

"Your pacing is making me dizzy," Jiji grouched, eyes on his folded newspaper. He spent every Sunday morning reading the *New York Times* from front to back, then the evening on the crossword puzzle.

"I'm waiting for a friend," I said.

"The girl or the boy?" He meant Delia and Theo.

"A boy. One you haven't met before."

"New boy comes over. He should meet me," he intoned.

Colin's SUV pulled up. The shiny luxury vehicle stuck out like a sore thumb in our neighborhood of Subarus and dented Civics.

"He's here." I grabbed my jacket and bent to kiss Jiji on the cheek.

"Are you hiding him from me?" He frowned.

"Don't be silly," I chided. "I'm hiding you from him."

Forget my house and the neighbor's lawn ornamented with toy T-Rexes devouring garden gnomes. I didn't want Jiji to scare Colin off. My grandfather could decimate a person with a few words. And probably, if his spy training were still active, his hands.

"Dinner is in the fridge. Mom should be home in twenty," I said.

I headed out right as Theo's car turned onto the street.

Just then Colin opened his door and rounded the hood. "Hey. There's no hurry. I was going to walk up and get you."

Of course he would come to the front door. Colin had great manners.

"It's fine. I'm ready to go." I'd never really been embarrassed about where I grew up or where I came from, and it had me unsettled how insecure I felt.

Theo parked behind Colin. Two doors opened, and he and Camille both stepped out of his car.

"Emma," said Theo, walking up to me.

Camille shuffled up behind him. "Hey," she said to me, reserved.

The sting of the fight with my dad came back. He'd called a couple of times, but I hadn't answered. My feelings hadn't changed—marrying Madison wasn't a good idea. Camille had been collateral damage, and I felt bad about that. I missed hanging out with her sometimes. But I wasn't sure if we could be friends still, if she even wanted to be friends.

Plus, she was dating Theo . . .

Camille stared at Colin, not talking. I guess we had both decided it was better not to interact.

Introductions flew around.

Theo tilted his head at Colin and smiled faintly, apparently confused. "Colin? Emma's never mentioned you."

"Yeah?" Colin studied Theo, his stance widening, shifting slightly in front of me. "Funny, she hasn't said anything about you, either."

"Theo and I are neighbors. We grew up together," I interjected, caught off guard. Why was this so awkward all of a sudden? "What are you guys up to?"

"We're heading to Thrillfest at the SIFF," Camille said, grabbing Theo's hand. "*Twins of Evil* is playing. Theo forgot the tickets. Which wouldn't be a problem if he allowed his phone to upload electronic attachments."

"Air gap," Theo and I said at the same.

Theo grinned. "See? Emma gets it."

"I don't, actually," I said. "I've just heard you say it enough."

Theo had two computers, which he was very prickly about people—mostly me—touching and downloading apps onto, citing security reasons.

"Well." Colin blew out a breath. "You ready to head out, Emma?"

"Yeah, sure."

We said goodbye.

I watched Theo and Camille amble up his driveway as we drove off. Theo threw back his head and laughed at something Camille said.

"He seems like a nice guy." Colin kept his eyes on the road.

"Yup. Theo is the best."

We passed the house on the corner with sea glass hanging from its ancient oak tree and turned left toward Anoush Deli—with the best shawarma in town.

He didn't say anything for a moment. "You seem to know each other well."

"Since before preschool. He's like a brother to me. I mean, we used to take baths together." Unbidden, a tiny glimpse of Theo and me in his room eclipsed my vision. When he was barefoot and freshly showered. How he'd wrapped his hand around my ankle. Had it lingered longer than necessary? Nope. I shook the memory away. There had never been anything between us, only what existed in my imagination. That was all.

"Sebastian and I have a friend like that. He lives down the street. Everyone calls him Gorilla."

"What's his real name?"

Colin rubbed his neck. "I have no idea." He said it like that was the most normal thing. My phone lit with a text. I glanced down at the screen, breath hitching as I saw Camille's name. I swiped to see what she'd said. **Things more awkward than that meeting on the sidewalk: trying to breathe normally while walking uphill.**

It was an olive branch of sorts, I thought.

More than two flights of stairs, I'm basically fighting for my life, I responded.

She answered with a smiling-face emoji. I put my phone away, sat back in Colin's car. I was enjoying the ride, feeling like things were changing. But for good.

It was dusk by the time we got to the carnival, and I huddled in my jacket, warding off the cool evening air as we waited in the funnel cake line. The rides glowed neon.

"Huh," said Colin, breath foggy.

"Something interesting?"

His hands were in his pockets, and he was glowering at the menu. "I always thought it was 'fun-hole cake.' You learn something new every day."

A laugh barked out of me.

We shuffled to the front of the line. Colin ordered and looked at me. I shook my head. "I'm good." I salivated at the smell of sugar and cinnamon but couldn't afford the six bucks. When had carnival food gotten so expensive?

Colin studied me and ordered two plates, plus a second soda.

I sensed what he was up to. "You must be very hungry."

He paid with a card. "Starving."

The order came up, and Colin handed me one of the sodas and a funnel cake. Warmth bled through the paper plate, along with a good amount of grease. I focused on the grains of sugar clinging to the funnel cake.

"Thank you."

We walked to a few foldout chairs and round tables nearby and sat down. Across the field was a row of blue porta-potties.

"Emma." He waited for me to look at him. "This doesn't need to be a thing between us. Don't make this a thing between us, okay?" He was talking about money. The fact that I had a little and he had a lot. His lips pressed together. "Please."

I gave a relentless sigh and relaxed. "Yeah, okay."

I broke off a piece of the funnel cake and stuffed it in my mouth. I'd been working so long, paying my own way. I'd even footed the bill for my own current violin. I'd saved for years to purchase a used Ming-Jiang Zhu.

He propped both elbows on the table and leaned in closer. "You sure?"

I nodded. "Promise." I drank my soda, the fizzy liquid sloshing against the combination of guilt and discomfort lodged in my throat.

The pleased look on his face shrank whatever reservations I had. "Good." He tore off a piece of his funnel cake. "So next time you'll let me come in and see your house."

"I didn't think you noticed."

"That you were watching from the window as I pulled up, then fled out the front door like someone was chasing you?" His expression became inscrutable. "When it comes to you, I notice everything."

"My place isn't as nice as yours."

Over his shoulder I saw a couple of kids staggering off the Tilt-A-Whirl, holding their stomachs.

"You forget that all the nice stuff in my house hides an unhealthy dynamic where sons are pitted against each other."

"The grass is always greener, isn't it?"

"Especially if you don't water it. I'm pretty sure my mom is cheating on my dad."

I nearly spit up my funnel cake. "What makes you think that?"

"Just a feeling."

"What if she was?" The truth hovered on my tongue.

His brow furrowed. "They'd get divorced eventually."

"If your parents are unhappy . . ." I searched for the right words. Words better than *It's for the best.*

More along the lines of *If they get divorced, your heart will be shattered, and you won't feel like there's a safe space in the world for you anymore. For a bit you'll think it was because of you. You'll grieve forever because you will never forget when you were a family. Holidays won't be the same. But regular days won't be either. But you'll be okay. Or at least I think you'll be okay. I'm not sure if I'm okay. But maybe we'll not be okay together. Divorce just makes you approach life differently. More carefully. It's like a first beesting. Finding out the world hurts you sometimes, and the bee didn't mean it, and neither did your parents, but it hurts all the same. It makes you wary.*

"Can I tell you a secret?"

I pushed my funnel cake to the side and leaned in. "I'm all ears."

"You know those family holidays where my uncle and dad get together and metaphorically mud wrestle the whole time? I actually love them. I love being with my family. Even though I know my mom is putting on a show, and my dad, too. I kind of like the pretending. It's the closest we come to being happy. Pathetic, huh?" He smiled, chagrined, eyes holding a hint of pain.

"It's not pathetic." I sat on my hands, heart rising in my throat. "Next time you come over, I'll let you come in. You can meet Jiji. Fair warning, he's going to not like you, but he doesn't like anyone. And I will show you my kitchen with saloon doors and the porcelain sink with a drain that breeds fruit flies in the summer."

His smile grew. "Sounds nice."

My whole body sighed. "It is. I think we have lead paint on the walls."

"I promise not to lick them."

"Has that been a problem before?"

His brow crinkled in amusement. "I'm not sure I should tell you."

"Now I have to know."

"Can't." He stood, picking up the plates and folding them in half before shoving them into an overflowing green garbage can. "Sebastian, Gorilla, and I made a pact." He cracked his knuckles. "So what do you want to do first?"

I patted my stomach, overfull of funnel cake and soda. "I don't think I can handle any ride moving more than one mile an hour."

"Games it is, then."

We headed toward them, and almost immediately, a carnival guy wearing a mesh tank top and gold lamé pants stepped in our path. "Shoot five ducks and win a prize for your girlfriend?"

"No thanks," I said, and Colin said, "Absolutely."

"We've got a taker!" Mesh Top hollered.

"This is a waste of money," I whisper-hissed at Colin.

Unicorns, Ninja Turtles, and marshmallows with huge eyes were strung around the booth and stared vacantly at the Ferris wheel.

"Four shots for twenty bucks," said Mesh Top.

Colin nodded like that was an extremely good deal and slapped a twenty-dollar bill onto the red-painted counter.

"You should just give me twenty dollars, and I'll sucker punch you in the face," I said.

Mesh Top frowned at me like, *Hey, lady, I'm trying to make a living here.* He slid a crossbow to Colin. "Shoot a duck, win a prize. Hit the red duckling, and you'll win the mega-sloth. It's that easy." His grin returned, and he pointed to the top of the booth, where a five-foot plush sloth clung to the ceiling.

I huffed out a breath and crossed my arms. The red duckling was about an inch in size, one eye shut in a mocking wink.

"Quiet. I'm trying to focus." Colin put both elbows on the counter and leaned forward, mini crossbow in hand.

His stance wasn't even right. Jiji had had me doing target practice with a slingshot since I was nine. We progressed to moving targets once I'd conquered shooting bullseyes on boards nailed to trees. Jiji strapped that board to his chest and told me to go to town while he darted behind bushes and leaped from ledges in surprise attacks.

Colin's timing was all off. The mechanical ducks clicked past in a steady row, and I calculated three seconds from when the Nerf arrow left the bow to when it would reach them.

Fewer than thirty seconds later Colin had exhausted his arrow supply.

"Tell you what, I'll give you a two-for-one deal. Eight shots for another twenty bucks," Mesh Top said.

Colin opened his mouth, but I cut him off. "How about a bet?"

An amused smile tilted Mesh Top's mouth. "What are you thinking?"

"One shot. If I make it, mega-sloth is ours."

"And if you don't?"

I pulled out my wallet. I had a fifty-dollar bill from the Presleys' clean plus three two-dollar bills my dad liked to give me sometimes. "This fifty is yours."

"You're on. Money on the table," Mesh Top said.

I slapped the bill down and picked up the crossbow.

"Emma—" Colin started.

"Quiet. I'm trying to focus," I said.

The ducks floated by.

Ah, there was the little red twerp. I waited until he was three clicks from dead center and pulled the trigger on the crossbow. The Nerf bullet hit the baby duck in the head, and its body tipped back.

"Kill shot." I placed the crossbow down and repocketed my fifty.

"I'm feeling very emasculated right now, and also strangely turned on." Colin trudged through the carnival, mega-sloth clinging to his back.

"Your timing was off. Common mistake." We came to the parking lot, to Colin's car, near the beer garden.

He opened the back door and pushed the mega-sloth through it, positioning him upright in the seat. "Maybe I'll be able to drive in the carpool lane now." He paused, twinkling eyes locked on mine. "My little sharpshooter. Who knew you were so dangerous?"

I wet my lips and felt my smile curve involuntarily. "My grandfather taught me. He also taught me how to make rain traps to collect fresh water, and how to forage for edible plants. He was either a spy or intensely interested in survival skills and espionage. Now the only survival games we play are messing with his medications. Kidding," I said as we loaded into the car.

My phone vibrated in my back pocket, and I ignored it.

He reversed the car and righted it, driving out of the gravel parking lot. "You got more time? I want to show you something."

"If it's the latest Gerard Butler movie, I'll pass."

He scoffed. "You'd be so lucky."

"Seriously. What is it about him? The accent?"

"That. And I don't know. He has something. An it factor. I mean, he's the total package."

I chuckled, and we continued driving through Seattle, soon pulling into a marina on the east side.

"You want to show me another boat?" I said as we got out of the car. Other than us, the lot was empty.

"A sailboat." Colin found a key with the number eight on his key chain. "Come on."

We wound around a warehouse. He unlocked a door, then opened it for me, and I walked in. The door shut and we were bathed in darkness, in the smell of cedar and varnish.

Lights flicked on, illuminating a large, imposing sailboat.

Living in Seattle, I'd seen sailboats on the water before, but never one up close like this. I put my hand on the aluminum hull and looked up.

"Beautiful, right?" He strolled forward, hands in his pockets. "It's mine."

"Yours?" I ran my palm along the boat as if petting it. I had never really thought of boats as pretty, but this one was—sleek and elegant.

He shuffled closer to me, hands in his pockets, and bent over my shoulder to whisper. "Mine." His breath was warm and sweet against the shell of my ear. "I've been building it the past two years. Nobody knows. Except for you. My dad gave Sebastian and me some seed money. Basically slapped a check down on the table and told us, 'May the best son win.' This is what I spent it on." He came closer. "Can I tell you a secret?"

I swirled to face him, cataloging his handsome features one by one. Chiseled jaw. Tousled hair. Those lips. "Yes, anything."

"I'm not going to Harvard next fall." His voice dropped low, intimate.

"No?" I froze.

He stepped even closer, picked up a lock of my hair and tugged it. "I'm going to sail around the world. No phones, no internet. Just me and the open water for a year," he said. "And nobody knows it but you."

My stomach sank; I deflated. Colin wasn't going to Boston. He couldn't be the letter writer. I shouldn't have been disappointed. I wasn't supposed to be looking for the letter writer anymore anyway. And Colin was my friend. That was all. No need for me to feel so dejected.

My phone buzzed in my back pocket again. I'd forgotten about it.

"Hold on." I checked the screen.

The call I'd ignored had been from Mom. Three missed calls and one all-caps text.

HOME NOW.

CHAPTER THIRTY-THREE

Colin eased to a stop in front of my house and put the car in park. "You sure you don't want me to walk you to the door?"

It was nearly midnight, and all the lights were on—not a great sign. Mom usually let me come and go as I pleased. She trusted me. She did not send me shouty, all-caps text messages demanding I return home. My stomach bottomed out. Had something happened to Mom? To Jiji? No. Her text was distinctly angry, distinctly directed at me.

"Thanks. But I don't want you to be caught in the cross fire."

I couldn't do that. Not to him.

"Text me tomorrow?" he asked.

Mega-sloth was in the back. I nodded and exited the car. Blood rushed through my ears as I made the slow walk up the stairs to the porch. Colin idled at the curb, waiting for me to open the front door and get in safely. My legs wobbled as I waved to him and pushed inside.

Mom was on the couch. No television on. No music. She was rigid, her eyes on me and the door as I shut it. This was serious. I stayed silent, letting her make the first move. She marched over, crossed her arms, stared too long, then visibly sniffed.

"What are you doing?"

"Smelling for alcohol. This is the only reason I can think of why you'd quit the Sherwood Institute. You must be inebriated and have lost your mind."

I grimaced. "Oh, that."

"Yes, that," she snapped. "The director emailed me this evening and asked if your decision was final. 'What decision?' I asked. Then he forwarded me your resignation."

"I can explain."

She gestured like I had the floor. "I'd love to hear it."

I couldn't tell Mom the real reason. How I'd watched her through the open door, rubbing her aching hands. How I'd sat beside her and imagined her life here alone with Jiji. How impossible everyday tasks would become if I went away to school. If she knew that, she'd be upset, feel guilty. She'd torture herself with what her health issues cost me. I wanted to be the least of her worries.

"There was this boy. My mentor, Ezra." As I said his name, fresh tears sprung to my eyes. "I liked him, and he . . . didn't like me back." The words sounded puny. Pathetic. I steeled myself. "I couldn't be around him anymore."

She threw out her arms. "You quit over a boy? That's just silly, Emma."

Chest tight, I offered a meek "I'm sorry."

She sighed the way she did when she thought I was acting impossible. "I'm tired, and I'm going to bed. But this conversation isn't over. Until then, you're grounded. School and work, that's all." She flicked out the words, then climbed the stairs and didn't look back.

I flopped down onto the couch, unsettled, my insides rocking like a boat on rough water.

Your mom still not talking to you? Colin texted me days later after school.

After I was grounded, I'd let Colin know the basics. That I'd quit the Sherwood Institute without her permission to help with the business.

I didn't tell him about Ezra, my fragmented heart, or how I was ruminating about the cool cello player and what he'd told me about Janey. He'd sworn it was all a terrible misunderstanding. Had I let my insecurities get the best of me? Worse, had I misjudged Ezra? Mom had called my actions silly. That stung—but felt close to home, too.

Hasn't said a word. We've eaten every dinner in complete silence. How's the boat? I was on my bed, my violin next to me.

The boat is good. In the water. Almost ready to take her out. All she needs is a name. Bad luck to sail without one.

I rotated to my stomach, elbows digging into the mattress, phone in front of my face. **Open to suggestions?**

I'm waiting, he said.

Please hold. I consulted Google. **How about something like this?** I sent him a photograph of a man, body slick with oil, in a Speedo with a captain's hat and a bottle of champagne on the helm of a sailboat. Underneath him, the boat's name was stenciled in Old English font: *Titan Uranus*.

Perfect. If only it wasn't already taken, he replied. **Actually, I think I have a name.**

Shoot, I said. My fondness for Colin was growing and growing.

Maybe you should make the first move. Tell your mom how you're feeling, came his answer.

I think that's kind of long for a boat name. But okay.

Emma . . .

I prefer to let the silence continue until this whole thing becomes water under the bridge.

I waited a moment.

Colin?

No answer. But there was a notification for a new email from the letter writer.

I chewed a thumbnail, debating. Last email exchange, I'd written him back. *I'm okay.* Two words the equivalent of cracking a door open, an inch of sunlight. Did I want to push through more? Let him back in?

Yes, the answer came clear through my murky thoughts. I was grounded and alone. I needed a friend. Just no more trying to figure out who he was. No more talk about future loves. I attempted to brand both into my brain.

Decision made, relief rushed through my throat. I exhaled slowly, smiled, and hit Open.

From: Letter Writer
(thechronosproject1@gmail.com)
To: Emma Nakamura-Thatcher
(ethatch121@gmail.com)
Subject: It has been eight days since we last spoke, since I last breathed

I'm glad you're okay.

I miss you.

From: Emma Nakamura-Thatcher
(ethatch121@gmail.com)
To: Letter Writer
(thechronosproject1@gmail.com)
Subject: Same

I miss you, too.

I'm grounded right now. And it's given me a lot of time to think. Have I mentioned I don't really like being alone with my own thoughts?

It's been work and school. School and work.

In biology we watched some movie about clones. Mr. Sampson, my teacher, is retiring this year and really phoning it in. Every Monday is Movie Monday.

The film was bad.

I can't even remember the name, but it got me thinking. About you and me, timelines, universes, and the possibility of a million Emmas. I wondered if you really know me. If I could stand in a room among a thousand girls who looked exactly like me. Same eyes. Hair. Body. Identical down to the pores on our faces. But with different minds and personalities. Would you be able to find me?

I don't know, is this crazy talk? Have I finally spent too much time in my own head?

From: Letter Writer
(thechronosproject1@gmail.com)
To: Emma Nakamura-Thatcher
(ethatch121@gmail.com)
Subject: Re: Same

I would be able to find you. I'll always see you. Head down. Heart tucked away.

Catch me up. Tell me why you're grounded and what happened before that. You thought you'd figured out who I was?

From: Emma Nakamura-Thatcher
(ethatch121@gmail.com)
To: Letter Writer
(thechronosproject1@gmail.com)
Subject: Re: Same

It's kind of embarrassing. I thought I had figured out who you were, but I was all wrong. What sucks the most is that I really opened up with him. He had helped me see my life differently . . . like, he convinced me to apply to Berklee College of Music. I'm shelving that for now. I quit the music program I've been doing, and my mom found out. Hence, the grounding.

Even worse? I'm not speaking to my dad right now, since I told him what I thought of his fiancée.

Then, because burning down my personal life wasn't enough, I went ahead and set fire to my professional life too. I popped off on a client's son because they forgot to pay me. He kind of deserved it, though.

But also I didn't like myself very much that day. In a strange reversal, he apologized to me right as I was going to apologize to him.

We're kind of friends now, I think. Which is weird because we're from two different worlds.

No, scratch that, two different planets.

From: Letter Writer (thechronosproject1@gmail.com)
To: Emma Nakamura-Thatcher (ethatch121@gmail.com)
Subject: Got another quote for you: Don't cut off your nose to spite your face

Telling your dad about his fiancée wasn't the worst idea ever. At least not compared to the parachute coat, pop-up ads, or Betamax. For real, though, look up the parachute coat.

I wish I could fix all this for you. But I gotta say . . . Berklee College of Music? That's big, Emma. Really big.

I remember the first time I saw you play the violin, and every time after. How I stared at you with quiet wonder. I have never seen someone so wholly themselves while holding an instrument.

Maybe don't let this one crumble to ash and blow away?

CHAPTER THIRTY-FOUR

Mom and I still weren't really talking by Thursday. We communicated only the necessities: logistics regarding Jiji, if I needed to stop at the grocery store, catching up on cleaning houses. I was doing the dinner dishes when I heard the whoosh of the saloon doors.

Out of the corner of my eye I saw her dipping into her purse for her Voltaren. I kept washing the plate, focusing on the suds, following the sponge as I circled it, trying not to let the silence suffocate me.

At length, a chair scraped against the linoleum. "Come sit," Mom said. "Talk to me."

I wiped my hands on a yellow dish towel and joined her at the table. Sadness welled in my chest, but I made myself speak. "I know you think it's ridiculous I would quit the Sherwood Institute over a boy, but I liked him so much."

My throat constricted, and my voice became flimsy. How could love be so wonderful and then so horrible? I didn't understand the meaning of all of it. Why the suffering? The thought of Ezra with someone else, that he might have liked Janey, been with her, had triggered some defensive action in me, had turned me into someone I didn't recognize. Insecure. Small. Afraid I wasn't enough.

Mom sighed, tilting her head. She offered me a small close-lipped smile, and I felt the final crack in the shell of our argument, the pieces giving, falling away. "Believe it or not, I understand how you're feeling."

"Yeah," I drew out slowly.

She didn't need to elaborate. She'd been humbled by heartbreak once. The walls of our house used to be littered with family photos. When Dad filed for divorce, Mom packed up the pictures and replaced them with still lifes of flowers. A lily had replaced the photograph of their wedding day. A chrysanthemum, our trip to Disneyland. A bouquet of roses, our Easter egg hunt. It was like she wanted to erase her life with Dad, but when she did, she erased some of my childhood, too. Growing up is supposed to be slow and natural, like gently peeling a Band-Aid off. But I knew the exact moment I wasn't supposed to be a kid anymore.

She reached over and placed her dry, cracked hand over mine. "You have so much potential, Emma. I don't want a boy to get in the way of that."

I nodded vacantly, pushing past thoughts of Ezra and landing on Berklee. Auditions were a couple of weeks away.

I still had time.

What if I auditioned? What if I got in? Would I go? The thought of leaving Jiji and Mom was unfathomable, undoable, a knot tied too tightly. But maybe I owed it to myself to try. I didn't want Future Emma to look back and have regrets.

"Am I still grounded? I really feel like I learned my lesson," I ventured, hope slipping into my bloodstream.

Mom studied me. "That depends. Is there anything else you're keeping from me?"

I tapped my fingers against the table, drumming up the truth. "I lied about going to Delia's and really went to a party the first weekend when school started. There was drinking there. I didn't drink, but honestly, I probably would have. I didn't get the chance. Someone threw up on my shoes, and I called Theo to pick me up. I also exchanged the underwear you bought me for something else." I paused, thought about the Seattle underground. "Two parties," I pushed out. "I went to two parties. Someone was smoking weed at the second one."

Mom ducked her head, trying to hide a smile. "I see. These parties were with that boy?"

"The second party, yes. Are you upset?"

She looked at me. "I'd rather you not drink, but I'm glad you told me." She rose and bent, kissing me on the forehead. "I'm glad you talked to me. You're not grounded anymore. Heartbreak is its own punishment. No more lying, though. You're lucky. Jiji wanted to test your urine for drugs. I told him no." On her way out of the kitchen, she paused, one hand against the saloon doors. "It only hurts right now. It won't forever. You'll see."

The next day, Friday, at the Sherwood Institute, I stopped and listened, pressing my ear against the door. Ezra was on the other side, waiting for me. I knew because I'd seen his car parked down the street. In the last twenty-four hours, since my conversation with Mom, I'd apologized to the Sherwood director. Cushioned between my sincere regrets and desire to continue with the program, I'd requested a new mentor.

The director had responded, welcoming me back with open arms. But said he couldn't accommodate my request. No can do. All the string mentors were taken; I had to stick with my original.

With a flick of my wrist, I pushed open the door.

Ezra unfolded from his hunched position. His sunken eyes flared to life. His lower lip was red, as if he'd been chewing it. "Hey. I wasn't sure if you'd really show up."

"Hey," I said back. I remembered how tongue-tied I'd gotten with Ezra the first time in this room. How my speech sped up, and my thoughts slowed. It amazed me that words came easier now. I no longer placed him on a cherry-lollipop pedestal. I laid my violin case on the ground and unsnapped the hinges, opening it. "I've been thinking about audition pieces," I said, unsure where to start, how to close the distance between us. This was a whole new level of awkward.

"For the record . . ." He drifted closer. "Janey and I are finished. Not that we were ever even together. But I've made it clear to her that we're done."

I exhaled, opening the tuning app on my phone and propping it on the stand. Finally I looked at him. "I believe you."

He wiped a palm down his face. "You'll never know how glad I am to hear it."

"It was less about you, more about me," I said, my voice garbled. I plucked at one of the strings on my violin. We hadn't had a session in weeks. My insecurities had cost me time. I was quietly mindful that I was behind and feeling anxious to catch up. "Anyway." I straightened, holding my violin by the neck. "I'm back now and I want to get to work. I've been practicing 'God Save the King.'" By Paganini. A notoriously tricky left-handed piece featuring dizzying pizzicato sections and double stops.

He scowled, then shook his head a little, like he was coming to. "'God Save the King' is a good choice. It's impressive on a technical level." He stopped short.

"But?"

"You're going to need three pieces." His dark eyes skittered up and down my body. "A range to showcase your abilities. Plus, I wouldn't put it past them to ask you to pick a jazz standard and improvise over it."

"A mash-up, then," I said. Already seeing the notes, how they might fit together. Wheels were turning. "A Bach sonata, maybe some Debussy."

He nodded intently, getting into the groove. This was where we were best together, talking music. "There's this guy. Doesn't get nearly the credit he deserves. I think because he focuses on composition rather than performance. But he has a cult following on YouTube. He did this mind-blowing transcription of Beethoven's Fifth." Confusion swept across his face. "I hate that I can't remember his name. I follow him. Hang on."

He was reaching for his phone but stopped when I said, "Augustus Tran."

I followed him too. Salivated over his videos. Talk about "God Save the King," it was like watching a modern-day Paganini. "He's brilliant."

Ezra cracked a smile. "The first time I saw him, I stayed up all night watching him."

"Obsessed with him," I said, stepping closer to Ezra, getting caught up. When I first found Augustus Tran, I was also eager to share. Delia had listened for a while, then gripped my shoulders and said very seriously: "I love you so much, probably the most a best friend has ever loved someone, but if you make me listen to any more of this, I'm going to use my scissors for something other than cutting."

Theo hadn't been much better. "I dunno. I can't tell the difference between what you play and him. Honestly, I think you're better." Which was sweet but also stupid. Me better than Augustus Tran? That was like comparing a duck to an eagle.

Ezra was grinning at me. My stomach flipped, the little traitor. My smile waned. A vent whirred with air, cooling me down. I dipped my chin and stepped back, vowing to keep my distance. "I don't think I'm Tran territory, but maybe something like that," I said evenly, submerging the mood in ice. I found it all very overwhelming being back at Sherwood with Ezra. I'd changed so much since running into him at the mall. But I still felt that tiny spark, a flame threatening to ignite with talk of notes and composers.

"Yeah." His eyes bounced to the mirror, then back to me. Mouth tight, he seemed disappointed, and it made me feel guilty. Why? I didn't know. "Let's warm up. Start with a sonata, and we'll work our way into 'God Save the King.'"

"Sounds good."

He backed off and slumped into a chair.

Then I played, letting the music fill up the room, all the hollow spaces.

From: Emma Nakamura-Thatcher
(ethatch121@gmail.com)
To: Letter Writer
(thechronosproject1@gmail.com)
Subject: My nose is intact

I looked up the parachute coat. Poor Franz. However, his invention did pioneer the batwing suit used for BASE jumping. So maybe one bad idea precedes a great one?

Have you been speaking with my mom? I feel like the two of you might be in cahoots regarding the whole music school thing.

From: Letter Writer
(thechronosproject1@gmail.com)
To: Emma Nakamura-Thatcher
(ethatch121@gmail.com)
Subject: Re: My nose is intact

Have I told you I think your mom is the smartest person on the planet?

From: Emma Nakamura-Thatcher
(ethatch121@gmail.com)
To: Letter Writer
(thechronosproject1@gmail.com)
Subject: Re: My nose is intact

Okay. You win, I decided to go back to Sherwood. I'm going to follow through with the Berklee application. I have one month to get in shape for the audition. Pray for me?

CHAPTER THIRTY-FIVE

"I'm going to fall in the water," I said, arms outstretched in front of me à la Frankenstein's monster.

After arriving at the marina, Colin had placed a blindfold over my eyes. I'd been game until he'd led me away from the warehouse and onto the wobbly dock, a seagull shrieking as if in warning.

"You're not going to fall." His oven-mitt hands gripped my shoulders, leading me.

I let out a humorless laugh. "Said the man without the blindfold."

"So cynical," Colin murmured. He stopped, hands lighter on my shoulders. "You ready?"

I nodded once. "Ready to be stunned. Ready to be irrevocably changed. Ready to never be the same."

"Hardy har har," he deadpanned. He whipped the blindfold off. His sailboat was docked, bobbing in the water. Blue stripes had been painted on the body along with a name: *Sharpshooter*.

"I know what you're thinking." A gentle breeze ruffled his sandy hair. "'He named his boat after me.'"

"I wasn't thinking that."

I was thinking exactly that, and it made my heart flip over and ache with want. If only. After graduation next semester Colin was leaving. Literally sailing off into the sunset, the world at his feet.

And I'd be here.

Probably.

It was best to keep things as they were. With my heart tucked away, as the letter writer had said. Things could get messy otherwise. This course of action was safer.

Lonelier, too.

Oof.

I punted that thought away.

His jade eyes darkened. "*Sharpshooter* is more about focusing on the bullseye, on what you want. Like I want to be free of my dad's expectations."

I gathered my emotions and stuffed them down. "On one hand, I am offended you didn't name your boat after me. On the other hand, I think what you're doing is incredible. Very brave."

He smiled. "Come on, let me show you around."

I shuffled in front of him up the ramp. "Am I literally walking the plank right now?"

"Pirate jokes are beneath you. Up you go." He grabbed my hips, hoisting me over the railing, then followed, steadying me again when we were both on the boat. I placed a hand on his chest, felt his wildly beating heart. His eyes fixed on my mouth. We stared at each other, unblinking.

I didn't know how to handle this new intensity between us, so I closed my fist and swung away. "So this is it, huh?" I peered around, looking underneath the steering wheel, shaking with restraint, then came back to him.

A moment ticked by before his hazy expression cleared. "Okay. I mean, yeah, this is it."

Colin gave me a full tour. The sailboat had all the bells and whistles: a cabin with a bedroom, a bathroom and shower, a water maker, autopilot, digital tank monitors.

Around sunset we took her out, cruising up Puget Sound. Colin dropped anchor right as the final rays dipped behind the horizon. Other boats drifted nearby, but it was quiet. We were surrounded by the dark silhouettes of Vashon and Bainbridge Islands, distant lights dotted along the shores.

"You cold?" Colin asked.

I was sitting on the deck and had pulled my legs up to my chest. Before I could answer, he opened a hidden door and pulled out a cashmere blanket and a bottle of wine. He wrapped the blanket around me and then sat next to me, shoulder to shoulder. He uncorked the bottle, took a swig, and offered it to me.

I sipped the wine and handed it back. "I can see why you like sailing."

The actual part of driving the boat was a giant adventure, leaning this way and that, unsure if you would be knocked overboard. But when you stopped, it was so peaceful, unhurried. I liked the solitude. He hadn't shown me any Wi-Fi equipment. There wasn't any cell service out here. "What happens if you have an emergency?"

Wind ruffled his hair, and the tip of his nose was pink from cold. "I'll use the radio."

Earlier Colin had spread out a map of his itinerary. He'd sail south, first stop Hawaii.

"Won't you be lonely? Aren't you scared?"

His eyes stayed on the water, and his throat bobbed on a swallow. "Yeah. I'm scared as shit. But I've been floating the idea around in my head awhile. Originally it started as a big fuck-you to my dad. But I don't know . . . since meeting you, the reason has changed. I need to do this. I need to prove to myself I can. I need to see what I'm made of."

"I can safely say you're going to find out."

He drank and offered the wine bottle to me again. "Go big or go home, right?" He rewarded me with a breathtaking grin, the faintest stain of purple on his lips.

"To going big." I held up the bottle and drank. "This is actually pretty good." I wiped a drop from my mouth.

"From my mom's private collection." He took the bottle from me.

I stared at him for too long, then rearranged myself to face him. Sitting crisscross, I twiddled my thumbs. "Since you mentioned it. About your mom . . . there's something I wanted to talk to you about."

His eyebrows shot up. "Uh-oh."

"It's probably nothing. But I saw something in her stuff. When I was cleaning. I wasn't snooping or anything."

He gently pried my fingers apart, heat traveling up my arms where he touched me. "I didn't think you were."

"But full disclosure: I have snooped before. I cleaned a house, and the guy wouldn't let me go in one room."

He blinked at me. "And that's how you discovered he was keeping someone chained in there?"

"Nope. Not even close. He had hundreds of photographs of Jane Fonda. Signed posters, VHS tapes, even leg warmers."

Colin laughed and drank again. "I never would have guessed that."

"She'd inspired his fitness journey. He'd become healthier and a triathlete, forever grateful to *Jane Fonda's Workout*." I paused. Inhaled. "Anyway, your mother."

"Yes, my mom."

I wrapped the blanket around me a little tighter. I had to tell him. I thought about myself if our positions were reversed. How I'd want to know what was going on.

Colin might get angry. I knew I would. He might even lash out. My joints locked, willing to bear the brunt of his anger, his hurt. Because that's what friends do. Like the time Delia had a panic attack at school, then sobbed after, cornering herself in the dusty nonfiction section of the library. I'd been helpless then, hadn't known what to do. Only that I should stay, even when she said I shouldn't, questioning why I liked her.

"I found a hotel key card in her stuff. A receipt, too. For two dinners and drinks. All while your dad was out of town. It's probably nothing." After I'd said it aloud, the notion sounded ridiculous. A hotel key card and dinner did not equate to an affair. I scrounged around to find a likely story. Colin watched me. "Here's what I think happened: Your mom went to a boozy dinner and was too drunk to drive home, so she crashed at a hotel."

"Or, more likely, she's cheating on my dad." Colin's lips pressed into a tight knot. "Because my dad cheated on her."

A sharp throb started in my chest. *Bang. Bang. Bang.* I hadn't been expecting that—that Colin would accept the information so easily. "I'm sorry." I was helpless, didn't know what to say.

"I wish I was surprised. She's punishing him. Sebastian and me, we're just collateral damage . . ." He broke off and threw the wine bottle over the railing in a precise spiral. Red liquid tumbled out, barely missing the deck. The bottle landed with a splash. Startled ducks launched from the water.

I hung my head, and a few tears fell. I didn't understand love or families. Why do some stay together and some self-destruct? When I was a child, love was black-and-white to me. Simple and easy. But it's so fragile and tender. Nobody prepares you for all the shades of gray. How complicated it is.

"Hey." He pulled my hands from my face and held them. "Are you crying for me? Don't."

I cried harder. I was crying for Colin but also for myself. For love, its hopeless complications. I missed the family I'd had with my parents. That security. The certainty that love stays.

Colin moved to cradle my jaw. He huffed out a sad laugh that bulldozed right over my heart. "Hey, hey. It's okay. It's okay," he said, stroking my hair. "It's like that quote, right? 'The wound is the place where the Light enters.'"

I pressed a hand against my mouth, stifling a gasp. I'd heard the quote before, from the letter writer.

My skin thrummed, and I so wanted to arch into his touch. To bend to him, to surrender. But I didn't trust myself anymore. I had been so sure about Ezra. Falling for Colin might end the same way. I needed to get my head straight. My heart, too.

I scooted back, and everywhere Colin's skin had touched

mine felt suddenly cold. The boat rocked. "I have to work tomorrow. We should get going."

I wrapped the blanket tighter around me, the fabric acting like a shield, containing the fear that when Colin left, he'd take a piece of me if I let him.

From: Letter Writer (thechronosproject1@gmail.com)
To: Emma Nakamura-Thatcher (ethatch121@gmail.com)
Subject: Picture me dumping Gatorade on your head

How does one get in shape for an audition? I picture you in a gray sweatsuit, running wind sprints, and doing burpees with your violin.

From: Emma Nakamura-Thatcher (ethatch121@gmail.com)
To: Letter Writer (thechronosproject1@gmail.com)
Subject: Training, in all forms

Yes, that exactly. I wake up at dawn and jog seven miles, then polish off a glass of raw egg whites.

JK.

Mainly, I practice until my arms and fingers ache. There is a lot of heavy breathing. But it is primarily a mental sport.

In other news, I called my dad. He asked me to come over for dinner. Which honestly kind of feels like a trap. I should have requested more-neutral territory. Like he might ambush me with Madison and Camille if he has home turf advantage—then wrestle me into apologizing. I am going to go, no matter what's lurking in the bushes. I'll view it as some kind of emotional training in resiliency. Have I taken this battle metaphor too far?

Anyway, the dinner is tomorrow. Time to face the music. (I wish I had the heart to laugh at the pun.)

CHAPTER THIRTY-SIX

"I'm sorry. You think what now? That Colin is the letter writer?"

Delia's voice was muffled by the fabric of my shirt. My car, made in the late, great eighties, had a tape deck, a dial radio, and a carpeted ceiling, but no Bluetooth. My hands-free technological workaround had been putting my phone on speaker and stuffing it in my bra.

I'd filled her in on the drive to my dad's.

Colin heading to Harvard. In Boston! Yes, letter writer.

But changing his mind to sail. No, letter writer.

Then quoting Rumi. Maybe, letter writer?

I circled Dad's neighborhood, searching for an open spot. Everything was taken nearby, and I parked between a van and a wagon a block away. "I'm not sure."

"Wait," Delia said. "Am I in your bra right now?"

I shimmied my phone out and held it, keeping it on speaker. "Not anymore. What do you think?"

"I think," she said at length, exasperation stretching her tone. "This has run its course."

"What do you mean?"

"I mean, what's your plan here? Every guy you meet, you're

going to try to figure out if he's the letter writer, then exclude him if he doesn't fit the clues?"

"When you say it that way, it sounds . . ."

"Crazy," she said. Silence greeted me at the end of the line, and then she started again, more gently. "At some point you're going to have to follow your heart. This guy, the letter writer, is in the future. You will never meet him. He is too far ahead of you, and trying to find him now . . . it doesn't make sense. This was fun. But you're here, and he's there." The magnitude of her words filled up the car, and I took a beat to absorb them. "You're super quiet. Did I lose you?"

"I'm here."

"Thoughts on my thoughts?"

I sighed and fiddled with the blinker. "I think you're far too wise for a seventeen-year-old."

"I told you my dads said I am the smartest and prettiest." I heard the voice of one of her dads in the background. "One sec," she said to him, then to me, "I have to go." She paused. "Seriously, Emma. Forget the letter writer. Think about what *you* want, right now, in this moment."

We hung up, and I sat in the car for a few minutes, digesting Delia's words. How she wanted me to take my future into my own two hands. I dragged in a stuttering breath. Did I need to know who the letter writer was to be sure about someone?

I was so absorbed in my thoughts, I didn't check for oncoming pedestrian traffic before opening my car door. The guy stopped short in the street, caught from plowing into the Buick.

"Sorry," we said at the same time.

He looked at me, a smile exploding across his face. "Hey, Emma, right?"

I climbed out and looked at him. He was Asian American. Cute with a flop of black hair, wearing basketball shoes and a grin with a dimple in his right cheek. There was a ghost of familiarity about him.

At my blank expression, he said, "Maybe this will ring a bell." He clutched his stomach, gagged, folded at the waist, and pretended to vomit all over my shoes.

Bell rung. I recognized the back of his head. "Ah, Kevin. From the party."

He straightened and pointed at himself. "Kevin from the party. How are you? More importantly, how are your shoes? Do I owe you a new pair?"

"I'm good," I said. "Unfortunately, the shoes didn't make it. We had a lovely ceremony for them on a hill, though. They're in a better place now."

He winced. "Shit. I'm sorry."

"All good," I said. "Although I might keep you outside of a three-foot radius." For the splash zone.

He nodded sagely. "That's fair." He jerked his head at the buildings. "You live here?"

"My dad does. Fifth townhouse down."

"Cool," he said. A car rolled to a stop near us, bass thumping. "That's my friend," Kevin said. "It was nice seeing you, Emma."

"You too." Kevin climbed into the car, and I waved to him as he drove off.

At Dad's, I pushed the door open and stalled, hearing him on the phone. His disembodied voice drifted from the kitchen. "She's seventeen," he said. Me? Was he talking about me? Obviously, he was. "I know you understand." A pause. "Yeah, I'm sorry too."

I swung the door open and shut it loudly. "Dad," I hollered after the slam.

"Gotta go. She's here," he said.

He came from the kitchen, phone in hand, strained face sinking into a smile when he saw me. "Hey, honey. You just get here?"

"Yep. Walked through the door just now."

"You hungry? I'm making us dinner."

I let my bag fall to the ground in a pool and followed him into the kitchen. Dad returned to the stove, where a carton of eggs lay open and a saucepan sat on the burner. He waved a spatula at me. "Sit. Let's talk."

My eyebrows pinched a little in the middle. "Where are Madison and Camille?" When I'd asked to see him and he'd said to come over for dinner, I'd figured they'd both be here. But the house was noticeably quiet and empty.

"They aren't here. We decided to cool things down for a while. Madison has been spending more time at her place. Her lease wasn't up yet." I raised my eyebrows, surprised, waiting for him to say more, but he didn't go on. Dad cracked a couple of eggs into a transparent dish and whisked them. "Will you grab the cheese and salsa?"

Without a word, I slipped from my chair, opened the fridge, and rummaged around. I placed the cheese and salsa next to him. I knew what he was making—breakfast burritos. The only thing he knew how to make well. The only thing he made me in the early days of the divorce. Thinking about Dad in his single days, I was swamped with guilt. He'd been so sad then, and I juxtaposed it against how happy he'd been with Madison. "Is this because of the ex stuff?"

"Ah, no." He grinned, but it didn't meet his eyes. "I knew

how close they were. I've met the guy. I like him. He's one of those types that everybody gets along with, fun and easygoing. It's not that." He dumped the eggs into a pan and scrambled them. "Want to do the avocado?"

I fetched an avocado, cutting board, and knife and sat back down. "So what was it, then?" I asked, slicing.

Dad spooned eggs onto tortillas along with sausage and salsa and a squeeze of lime. He put the two plates in front of me, waiting for me to garnish with the avocado. "I got to thinking after our talk. Maybe we were rushing things." He wiped his hands on a towel.

"So it *is* because of me. What I said?" I took a bite, and the lime stung my tongue.

"Of course not." He sat beside me and dug in. "No, like I said, I knew Madison was meeting her ex for the movies that night. It's something they've always done together, and I like that they have a good relationship. It's healthy. But your warning, it made me think about the bigger picture. About Madison, and the wedding, and how everything was going to change. Madison and Camille, they're amazing . . . that is, of course I knew what I was gaining, but I hadn't really stopped to think about what I might be losing. So no wedding for now." He nudged me. "You know you're the most important thing to me, right?"

I blinked at my plate. "I know that."

"Good. That's good. Let's agree not to give each other the silent treatment again, all right? I really missed you." At my nod, he went on. "The time away from Madison has been good for me." Dad became more animated. "I'm about halfway through my new book . . ."

For the rest of the meal, we made small talk. *How's school going? Good. How is cleaning houses? All right.* I told him about Sherwood, about Berklee. The upcoming college audition. Ezra and I had been practicing going on a couple of weeks now. And to be totally frank, it wasn't all bad. Our intent was singularly focused on creating an epic mash-up. The piece had taken on a life of its own. Both of us chasing the music, obsessed with catching it. Everything seemed like it was sliding into place. As for what I would do if I got into Berklee? That I was unwilling to confront just yet.

Dad listened quietly, leaving spaces for me to fill in the blanks. The only thing I left out was Colin. I wasn't sure how to describe him. *There's this guy whom I've been spending a lot of time with. It's actually a funny story. I clean his house, that's how we met. But we've been doing all sorts of things together. Like placing sketchy bets with carnival yellers and going on evening sails on his secret boat. I could see myself falling for him, but I'm trying really hard not to, because he's leaving at the end of the school year, and I've recently sworn off dangerous feelings for people who may or may not be my great love from the future.*

I helped with the dishes, and after, Dad jerked his head, motioning outside. "Walk?"

"Sure," I said.

We slipped on our shoes and wound around the townhouse to a paved path that bordered a wetland. The evening was cool, quiet, and calm. Way down the path, a couple of kids in matching rain jackets splashed in puddles, screaming in delight.

"Nice night." Dad had stuck his hands in his pockets and hung his head, content to listen to the evening coming. "No rain for once." It had been one of those late-fall days when the sun was out but the air was brisk.

"Yep." I chewed my lip, thinking. There was a lot on my mind. Dad had done what I suggested—he'd taken a step back, decided to proceed with caution. So why did everything feel so wrong? "I'm really sorry about you and Madison."

He looked up at the sky, then at me. "Don't worry about it. It's fine," he promised.

I texted Camille when I was back in my car. **Our parents aren't getting married.** It was a bad opening. But I needed to ease into what I really wanted to say. **Can we still be friends?**

She replied within seconds. **I know. Mom told me yesterday. She made me take a vow of silence until your dad spoke to you. WTF.**

It was because of me. **I'm so sorry,** I said, and it was a global apology. *I'm sorry I said anything to my dad in the first place. I'm sorry your mom is hurt. I'm sorry if you're hurt.* It wasn't my intention to cause pain. In fact, my intention had been the opposite—to do no harm.

Me too, she said. **We're still cool, though, right?**

A little relief. **Yeah,** I said. **We're cool.**

I started my car and drove away, relieved to be back in touch with Camille, yet heart still heavy—and even heavier when I realized the way my dad had said the word "fine" was the same way Mom did when she was trying to pretend that her hands didn't hurt.

From: Emma Nakamura-Thatcher (ethatch121@gmail.com)
To: Letter Writer (thechronosproject1@gmail.com)
Subject: When you hurt the person you love the most

I saw my dad today. Part of my grand rebuilding tour after my classic but poorly done burn-everything-down rampage. The talk was good. We're solid now, I think. He said he's slowing things down with Madison, and they're not getting married. It didn't feel like I thought it would.

How can I explain?

When I was a kid, I was super into tiny things. I'd spend hours molding little foods, people, and perfume bottles out of clay. I desperately wanted this Polly Pocket set for Christmas, and my mom got it for me.

I played with it for a day, then stopped. Because I realized the fun was in making the items. Joy is in creation, which is probably why I love music so much. I've been working on my audition piece and have kind of realized I may love composing even more than performing. You know, making something from scratch.

So, the Polly Pocket gathers dust for a few weeks, and I come down the stairs to see Mom looking at it in this weird way. Kind of half disappointed, half heartbroken. She said, "I'm so sorry you don't love it." Like, genuinely sorry. Not manipulative at all. And I realized she must have spent a good chunk of her paycheck buying it.

I felt the same way seeing my dad this evening. A shit sundae of crummy, disappointment, and guilt-whipped topping. No cherry. I guess that's how you feel when you get what you wanted, only to realize that in the process you hurt the person who gave it to you.

CHAPTER THIRTY-SEVEN

The night before my audition, I squeezed in a final practice with Ezra.

He'd texted me earlier: My brothers got sent home from school and my aunt has to work. Any chance we could meet at my place?

Nerves rising, I stilled outside his door. On the other side were vaguely prehistoric noises. As if someone had unleashed a set of juvenile pterodactyls inside, and they were overcaffeinated but also learning to fly. I gripped my violin case and a bag of cookies in one hand and knocked.

The noises ceased as Ezra swung open the door. He looked more tired than usual and had just-climbed-out-of-bed hair. Two sets of dark eyes peered around the corner. "Hey. Thanks for coming. You find the place all right?" He stepped aside for me to enter. He wore jeans, no socks, and a worn tee that said I'm with the Band. I was just as casual, in a white V-neck and denim too.

"Oh yeah," I said, slipping through. "A charming man with a full-face tattoo pointed me in the right direction."

Ezra lived in a huge apartment complex, in unit M, farthest from the entrance.

Ezra closed the door. "That's Justin. When we first moved here, he only had his neck done. He added the Mother Teresa on his cheek last month."

"She'd be so proud, I'm sure."

I stopped, craned my neck this way and that, letting my eyes wander.

Not much to see.

Neutral carpet that branched off into a small living room with baseboard heaters. A galley kitchen with laminate flooring and countertops. A hallway lined with bedrooms and light hollow doors. Pretty generic. It was familiar somehow, like the places my dad had inhabited over the years.

But this place was lived in. Coloring books and markers were scattered on the chipped table. Mismatched frames housed photographs and hung crooked on the walls. The couch was lumpy, and the air smelled nice. Like laundry and home-cooked meals. People loved and laughed in this apartment.

"I brought cookies to share." I made eye contact with one of Ezra's brothers and winked; the other was hiding behind him.

"We can have those after dinner," said Ezra. "You hungry?"

"We're having macaroni and cheese," one of his brothers said, stepping from his place around the corner.

"With hot dogs in it," said the other with the slightest lisp.

Goodness, they were cute little devils. Big eyes, full cheeks, and hair whipped up by cowlicks. How had these adorable creatures been capable of all that noise?

"That happens to be my favorite."

"This is Lucas and Levi," Ezra said, walking around and gripping their shoulders.

I shook their hands. "Nice to meet you."

As subtly as possible, I wiped my palm on my pants; one of the boys had sticky fingers. I preferred not to speculate from what. I set my violin down.

"Ezra made us put on pants," Levi said. He had a tiny mole just under his left eye.

"He also said when you come over that we have to pee with the door shut," said Lucas.

"And poop," Levi added.

"Remember what we talked about? You don't have to tell everyone everything I tell you," Ezra said evenly.

We sat around the table, and Ezra dished up the food. "You don't have to eat if you don't want to." He placed a bowl of mac and cheese in front of me. Bits of hot dog dotted the yellow.

"Oh, I forgot I drew you a picture." Lucas popped from his chair and ran to the living room. He shuffled through a pile of papers, pulled a sheet from the bottom, ran back, and thrust it at me.

"It started off as a corgi." He sat and shoveled mac and cheese into his mouth.

At the word "corgi," my eyes went wide. I stilled, spoon halfway to my mouth.

The letter writer had mentioned corgis once.

A coincidence. I flicked the thought away.

"Anyway," Levi continued, "I couldn't get the body right, so I turned it into a rocket ship."

I had the picture turned the wrong way and adjusted it. Ah, I saw the rocket ship, smoke billowing from underneath it, which also resembled a very large . . .

I made eye contact with Ezra. A wisp of a smile appeared on his face. I fought my own smile, but finally it gave way. The joke passed between us. But then I let my smile fade, wary of sharing anything with Ezra again.

I can only describe the rest of the meal as competitive. Where I was used to quieter meals, punctuated by silverware clinking against plates, Ezra and his brothers ate loudly, talked with their mouths full, interrupted one another's sentences, and licked their bowls clean. After we devoured the cookies, Ezra made some sort of elaborate nest out of couch cushions for the kids to swan dive onto from a chair while we did dishes. Then he flicked on a movie for his brothers, a show with many flashing lights and a singing man in a loincloth.

"C'mon." He led me down the hallway to the last door. To his bedroom. A lazily made twin bed was jammed against a wall. In an opposite corner was his cello. Pinned to the walls were a few posters of indie bands.

He closed the door with a soft click. The television muted. "Thanks for coming out here today."

"No problem."

I was alone with Ezra in his room. Pre–mall encounter, pre–Seattle underground, pre–Sherwood Institute, and pre-Janey, I would've died for this. Died.

I'd been a different girl then. I shifted my focus to something more neutral. "Do you mind if I ask what they did to get sent home from school?" Sure, they were energetic, but I couldn't imagine Lucas and Levi doing anything so wrong.

He did a quick face scrunch. "Officially, the form says 'inappropriate use of math supplies.' They bet another kid he couldn't fit five beans in his nose. They lost. The kid fit six and spent all day in urgent care. Lucas and Levi had been warned before. Twice, actually. They can go back tomorrow. I spent all afternoon lecturing them not to put stuff in their noses or other kids' noses. It's a fifty-fifty chance they'll make it through the rest of the year."

"I can't imagine them doing anything like that. They're so cute."

He raked a hand through his hair. "Don't let them fool you. They're supervillains."

"Adorable supervillains," I qualified.

The corner of his mouth curled up into a semblance of a smile. His phone dinged, and he pulled it from his back pocket, frowning at the screen. "Blue thought of another band name. Hot Green."

"It's better than Exploding Uteruses."

"Not by much." He leaned against the wall, gaze sweeping me from my head to my toes. Who was Ezra to me now that our playing field was even?

I laid my violin on his bed. Music sheets with his handwriting were strewn on the floor. "So you're really doing it? Hitting the road next year?"

"That's the plan. For at least a few months. Maybe just over the summer." He was watching me. "I don't know. I go back and forth. New England Conservatory is a lot to give up."

I pulled my ponytail over my shoulder and played with the strands, rolling his statement around in my mind. An errant, unwanted thought popped up . . .

Ezra *could* still be the letter writer. He'd sold only one of the albums. Maybe there were more, one that was so important, he'd never let go of it. Maybe he ended up in Boston afterward . . .

A fist banged on his bedroom door right before it sprung open. "Ezra." Lucas stood in the doorway. "We're hungry again, and I have a booger on my finger."

"Gross." Ezra's full attention was on his brother. "Go throw your booger in the trash and wash your hands."

"It's not my booger. It's Levi's."

Ezra hung his head. A million silent curse words poured from his mouth. He took Lucas by the shoulders and steered him into the bathroom.

I heard the faucet turn on, Lucas chattering away, asking questions about sharks, and Ezra's dulcet tones as he patiently answered. "No, sharks don't live in fresh water . . . No, sharks can't come up through bathroom drains . . . Not the toilet, either."

I smiled to myself, my thoughts circling back to the letter writer, if Ezra might be him. One day.

But then Delia's voice coasted in, what she said to me on my way to my dad's that night, the question she'd planted.

Forget the letter writer. Think about what you *want, right now.*

CHAPTER THIRTY-EIGHT

That night I barely slept.

In the morning Ezra was as jittery as I was backstage at Sherwood, waiting for the student before me to finish playing his oboe.

I checked my phone again, rereading the series of good luck texts from Colin last night:

> Break a leg, or actually, I hope you don't. (Why does anyone say that?!)

> Or maybe it's OK if you don't need your legs to play the violin.

> Just kill it, or if they don't like it, kill them.

> Sorry, did I go overboard with that?

The final note of the student's performance fell flat, and he exited, head low and posture deflated as he passed us to burst through the stage door.

"Just remember," Ezra said. The backstage lights were dim. Cast in shadows, his profile was sharp, jaw accentuated. "Ease in on the sonata. Pace yourself. Let it build."

I nodded, hyping myself up. Emotions flooded me. I wanted Berklee. I wanted them to say yes. Even if I wasn't sure I could go, I needed to know I was worthy of it. "Yeah. Okay. Thanks."

I walked onto the stage, my steps echoing in the near-empty auditorium. The admission panel had been set up in the tech booth. Representatives from all the major schools were present. Berklee was on the left.

I gripped the microphone. "Um, Emma," I said, pulling away at the feedback. I waited for the sound to die and spoke softer. "Emma Nakamura-Thatcher. Composition and violin."

My palms were already starting to sweat. I stepped back, dragged the music stand before me, and placed my pages on it. Someone on the panel cleared their throat. A door offstage opened and shut, most likely the next student readying for their turn.

My insides were chaotic. All the notes I'd practiced jumbled in my head, and I froze, forgetting how to play.

"Go, Emma!" a deep voice shouted. It was one I recognized. One I'd been hearing since elementary school. My gaze jumped from the panel to the right. To three figures standing in the third section, middle row—Camille, Theo, and Delia.

A smile exploded across my face, and my heart twisted in my chest. What on earth? Camille put two fingers in her mouth and whistled. Delia clapped. I locked eyes with Theo, and we did that thing where we spoke without words. *You're here?* He nodded, jerked his head toward Delia. *She told me.*

The representative from Juilliard scowled, swiveled around, and shushed them, finger pressed hard against her lips.

The trio sat down, settled in, and Theo gave me one of his *Give 'em hell* nods. The kind he did when he was gaming, before raiding dungeons or running headlong into battle.

I tucked my violin between my chin and shoulder. Closed my eyes and found the first note in the piece. Ever so slowly I drew it out. Teasing, letting the music pool. Memories flashed against the backs of my eyelids. Seeing a violin for the first time. Learning to play notes. Wondering at how they fit together. Feeling the inside of me shift. Change.

The music was me. I was the music. Everything else faded away. I was home.

When I was finished, I was a little dizzy. I took a jerky bow, said my name again, and watched as Camille, Theo, and Delia left. I'd text them later, I promised myself. After the adrenaline had run its course. I hurried off the stage.

I buzzed up to Ezra. How had I done? His face didn't give anything away. "I should have done something more textbook. Maybe they wanted a more traditional piece," I fretted, confidence falling away.

"No." He began to shake his head. "No. That was amazing. *You're* amazing."

"Really?" My face broke into a smile.

"Really." He laughed quietly. He gripped my shoulders. "You're going to get in. They're going to be begging you to go."

I looked at him. He stroked my jaw with his thumb. My breath stalled. Butterflies swarmed my tummy. I tunneled back to that night in the alley. When he'd kissed me, his lips tasting of cherry sucker. Without a word, he leaned down.

But then . . . my whole body reacted, and I moved away from Ezra, a physical rejection of his touch. We stood facing each other, the world around us falling in a silent hush.

The painful truth was that it could have been us. Right now. Right here.

But whatever we'd had wasn't there anymore. That spark had been slowly rubbed away by the night in the park, twisting my ankle, tacos, Slim Jims, polar swims, tea with Mrs. Sydney, sunset boat rides.

A frown line formed on Ezra's forehead. "Emma. I thought—"

"Colin." His name was the only word my brain would form.

He reached out, traced his finger against my cheek, and I let him—because I understood what it meant: an acknowledgment, and a goodbye.

"Colin," he said numbly, and it was the only answer I needed to give him.

I was still a little shaky getting back into my car. The adrenaline from the audition was wearing off, but something new was replacing it, something much scarier, more exciting, too.

I was done fighting these feelings that were building in my heart.

I parked at a 7-Eleven and went in, my unfocused gaze landing on something bright and yellow near the cashier. With one hand, I grabbed them all and dropped them on the counter, buying the whole lot.

. . .

Everything was in sharp relief as I pulled up to Colin's house. I walked up the driveway and knocked on his door, ready to . . . just ready, I guess.

The door swung open. I caught a blur of sandy hair before closing my eyes and thrusting the bouquet of Slim Jims at Colin.

"Thanks. It's what I always wanted. Nonperishable meat," a dry voice, not Colin's, said. The beef stick bouquet was plucked from my hands.

I opened my eyes and saw Sebastian. My sails deflated. "You're not Colin."

"Fortunately." Sebastian scowled at me and offered back the Slim Jims.

"Emma?" Colin appeared behind Sebastian. "You're here." His smile was quizzical. Happy. "How'd the audition go?"

"Awesome." I brushed past Sebastian. "These are for you." I thrust the bouquet at him. But then I thought how silly it was. "I mean, unless you think it's stupid." I started to retract the offering, but Colin grabbed it.

"No way." He fisted the bouquet in his large hand and let it hang by his side. "It's what I always wanted."

I smiled, goofy. Lovestruck.

Sebastian looked between us. "You two are strange."

"Sebastian." Colin didn't take his eyes off me. "Don't you have something better to do? Like mine diamonds from your asshole or yell at old ladies crossing the street too slowly?" The corner of his mouth lifted into a lazy smile. "He actually did that once."

"As a matter of fact, I am heading out." Sebastian reached past me to a set of keys thrown on the foyer table, his body positioned in front of Colin. "Don't break his heart," he said low.

I swallowed thickly but didn't say anything.

Keys in hand, Sebastian disappeared out the door. I heard the garage open and shut, then tires against the driveway. Headlights flashed through the windows.

Sebastian was gone.

I was alone with Colin. And I knew what I wanted.

CHAPTER THIRTY-NINE

I was in Colin's room. He was feet away from me, standing in the middle of the carpet. I could feel the press of his eyes on my back as I studied his shelf. "It's weird being in here without my cleaning supplies," I chattered inanely. I felt a little naked. A lot vulnerable.

"I like having you here. In my space," he admitted quietly.

I quirked an eyebrow at him and returned to the shelf, sliding the Winnie-the-Pooh book out. "Big fan?" I asked, remembering how odd I'd thought it was, a little childhood relic nestled between the rowing trophies and signed baseballs.

"Isabella gave it to me. She was my favorite nanny, ages three to six. We listened to it all the time. It had been hers when she was a little girl."

Listened? That's when I felt it. It wasn't a book, but a box. I opened the cover, and inside was a shiny disc. "It's an album." I shivered at the implication, what this might mean.

My most treasured possession is an album.

My heart began thumping extra hard, even as I scrambled not to read too much into it.

Delia had been right that the letter writer was years away. I'd been chasing something I'd never catch. I should not be thinking these thoughts. But . . . how could I not? I wanted Colin, but as long as he was in my life, I'd always be searching for the letter writer. Hoping the person I was with might be him. Anxiety stirred low in my belly.

"I don't have anything to play it on anymore. But I keep it. Sentimental reasons, you know?"

I didn't say anything for a few loaded seconds. "You'd probably never give it away." I traced Pooh's figure on the front, his round belly. Eeyore was in the background, under a tree, glum as usual.

Colin plucked the box from my grip and slid it back onto the shelf. Slowly he ran his warm hand up my arm, over my neck, and cupped my chin, angling my head to stare directly into my eyes. "Hi," he said.

My stomach knotted into a pretzel. I might've melted to the ground if he hadn't been holding me up. I smiled, shy. "Hi."

His hand moved to my hair, and I pressed my hands to his chest. I stared at his throat, his Adam's apple, then let my fingers inch up until I was fisting his sweatshirt. A silent plea to stay. To kiss me. I gazed at him, letting this intensity between us finally run loose. His eyes had turned a darker, hungrier shade, ready to devour. I marveled at our closeness, the way our breaths tumbled together.

"Is this moving too fast?" he asked, his words catching. He swallowed. "We can watch a movie or something. I mean, I'll probably need a very cold shower, and you'll need to put on a sack or something." He squinched his eyes shut. "Honestly, though? I'm not sure a sack would do it."

Standing on my tiptoes, I kissed him right on his throat, over his hammering pulse. He groaned and tilted down, lips covering mine. His mouth parted. His nose brushed the tip of mine. The kiss deepened and flowed; his hands were everywhere, fingers running down and then up into my shirt, caressing my bare skin above my waistband. He broke away only to rain more kisses down my neck.

I was dizzy and lightheaded, tingling everywhere. Then his leg was between mine, and we were moving. Stumbling backward to land softly on his bed.

His lips skimmed tenderly down my jaw, neck, throat, down, down, down.

All the while, he murmured little words of praise. "You're so beautiful. You're perfect." Around my stomach, he switched to confessions. "It's hard to breathe when I'm around you."

I could only answer with little sounds.

Hums.

The first notes of a new song.

My shoes were off. My shirt hiked up above my belly button. Colin was sprawled on top of me. My arms were around his neck. We were kissing and more—groping, rubbing, fusing.

I needed him. Colin. My Colin.

Somewhere in the depths of the room, my phone pinged.

He propped himself up on his elbows. "Need to get that?" His eyes were hazy.

"No." I felt the scruff of his jaw and kissed him. He growled and pressed against me harder.

My phone pinged again. I remembered my mom, her *HOME*

NOW text from a few weeks ago, and it was like being doused in cold water.

I broke away and said, "Yes."

"Okay." He kissed my neck quickly, and I relaxed, caught in a tidal wave of sensation. It felt like my whole body was a giant nerve ending.

Again my phone pinged. I pushed on his chest, and he rolled away onto his back. A beat passed as we caught our breath.

I started to get up, but Colin was faster. "I got it. Stay right there. Don't move."

I'd dumped my purse on the floor, and Colin dipped his hand inside, finding my phone. "Got it," he said. Then I watched as his brow slipped, seeing the screen. "New message from Letter Writer. Who's that?"

I blinked and sat up. He handed the phone off to me.

The new message alert included the subject line *I will never stop loving you.*

"Nobody."

I said it too quickly.

What a mistake. I shouldn't have said "nobody." "Nobody" made it sound like I didn't want Colin to know who the letter writer was. Like I was hiding something.

But I couldn't tell Colin. *Letter Writer is in love with me, and he's from the future.* I'd sound like a maniac.

His smile grew quizzical, distant, busted up. "Pretty important nobody if you set your phone to alert you when they email."

"You're right." I felt the situation running away from me, and I fought to catch up. "He's my friend."

"He?"

By Colin's face, I knew I'd made it worse. I grabbed his hand and pulled him closer. He towered above me. "A friend." I looked up. "Promise. It's not what you think. He's like a pen pal. We've never even met in person. This could all be an elaborate catfishing scheme. He could be, like, twelve and living in Costa Rica." I'd tried to make a joke. Upset, I felt my face redden, then imagined how my pink cheeks translated to Colin. A flashing guilty sign.

Colin narrowed his eyes, my words reverberating around us. "How long have you known each other?"

"A couple of months, maybe."

"Do you care about him? It seems like he cares about you a lot. Based on that subject line: 'I will never stop loving you,'" he rasped out as if to say it caused him physical pain.

The air was tense and thick all of a sudden. I chewed my cheek. I didn't want to lie, and my silence spoke volumes.

He let go of my hand, and his expression grew serious. "Here's the thing, Emma. I've watched my parents cheat for years. I've watched how they hurt each other. All my life I've come up short. Been second." He exhaled a shaky breath. Hands on his hips, he stared up at the ceiling. "I don't want to be second to anyone, and . . . I care about you. A lot. But I can't be with someone I don't trust."

I shook my head wildly and stood, hands balled into fists. Desperate emotions welled up in my throat. "No. You've got it all wrong."

He wouldn't even look at me. He took a long, defeated breath and pinched the bridge of his nose. "I think you should go."

My eyes went wide, and I stared at him in shock, trying to figure out what to say. How to make it better. I couldn't tell him the truth. That the letter writer was from the future. That I'd even wondered if it could be *him*. There was no way he'd believe me. Plus, what would the point be? I'd go out on a limb just to have the branch break when Colin left me for a sailing trip around the world next year anyway.

He busied himself in stony silence. Slipping on a sweatshirt, fisting his boat keys.

After this I knew where he'd go. To the sailboat. To lose himself on the water, like I would in music. I knew him well enough now to know that he'd take *Sharpshooter* out, take his problems to the sound.

I had begged once before, heart on my sleeve, when I went to my dad's during the divorce. I'd cracked myself open completely.

I couldn't bring myself to do it again. To ask Colin to believe me. It was too much.

Come home. I heard the echo of myself on my dad's couch. His voice telling me he couldn't.

Self-preservation told me to walk away.

So that's what I did.

CHAPTER FORTY

Chin tipped low, I careened through the hall and down the stairs to burst outside.

Cold December night air stung my lungs, piercing my insides like a thousand needles.

I wasn't okay. Clouds rolled over the moon, and I pressed my hands to my chest, decimated. Absolutely train wrecked.

I'd had Colin. I'd chosen him and what had happened?

With shaky hands I unlocked my car and sat in the driver's seat, squeezing my eyes shut and opening them. Tears rolled down my cheeks. I swiped them away, angry, humiliated, and brokenhearted. What a bitter combination.

I drove home, and it was late when I parked in the driveway. The lights were out, and I felt small inside, shriveled. My throat was hoarse from crying.

In the kitchen I rooted around in the freezer. Frozen vegetables. Some biscuits from the mid 2000s. A pound of meat with an orange sale sticker. At the bottom, a carton of ice cream with freezer burn.

That would do. I stood on my tiptoes and reached for a bowl.

"Emma-chan."

At Jiji's voice I startled and dropped the bowl. It cracked and then broke into three even pieces. I clutched my chest. "I thought you were sleeping."

He wore his plaid robe, neatly folded, left over right, tied at the waist. "I heard a noise. I thought we were being robbed." He shuffled in, picked the bowl up, and placed the pieces on the dining table.

Dad had bought the bowls for us when he was on a research trip to Vermont. He came back and had a big story about how he'd spent a whole day in a potter's studio.

My nose tingled. I started crying again.

"Eh," Jiji said. He got down another bowl and scooped me out some ice cream. He slid the bowl in front of me along with a spoon. "This will upset your stomach. It's too late for milk. Not good for the digestive system."

I sniffled. "A bad digestive system is the least of my worries now." I could see Colin's image so clearly. His tightly restrained profile. His mouth asking me to go.

"Eh," he said again. Jiji puttered around the kitchen, opening drawers and getting a newspaper from the recycle bin. I watched him spread the newspaper on the table and put the broken bowl on top. It was soothing watching his unhurried movements. I could always rely on him, steady in the face of a storm. "This is nothing that can't be fixed."

Part of me ached, wanting that to be true for this bowl, and for everything else.

I wasn't sure how to explain to Jiji that the broken bowl was just the last domino falling. How I felt whittled down to a nub.

Maybe Jiji could sense it. I didn't need to say the words. I remembered him when we played outside, lost in the forest. How he pressed a finger to his lips and whispered, "Follow me. I know the way through these woods." He always led me in the right direction.

Now he sat in a chair across from me and lined one jagged piece of the bowl with glue. Then the other and the other. I watched him and let the ice cream melt. I hadn't been that hungry to begin with; I'd just been looking for something to soothe my throat, my soul. Watching him work was a better balm.

He held the pieces together, allowing the glue to partially dry. "You had your audition today," he said. "It didn't go well?"

I stirred my soupy ice cream, watching the chocolate mix with strawberry and vanilla.

The audition felt far away, another life.

"No. It went well. I might get into Berklee." I smiled weakly at him, floating the idea. His facial expression stayed the same, stoic and unbothered, ready for me to explain more. "But of course, I wouldn't go even if I did."

"Why is that?"

Quietly, I told him. "I couldn't leave. You and Mom need me."

He sighed and glued another piece of the bowl, letting the parts set in his hands. "Do we?"

I straightened. "Yes."

Who would divide Jiji's pills, put them in the day-of-the-week container, and check he'd taken them? Who would fetch his hearing aids or remember to charge them? Who would start dinner or wash the dishes? Or fold the laundry? Who would cover shifts for Mom when her hands ached too much to go to work?

Jiji set the bowl in the middle of the table. "All fixed," he announced.

"It's not the same." The cracks were evident; liquid would leak through, so we'd never be able to use it again. "We should throw it away."

"It's a beautiful bowl, even if it's been broken." He believed in wabi-sabi. Finding the sublime in the damaged was part of his worldview. But I'd never quite adapted to the philosophy. "Don't touch it for a day." He stood and placed a hand on my shoulder. "I survived in the desert. Four days with no food or water."

I stared at him, bewildered. "Okay?"

"If you want to go to Berklee, I would miss you, but I would be okay." He patted my shoulder. "Don't stay up too late."

By rote, I cleaned up. I should have gone upstairs. Washed my face, put on my pajamas, nestled under my covers. Gone to sleep. I had to work tomorrow. Life doesn't stop when your heart is breaking.

But instead I sat back down at the table alone. Heart compressed, as if my rib cage had shrunk. My soul strained, restless, aching for company.

Wanting to make sense of it all, I grabbed my phone, cleared the notification from the letter writer, and opened his email.

From: Letter Writer (thechronosproject1@gmail.com)
To: Emma Nakamura-Thatcher (ethatch121@gmail.com)
Subject: I will never stop loving you.

Oh, man. A shit sundae. I wish I could unsee that.

I've been thinking about you and your dad. About what happened when you were younger and recently. How the two are related. And I want you to know you are right. What you think is true.

Love is cruel. Love is unkind. Love is a beast. A yellow-eyed, hungry werewolf. Ready to tear you apart. Ready to burst from your skin. Ready to race under a bloated moon, pant, chase, devour, and conquer. Only to leave you in the sunrise, sickly and pale. Broken and humbled. Licking your wounds. Mourning what might have been. What glory has slipped through your hands?

But honestly, would you trade those days of being a family for never knowing what it felt like at all? Would you trade falling in and out of love as well? I know I wouldn't. I guess that's what I want you to know.

I am glad to have loved you. I am glad that
I will never stop loving you. No matter how
much it guts me. No matter how big the wound
becomes.

It's a beautiful thing to open your heart.
Someday I hope you'll say, like I say to myself:
The hurt was good, the hurt was worth it.

Loving you has been an honor, the single
greatest thing I've ever done. I don't regret it.
Any of it.

Because—here comes another truth—love
doesn't ever end. Not really. Love contracts and
expands, but it is never truly gone.

Don't you see?

This is the answer to your wish. This is how love
endures. This is how love lasts. You choose it,
and you believe in it. You believe.

This is what brings me back. This is why I return
to you.

Over and over again.

CHAPTER FORTY-ONE

After my folks divorced, after my grandmother died, I started to anticipate loss. I embraced the idea that all love eventually leaves. It was inevitable. So why try to hold on? It's why I'd pushed Ezra away. Why I'd let Colin push me away.

This whole way of thinking was insanity, of course.

And it was why I was bad at love.

I finished reading the letter writer's email. Then I read it again, breathing in and out, my heart thundering, digesting his words.

And at the same time I felt my whole life, my whole way of thinking, rearranging.

When I was first learning the violin, I sucked. Of course I did. I'd practice in the living room, bow screeching across the strings, turning out wrong notes. I'd grow so frustrated that I wanted to throw the violin down on the couch and walk away.

But I always came back, the music calling to me, and I'd learned it takes practice to be good at things.

It takes practice to be good at love.

The letter writer was right. It was clear as glass to me. Why hadn't I seen this before? In the quiet, in the dark, I had this revelation. Love needs to be cultivated, gathered, and sheltered. You have to keep choosing it.

That's how you make love stay.

I sat there. In the dark, at my kitchen table, phone in my hand, for I don't know how long. The truth spreading around me like sunshine after a thunderstorm. And there was only one person I wanted to share this revelation with.

Colin.

My heart was knotted in my throat as I called him.

An automated voice answered. "The person you are trying to reach is out of service."

I remembered. He would've gone out on the boat.

I grabbed my keys in a desperate whir of regret. I should not have let Colin push me away. I should have stayed. I should have told him, *I choose you. I want you. Let's plant something new and watch it grow.*

My car was a beacon, and I slammed into it, punching my keys into the ignition and cranking. The engine sputtered to life only to die on a whimpered protest. My stomach dropped, and I beat my forehead against the wheel. *No. No. No.*

Shoulders slack, I crumpled, feeling helpless. Hopeless. But then my eyes lit on something.

It was one o'clock in the morning. I flung myself out of my car and stomped to the garage. The paint was peeling, and we always left it unlocked. There wasn't anything worth stealing. Some rusty power tools, a folded-up treadmill that didn't work, and my old bike.

My old bike.

I pulled up the door and there it was, outlined under the canvas drop cloth we'd used when I painted my room periwinkle at age twelve. The last time I'd ridden it was in the rain. To my dad's, heart aching and open and wanting, then eventually crushed. I'd been happy covering it up, blunting the painful memory.

I felt along the tires. Deflated. Drawers lined the back of the garage, and I yanked them open, giving a determined nod when I found the pump.

Relief flushed hot through my blood when the tires stayed inflated, no leaks. Time hadn't worn the rubber completely away.

Back upright, I fingered one of the iridescent tassels. I used to ride and watch them twisting in the wind, sparkling in the sun, tendrils of magic.

For so long I hadn't let myself feel this way. I channeled it all into pumping my legs as fast as I possibly could. There was so much to say to him. I'd start with *I'm sorry* and then explain everything. Who the letter writer was to me. Beg him to accept the crazy truth and come back to me.

It wasn't raining, but I did splash through puddles, navigating the empty, dark roads to the marina. An hour passed. My quads were on fire, and my cheeks and knuckles were stung numb by the frigid air. Leaning my bike against a metal railing, I peered at the docks floating in the inky water. I smelled the salt in the air, a hint of diesel, and saw Colin's boat slip.

Empty.

I was too late. He'd sailed away. *He'll be back,* I thought. But then again, maybe not. What kept him here, anyway? Colin was gone. Maybe forever.

CHAPTER FORTY-TWO

For two weeks afterward there was only extreme sadness and a dull numbness. And silence, as in no word from Colin.

Feeling very self-destructive and desperate, I called him two, three, four times a day. Drove by the marina after school. Played the violin on the dock, next to his empty slip. I worked, too. Cleaning and scrubbing until my hands were raw. I took care of Jiji and didn't admonish him when he asked for extra salt. Time moved by at a sluggish crawl. Heartbreak consumed me.

And I slept. A lot.

"Have you been drinking?" Mom asked one night at dinner.

"What? No." I straightened. I was picking at my food. Everything tasted like sand in my mouth; the blood inside my body felt cold. "Why would you say that?"

"You're not eating. Maybe you are really using drugs. You think she's using drugs?" Mom asked Jiji.

"Urine test is the only way to be sure." Jiji slurped his soup.

"I'm not drinking, and I'm not using drugs."

"What's wrong with you, then?" Mom snapped.

I pushed from the table. "Nothing. I'm tired. I'm going to bed. I'll do the dishes in the morning." It was supposed to snow the next day, and I was counting on the bad weather. School would be canceled. Winter break was right around the corner, and I planned to hide myself away.

She didn't call after me.

I dropped off and went to sleep.

I woke to no snow and instead to noise—the clatter of dishes, and an unfamiliar voice. At least, an unfamiliar voice in *this* house. Six years had passed since I'd heard the deep baritone bouncing off the walls.

Dad?

Rumpled and confused, I drifted downstairs to the kitchen. Pushing open the saloon doors, I blinked once, twice. Was this a mirage?

Dad was there. Mom, too. Both were at the counter, littered with take-out boxes. Jiji sat at the table. Fried eggs, maple syrup, and onions punctuated the air.

"Morning!" Dad said, his enthusiasm pushing through my brain fog. He lifted two plates full of scrambled eggs, bacon, and potatoes—standard diner fair—and set them down at the table. One in front of Jiji, the other in front of an empty chair. "I got you chocolate chip pancakes. Come on, sit. Eat while it's hot."

I stayed near the doorway, anxiety ratcheting up a notch. My parents hadn't been in the same room since my freshman recital. I remembered it acutely. When they'd sat on opposite sides of the auditorium, then waited in the lobby, even farther apart, for me to come to them. I'd suffered a minor panic attack, deciding whom to go to first, like I was choosing which parent I loved the most. "What are you doing here?" My throat was dry, dehydrated. From crying off and on all day yesterday.

"I am here to help." Dad had his back to me, dishing up more food. He opened the utensil drawer. "Where do you keep the napkins these days?"

"What is this?" I looked to Mom, who had always been the more practical of the two.

"Cabinet right above you," she told Dad, then turned to me. "Your grandfather called your dad. He came over this morning. We had a family meeting." She sat down as Dad placed the last two plates on the table.

A family meeting? Without me? And so early? The whiplash kept coming.

Dad sank into a chair. "Come on." He unfolded a napkin and laid it across his lap. "Let's talk, kiddo."

My butt landed in a chair, and nostalgia swept through me. We'd had Christmas dinners here together. Served mashed potatoes at Thanksgiving. Blown out candles on birthdays. My grandmother had been alive then, and we'd squeezed the five of us around the tiny table, a small but mighty force. After the divorce we'd dwindled to four, then three. Mom didn't make turkey for Thanksgiving after that. The effort didn't make sense, there would be too many leftovers, we couldn't possibly eat them all.

"You called him?" I asked Jiji.

My grandfather didn't like my dad much anymore. "You do not change spouses like sets of clothes," he'd told my mom during the divorce.

"Hai," Jiji said. "Adrian." He called my dad to attention. "You get me an omelet with ham and cheese next time."

"Sure thing, Masa," Dad said with a smile, biting into a piece of toast.

My dad didn't like Jiji much anymore either. He'd called him rigid, and once, a general in a biting, super-condescending way.

"I don't understand." I shook my head, befuddled. How were we all sitting at the same table, having a meal together?

Mom speared a bite of scrambled eggs. "Jiji told us about Berklee. Your concerns about leaving."

My stomach melted. "Oh, I shouldn't have said anything. It's not a big deal. I mean, I haven't even gotten in. I probably won't."

"*When* you get in, we will need help," Jiji said. "That's why I called your father." He turned to Dad. "Along with the omelet, I would like sausage."

Dad nodded. "Sure thing." He addressed me. "Just like this morning, I can check in on Jiji. I'll cook meals or order food and make myself available to take your mom and grandfather for doctor's appointments. My writing schedule will be flexible. It'll be kind of like when you were a baby. Maybe I'll go back to writing later at night."

"And I'm thinking we'll find a nurse for Jiji," Mom added.

"We can't afford that," I whispered to her.

Dad cleared his throat. "I can. And your mom is going to allow me to help."

Jiji scowled. "I don't want a nurse. No strangers in the house."

Mom smiled gently at me. "We'll keep discussing it."

I took in the scene.

Mom was wound as tight as a rubber band, Jiji even tighter. Dad had a nervous jailbreak air about him, like he couldn't keep still and was waiting for the best opportunity to escape.

This whole notion was madness.

"I appreciate it. But I don't think this is going to work."

"Of course it's going to work," Mom said.

"No. We should just keep things separate. I can handle taking care of you and Jiji myself."

Dad didn't need to get involved. It would be more of a headache.

"It's already in motion, kiddo," Dad said. He scraped the last bite from his plate.

Tears clouded my vision, and I tried to figure out why. My thoughts turned inward, questions passing through me. Why hadn't it always been this way? Why had it taken so long for us to sit down together? Why was I so afraid of everything changing?

The hard truth? I was afraid of going away to school. Maybe I'd been clinging to Jiji and Mom as an excuse not to go. I suddenly felt unanchored. "But . . . but why?" was all I said.

Mom shared a look with Dad before coming back to me. "Because we love you. And we're going to work this out."

I walked Dad to his car. Lawns were frozen and everything was kind of still. Stagnant. But I . . .

I realized I felt alive again. Alive—and uncertain.

"You sure this is a good idea?" I asked, stopping.

"You know what they say, the road to hell is paved with good intentions." He shrugged and opened his hands. "I'm kidding. Sorry, it's probably too soon to make jokes."

"Way too soon." I started walking again.

"But seriously, I didn't know you two were having trouble making ends meet. I'm going to make it a habit of communicating more with your mom. But you have to meet me halfway. You need something, you say so."

I swallowed, nodding and agreeing. "Jiji is going to be difficult. He'll try to take advantage because you don't know certain things. He shouldn't have ham-and-cheese omelets. If anything, he should have a veggie omelet with a light feta."

"I consider myself officially in Jiji training. We'll practice the rest of this school year. You can send me lists. I'll get the hang of it."

"He doesn't like you," I said.

"Please," he said. "I once had an editor leave me four hundred in-line comments on a manuscript. If I can handle that, I can handle one sly old man."

I laughed.

Dad smiled.

We came to his car. I chewed my cheek, still feeling a heaviness. I knew where the weight originated. Madison and Dad. I'd gotten a lot of things wrong, and one of them was telling Dad not to get married. "Hey."

"What's up, kiddo?"

"I want to talk to you more about Madison."

"Okay." He visibly tightened.

"I was wrong about her." I paused. The truth had solidified like a block of cement in my chest. I'd been so afraid of love, of being hurt, that I'd manifested that fear, used it as a blunt instrument against the world. Batting away Madison from my dad. Colin from myself. Ezra, too. So much was unfixable. But this . . . this I could repair. "About you getting married again. I want you to."

He softened and smiled weakly. "I don't know."

"I like Madison," I said urgently. "What I said wasn't about her. It was about me . . . I just didn't want you to get hurt again. I didn't think love could last. But I made it worse. Please," I said. "I want you to be happy." I opened my hands, wanting to fix what I'd broken. "Think about it?"

He inhaled and promised to. We ended with a full hug.

He said he'd be back tomorrow to take Jiji to the doctor.

And I said okay.

On the walk back to the house, my steps felt light. As if something inside me had lifted and flown away.

From: Emma Nakamura-Thatcher
(ethatch121@gmail.com)
To: Letter Writer
(thechronosproject1@gmail.com)
Subject: My heart IS clay

Deep breath. This is hands down the hardest email I've ever had to write. So I will say it quick, like ripping off a Band-Aid. I think we should stop writing to each other.

Let me explain.

At first I didn't believe you. Believe *in* you. And once I realized you were real, I wanted so badly to find you.

The last few months I've searched for you in every boy I've met, seeking forever. Eternal, elusive love. I still don't know if forever exists, but that wasn't the reason you were writing, was it?

I was never meant to fall in love with you. I was meant to live my life. It wasn't about finding you, but about finding myself. The Emma I buried when my parents divorced. The one who rode her bike in the rain. Who picked up a violin, having never played it, and believed enough in herself to figure it out. The Emma who was not afraid to take risks and get hurt in the process from time to time.

Thank you. It's been wonderful to unearth her.

Have you ever seen *Dumbo*? Honestly, I kind of hate that movie. Theo's dad made us watch it when we were too spooked to sleep after watching *The Sixth Sense*.

Anyway, in the movie Dumbo has this feather that he thinks makes him fly, but really, he never needed the feather. He could always fly.

I think that's what you've been to me, a feather. Someone I thought I needed to find, but I didn't after all. That's not why you wrote me. Is it? You wrote me because you loved me, because you wanted me to take risks, open myself up again.

So to that end, now that I am crying—like, a lot crying—I'd like to say: I'm good now. So good. I guess I'm ready to be hurt. And so weird, I'm a little excited about it.

All my love,
Emma

P.S. I may be crying, but I am also smiling wide and bright.

From: Letter Writer
(thechronosproject1@gmail.com)
To: Emma Nakamura-Thatcher
(ethatch121@gmail.com)
Subject: I would never chain you

I remember the movie.

You would think, living in the future, I should have seen this coming. I'm so proud of you. You're right, it is time. Now I'm crying too. But manly tears. I joke only because I ache. Humor blunts the pain.

I suppose I should have always known I'd have to let you go at some point. I wish it weren't this soon. But you were always a quick learner. So much smarter than me. Such a clever, beautiful girl.

Your heart is wild and free, and I know it will lead you to do the most wonderful, soul-crushing things. Do me a favor? Keep going. Let the world greet you. You'll find open arms, I promise.

I cannot wait to see what you become.

I love you. I love you to the point of madness. And I always will—yesterday, today, and tomorrow.

Conquer the world, Emma. I'll be watching.

P.S. You are wrong about one thing. Forever does exist. You and me, this moment, we are time itself. Eternal.

From: Emma Nakamura-Thatcher (ethatch121@gmail.com)
To: Letter Writer (thechronosproject1@gmail.com)
Subject: Last email, I swear.

Always. Until the end of time.

Inbox: undeliverable: thechronosproject1@gmail.com: Last email, I swear.

Address not found

CHAPTER FORTY-THREE

Each step I walked up Colin's driveway, I was hit with a memory:

Dragging my vacuum across the cobblestones, thinking the air smelled better in this neighborhood. Meeting Colin and Sebastian. The time Colin made me a turkey sandwich. The other time when he helped me clean. The way he sat with Mrs. Sydney and listened.

I hadn't seen him coming. What a force he'd been.

I rang the bell, my insides wobbly. This was the most insane thing I'd ever done. More insane than riding to the marina in the wee hours of the morning.

In a final gamble, I was going to ask Colin's family for help.

The door swung open, and for a moment I was lightheaded, thinking it was Colin. That he'd come home. But on my second blink, to my utter devastation, I saw it wasn't Colin.

It was Sebastian.

"Oh, it's you." He seemed just as disappointed to see me as I was to see him. "I thought you quit."

Once I'd told her I didn't want to clean the St. Jameses' house anymore, Mom had hired another cleaner, a sweet lady named

Rebecca, who'd been thrilled that she could bring her baby with her to the job site.

"I'm looking for Colin."

He leaned against the doorjamb. He wore loose basketball shorts and no shirt despite the weather having dipped into the thirties. A medallion hung around his neck, and he crossed his arms. "He's not here. Hasn't been home in a while. I told you not to break his heart. Now I'm going to have to destroy you," he said, no trace of sarcasm.

I squinted at him, searching his face to see if he was serious. "Do you really think that's okay to say to someone? Like you just wake up every day and float through your life, mouth unchecked?"

He stared back at me, unfazed. "Mostly, yes. Wouldn't you do the same if you were me?"

"There is something broken inside you." I licked my lips and smoothed them together, regrouping. The conversation had veered off course. "Do you know where Colin is?"

His expression shut down, and he peered at his nails. "Maybe."

"Would you be able to get him this letter?" I pulled the envelope from my bag.

"Maybe," he said again.

"Then . . . here." I waved the envelope at him, a lump forming in my throat and expanding. "Take it. Please. I'm trying to make things right."

He wrapped reluctant fingers around the paper.

"Thanks." I stepped away. "There's extra stamps on it."

"What's it say?" he hollered after me.

I walked faster and didn't answer.

That was between Colin and me. No one else.

• • •

It was silly checking the mailbox the next day. There was no chance Colin had received my letter, wherever he was, and written back in the last twenty-four hours. Hope ballooned in my chest anyway as I opened the box, then abruptly burst when I saw it was empty.

I knew I'd check again tomorrow.

I took my time walking back to my house. Snow started to fall. Big flakes that obscured my vision—and that's when I saw him.

On my porch, hands in his pockets, peering through the door.

A warm wave of awareness passed through me upon seeing his back. The shoulders I'd hugged, the hair I'd run my fingers through. The way he moved was hardwired inside me.

Speechless, I approached, the sight of him like a lifeline yanking me forward. "Colin?"

He turned. "Emma." His panicked expression ebbed into relief. "You're home. I rang the bell and no one answered."

Jiji was inside but didn't have his hearing aids in.

My thoughts stuttered. It seemed impossible that Colin was here.

"You got my letter?"

But it was too soon. How could this be?

"What letter?" He jogged down the rickety stairs, the brown paint peeling. Snowflakes caught in his hair, in my eyelashes. He was wearing a sweatshirt, puffy vest over it. I'd cocooned myself in a thick sweater and thin leggings. My hair was in a messy topknot, face clear of makeup. I hadn't planned on company.

"I wrote to you and gave it to Sebastian yesterday." I shook my head, bemused, forgetting the cold and snow. Colin was here. It was wild. Absolute madness. "It doesn't matter. What's going on? I don't understand. You've been gone for weeks. Where have you been? How'd you get here? Where's your car?" I craned my neck, searching the street. All the vehicles I recognized as the neighbors'—a beat-up Subaru, a dented Honda CR-V, a red truck with decades-old, fading political stickers.

"I went up north, docked in Vancouver, in British Columbia. I just got back today and caught an Uber. You're all I've been thinking about. I'm not going to give up." He inhaled and exhaled a huge breath, growing determined. "I'm here to fight for you."

He was joking.

I laughed, and his nostrils flared.

"Oh, you're serious."

Despite his size and likeliness to win, Colin wasn't a fighter. At Mrs. Sydney's house I had seen him usher a fly gently out the door. *There you go, little buddy. Go find a nice girl fly and garbage can. Make a home together, a million babies, too. Live forever.*

A single confirming nod. "Who is it? Your neighbor? That guy in the leather jacket?" He stared at me, eyes burning, for five endless seconds. "Tell me. I'm losing my mind."

My pulse spiked. "There isn't anyone else. The email you saw was from an old friend. It was true when I told you I'd never even met him. But more importantly, we're not talking anymore. I should have cut off all the communication sooner, when I realized how much you meant to me. I wish I'd handled all of this differently."

He pinched the bridge of his nose, then his eyes came to

mine. His breathing was still slightly irregular, his voice still slightly strained. "Sebastian told me I should kick their ass."

"That's so . . ." I struggled to find the right word. Sweet? No. "Unnecessary."

"Really? I had this whole chest-heaving plan to pound at your door until you let me in. Then punch whoever you were with and carry you away over my shoulder."

I smiled, the truth exploding inside me. Colin was here for me. I took one step closer to him, eyes traveling his face, drinking him in. "Well, my eighty-one-year-old grandfather is inside. It might seem like an uneven match, but I'm pretty sure he knows that trick to incapacitate a person just by pressing a certain spot on their neck."

Our toes were nearly touching. His feet were in sneakers, mine in my mother's Crocs.

"I had this whole plan. I've been hyping myself up all the way from BC to here." He smiled down at me, encircled my wrists with his hands, tugged me closer. I could feel the warmth radiating from his chest. "Tell me about the letter you gave to Sebastian."

Snow had melted inside the collar of my sweater, and a cold droplet curved its way down my neck as my throat knotted, remembering. "I wrote to you. Basically, apologizing for how we left things and asking for another chance." His eyes were a potent mixture of hope and happiness. "I thought you were gone forever . . ."

"No." He rubbed his thumbs over the outsides of my hands. His jaw flexed. "I was always going to come back. I was getting my head together. I've never felt this way about someone. I wanted you back and called my brother. He told me to turn around, then told me I should punch the other guy. He's terrible at advice. He once told me shaving without foam would make me tougher." He swept a loose lock of hair behind my ear. "You're all I've been thinking about. I was up north and saw killer whales. They came right up to the boat, and all I could think of was how much I wished you were there with me. I'm sorry. I shouldn't have let you walk away."

My heart skipped a happy beat, relieved tears pushing from my eyes. "I'm sorry too. I shouldn't have walked away."

Tentatively he smiled. "We're starting over."

"I'd really like that."

His hands skated up my arms to my shoulders, and he pulled me into him, tucking my head into his chest. The snow was really coming down, but I didn't care. I was warm. I was safe.

"Killer whales, huh?" My words were muffled by the fabric of his vest.

"It was amazing and terrifying. They are huge in real life," he said into my hair. "I'll take you there. It's only a day or two ride."

"Yes, I want to." I peered up at him. "But first you should meet someone."

Jiji sat fully upright in his favorite chair, appraising Colin with sharp eyes.

Introductions had gone well. Sort of. Jiji had shaken Colin's hand but then, in some sort of geriatric ex-government power play, had not invited him to sit.

Jiji tilted his head, considered Colin at length. "You picked Emma up before in a fancy car. A BMW."

Colin cleared his throat. "Yes, sir."

"I don't like your vehicle. It is too flashy."

He swallowed. "Yes. Too flashy. Absolutely."

Colin had devolved into some sort of primitive state where he could form only one- or two-word sentences.

"In Japan, having your hands in your pockets is rude."

Colin instantly removed his hands from his pockets. "Yes, sir."

Jiji slid his newspaper and pen on the coffee table toward Colin. "Write your social security number down."

I pushed Colin's arm away as he reached to take the newspaper. "You don't have to do that." I placed the paper and pen back in front of Jiji. "We're going to go upstairs for a little bit."

"Door open," Jiji called.

One might think I'd be nervous showing Colin my house and room, and one would be right.

I had this buzzing feeling in my limbs climbing the stairs, Colin at my heels. Before entering my room, I pointed at the four doors on the landing. "That's my mom's room, Jiji's room, the bathroom, and . . . this one is mine."

"I wish I wasn't wearing sweatpants the first time I met your grandfather. I might regret it for the rest of my life. I think all the blood drained from my body."

"You called him 'sir,' like, eight times."

He shifted. The little landing looked even smaller with Colin scrunched onto it. If he reached up, he'd be able to touch the ceiling. "He's kind of scary. What did he do before he retired? Was he a butcher? Did he work with knives? I bet he worked with knives."

"Well, we tell everyone he worked for a phone company, but really he consulted with the government on foreign jobs."

Colin's forehead scrunched. "Oh my God, that's worse, he was obviously in the CIA. I'm on a government watch list now, aren't I?"

The possibility was high, but I decided to keep that to myself. I smiled, bright and reassuring, at Colin. "I think he liked you."

"I think you're hopelessly optimistic." He went quiet, doing a top-to-bottom sweep of the space, then trained his focus on my bedroom door. "You going to show me your room?"

I jumped into action, Colin following me as I pushed inside my room.

He stopped short of the threshold. "So this is it. Where it all happens."

I watched him take it in: The unmade double bed in the center with a quilt my grandmother made. My chipped white nightstand that I'd found at a thrift shop and that Delia had decoupaged with music notes. My shelf littered with the little clay creatures I used to make; the lump of laundry in the corner; my desk, where I had never done homework and mostly watched time-lapse videos of the world's messiest houses being cleaned. Finally, my music stand and violin, which drew him farther in. He touched one of the strings.

"It's not as big as your room." I gave him a half-hearted smile, pulling my quilt up and hastily making my bed.

"It's great." He sidled up to me, cupped my cheeks. "Thank you for letting me into your world."

I smiled, laughing through my tears.

The past was in the past. And in the future, who knew what would happen?

But this moment, right here, with Colin, was perfect, and I let myself feel all of it.

This happy for now.

EPILOGUE

Dad is married in the spring, in late March, during a vicious thunderstorm, but it doesn't matter. Madison doesn't even blink when tree branches thrash against the large windows of the public library. She is elegant and glowing in an off-white satin dress, holding a bouquet of ranunculus as she walks between the stacks to the crooning of Al Green.

"I'm so tired of being alone . . ."

After the ceremony everyone heads to the community room for appetizers and dancing. The light is yellow and warm, and the mood is jovial.

Colin is my date. He cleaned up nice and insisted on picking me up at home beforehand to show Jiji he owned a suit.

Since their first meeting, Jiji has warmed up to Colin. Like, it was a big deal when he invited him to sit on the couch. His exact words were: "Why are you always standing? Do you have somewhere to go? Come, sit for a while." The rest of that day, Colin acted as if he'd won a prize.

Real life has become very different from just a few months ago. In fact, it's changed in ways I could not have imagined. All for the better.

I received my acceptance letter from Berklee yesterday, and it's now settled—I will head to Boston in the fall. Jiji insisted we should drive across the country and have one last adventure together. I burst into tears at the suggestion.

Colin and I will do long distance for a while. He's still planning on sailing the world. I think it will be good for us. I'm kind of into writing letters now.

"This is quite the party. Who knew your dad used to be in a band?" Theo is next to me, sinking his teeth into a stuffed mushroom.

"Easy with those," I tell him, smoothing my hands down my dress. Honestly, I can't stop touching it. It's vintage, daffodil yellow, with a crinoline underskirt, sweetheart neckline, and halter top tied in a bow. A special gift from Mrs. Sydney's closet. "They're full of cheese."

He finishes and rolls the toothpick into a napkin. "So?"

I scan the room, make eye contact with Colin, and wave. He's deep in conversation with Camille's dad, the painter and—as it turns out—fellow amateur sailor. I abandoned ship once they started talking about trade winds. My guy could be adorably nerdy about knots sometimes.

"So." I turn back to Theo. "I'm talking about you being lactose intolerant. Isn't that thing going to make your insides explode? Don't you think it's too soon in your relationship for Camille to witness that?"

They were still together and would probably walk down the aisle to the *Jurassic Park* soundtrack.

"I'm not lactose intolerant." He plucks another cheese-filled mushroom from a passing tray and swallows it one bite, as if proving a point.

A camera flashes; Camille and her mom are taking pictures, the backdrop the thrillers section, right in front of the *T*'s, where Dad's books are shelved.

I square up to Theo. "Yes, you are."

Why am I arguing with him about this?

"I'm not. I stopped eating cheese after you barfed it up when you were sick." He pounds his chest. "Out of solidarity. Wait. You're over that, aren't you? Is watching me eat cheese going to make you gag?"

"I'm not going to gag." My heart speeds up, and I have an eerie sense of déjà vu, followed by an insane thought that I immediately shake away. "I just . . . I thought you were lactose intolerant, that's all. You think you know someone."

"Guess we don't know everything about each other," he says with a small smile. "On that note, there's something I've been meaning to mention."

My brow is still furrowed, stuck on the fact Theo isn't lactose intolerant. "Yeah?"

"I changed my mind. I'm going to Boston—well, Cambridge really—to MIT."

The music fades away and I take a beat absorbing this. *Boston.*

The city name presses into my side like a hot iron, and at the same time adrenaline begins to course through me.

I am going to Boston too. Theo will be there. The letter writer lives in Boston. Dusty puzzle pieces begin moving in my mind.

"When did this happen?" I manage to ask.

"A while ago," he says. "I've been underwater, handling the emotional fallout from my mom. She was all set on Caltech and me staying on the West Coast." Then he gives me a funny look. "Weirdly, you had a hand in my decision."

"I did?" My heart feels like it's going to pound out of my chest.

"When you brought up time travel, it got me thinking. Like, why *couldn't* it be possible? I want to explore the universe, and with MIT the options are limitless. They actually have a program dedicated to studying Einstein's special theory of relativity."

I balk in confusion. "This is a lot to take in. A big turnaround."

"The universe is vast, Emma. We are but mere particles of light in human shapes drifting in space," he says to me, mouth turning up in a teasing half grin. "The program is small, as in a couple of dudes working on it in a forgotten basement somewhere. They've been calling it TARDIS, which is the most unoriginal thing ever. We need to figure out a better name. I'm definitely going to get laughed at a lot. This is the wildest thing I've ever done."

"You should call it the Chronos Project," I whisper, then slap my hand over my mouth.

His face screws up. "Chronos? As in the father of time? That's pretty cool." He scratches the back of his head in a way that's all too achingly familiar. "Anyway, sorry I didn't tell you before. I think my mom is mostly under control now. She spent all night making this scrapbook of you and me as kids. You should see it, it's all our greatest hits. I'm pretty sure it'll be my favorite thing ever. And that says a lot, since you know I have original Superman memorabilia."

I remember the box of photographs in his family room closet.

Then I imagine his mom arranging each one in an album.

A treasured possession. A *most* treasured possession. I am

thunderstruck. The absolute madness of it. Could Theo be the letter writer? Is it even a question now? The truth sears a path across my chest.

"Are you okay? You look pale." Theo flags a waiter for a glass of water and presses it into my hands.

Icy condensation coats my palms, and the cold grounds me. I look down into my glass, afraid Theo might see the confusion in my eyes, the turmoil. "I'm okay. What happens if you figure it out? Would you go back in time?"

"I don't know. I'm mostly focused now on proving everyone else wrong. You don't want to mess with the space-time continuum. But now that you ask, I suppose I would. If I had to. It would have to be for something important."

For someone you love, I think, but don't say it.

We are time itself. Eternal.

He fetches his own water glass. "Here's to the future and to all our crazy dreams."

I automatically clink my glass against his and school my features. "You're going to do it. I know you will." I rally behind him, because that's what he's always done for me.

A doubtful smile. "We'll see."

He drinks, and I see him share a look with Camille over his glass. The kind of look he used to send me: warm, alive, knowing. They've only grown closer the last few months. Theo and I, further apart. I remember time is malleable, ever changing.

Maybe since he wrote, our paths have shifted. The Theo that loved me and wrote to me from the future might not exist anymore. He doesn't know the Emma that goes to Berklee. And maybe I don't know the Theo that invents time travel. The Theo that doesn't need to reach back to rescue his childhood friend. Because this Emma goes to Berklee. This Emma is heading into the unknown. Nothing is ever certain. Except . . .

Theo is with Camille.

I am with Colin.

I push past my sense of bittersweet loss. "Are you happy?" I ask him. The same question the letter writer asked future Emma. I poise, ready for his answer.

"I am," he says, and I can see he's telling the truth. "You?"

I turn to look at Colin, who's finished his conversation with the painter-sailor and is heading toward us. In my ears I can hear the echo of his boisterous laugh, the way his voice deepens when he says my name. The connection between us is as strong as ever. I want Colin. Berklee. Music. And it's all within reach. These things that bring me joy. "Yeah."

As soon as Colin is close, he catches my wrist and pulls me into him.

"Hey, man." He dips his chin to Theo. "Dance?" he asks me, eyes soft, devoted.

I grin up at him. "Up to you. You know I have two left feet. How much do you value the use of your toes?"

His hands come to my hips, squeeze. "Worth the risk."

We sway. My cheek presses against Colin's solid chest.

I watch Theo find Camille, twirl her under his arm, and rock with her to the music.

"Thank you," I mouth to Theo, but he doesn't see.

And that's okay.

He wouldn't understand what I'm thanking him for anyway.

ACKNOWLEDGMENTS

Thanks so much to everyone who's read, recommended, or reviewed my books. You are why I get to do what I love every day. But a book doesn't become a book through writing alone. This book exists because of the talent and dedication of so many amazing people.

My deepest thanks to Sarah Barley, my editor, who understood that getting the details right matters—thank you for caring as much about email addresses and flap copy as you did about every sentence in between. I appreciate your patience, insight, and attention to detail.

Thank you also to Alma Gomez Martinez for keeping everything organized and moving forward.

To Erin Harris, my agent, who understood what mattered most and helped make it possible—thank you for ensuring this book found its way to exactly where it needed to be.

To Justin Chanda, whose early enthusiasm and support opened doors for this book, thank you for creating a space at S&S Children's for my work.

I'm grateful to the talented team who brought this book to life: Laura Eckes and Sammy Yuen for the beautiful jacket design, Ben Giles for artwork that perfectly captures the story's spirit, and Hilary Zarycky for the elegant interior design.

Thank you to Amanda Brenner, our production editor, for keeping everything on track; to Erica Stahler for meticulous copyediting; to Sophia Lee for careful proofreading; and to Chava Wolin for overseeing production with such expertise.

ACKNOWLEDGMENTS

Katie Boni and Antonella Colon, thank you for your publicity efforts. Cassandra Fernandez, Karina Itzel, Erin Toller, and Michelle Leo and her team—I appreciate all your work in getting this book into readers' hands.

To Joelle, whose contributions behind the scenes helped bring new dimensions to this project—thank you for your creativity and collaboration. Working with you has been such a gift.

Finally, to my family. To my husband, who never complained about late-night writing sessions. Your support means everything. To my children, who understood when I needed quiet time to write and who remind me daily why stories matter. And to my parents and siblings, who have encouraged my writing from the beginning. And especially to Liz, thanks for always asking to read. It means more than you'll ever know.

Thank you all for making this book possible. I am ridiculously lucky.